"How'd your family get-together go?"

"It went well," Carly replied. "I told them about you being alive. And here in Chicago."

Micha had suspected she might. "How'd they take it?"

"Well. You know how much they liked you. Several people asked why I didn't bring you with me."

"What did you say?"

"I changed the subject. Honestly, Micha, I'm still not sure how I feel about all this. Having you back and here with me is wonderful, but it's also scary as hell."

"Scary? How so?"

"Losing you hurt, Micha. It took me a long time to pick myself up and climb out of that deep, dark place."

"Would you rather I hadn't come back? Would you..." He had to swallow hard to keep his voice from breaking. "Would you rather you still thought I was dead?"

"Of course not. But I'm still struggling with the fact that you waited two entire years before even attempting to contact me. I know you have your reasons. But what you don't understand is this. I can't go through that again. I wouldn't survive losing you a second time."

"I'm sorry," he murmured.

* * *

Colton 911: Chicago—Love and danger come alive in the Windy City...

* * *

If you're on Twitter, tell us what you think of Harlequin Romantic Suspense! #harlequinromsuspense

Dear Reader,

Another Coltons book! Yay! As you know, I adore the Colton family. Writing about them reminds me of watching the TV show *Dallas* back in the '80s. Never a dull moment.

In this book, I got to tell the story of Micha Harrison and Carly Colton. It's a book about redemption and learning to trust again and knowing love won't ever fail to heal old wounds. It's got a lot of suspense as we try to figure out who wants Carly or Micha (or both of them) dead and whether or not it's tied to the potential serial killer who murdered Carly's father and his twin brother. The rest of the Colton family comes to visit, too. I truly enjoyed writing this story. I hope you enjoy reading it.

Karen Whiddon

COLTON 911: SOLDIER'S RETURN

Karen Whiddon

HARLEQUIN

ROMANTIC
SUSPENSE

Special thanks and acknowledgment are given to
Karen Whiddon for her contribution to
the Colton 911: Chicago miniseries.

HARLEQUIN®
ROMANTIC SUSPENSE™

Recycling programs
for this product may
not exist in your area.

ISBN-13: 978-1-335-62889-3

Colton 911: Soldier's Return

Copyright © 2021 by Harlequin Books S.A.

For questions and comments about the quality of this book,
please contact us at CustomerService@Harlequin.com.

Harlequin Enterprises ULC
22 Adelaide St. West, 40th Floor
Toronto, Ontario M5H 4E3, Canada
www.Harlequin.com

Printed in U.S.A.

Karen Whiddon started weaving fanciful tales for her younger brothers at the age of eleven. Amid the gorgeous Catskill Mountains, then the majestic Rocky Mountains, she fueled her imagination with the natural beauty surrounding her. Karen now lives in north Texas, writes full-time and volunteers for a boxer dog rescue. She shares her life with her hero of a husband and four to five dogs, depending on if she is fostering. You can email Karen at kwhiddon1@aol.com. Fans can also check out her website, karenwhiddon.com.

Books by Karen Whiddon

Harlequin Romantic Suspense

Colton 911: Chicago
Colton 911: Soldier's Return

The CEO's Secret Baby
The Cop's Missing Child
The Millionaire Cowboy's Secret
Texas Secrets, Lovers' Lies
The Rancher's Return
The Texan's Return
Wyoming Undercover
The Texas Soldier's Son
Texas Ranch Justice
Snowbound Targets
The Widow's Bodyguard

Visit the Author Profile page at Harlequin.com for more titles.

To my beloved husband and daughter.
I love you both more than I could ever express.

Chapter 1

The sun shone bright yellow in a blue sky speckled with fluffy white clouds. Happy clouds, Carly Colton thought. The kind she used to imagine were animals and ships when she was a child. All around her, birds were singing cheerful songs and the still-crisp air carried the promise of warmer temperatures to come. Typical spring in Chicago. One minute, cold enough for snow flurries; the next, warm enough to cause trees to start to bud and flowers to bloom. Finally, nice enough weather to enjoy the outdoors, to take more walks, maybe even visit the lakeshore.

Despite being outside, in the warm sunshine, Carly couldn't stop looking over her shoulder. The beautiful April day did nothing to lessen her unease. For the past six weeks, whether shopping or taking a walk, she'd been certain someone was stalking her, even though she'd never actually been able to catch sight of them.

It was more of a gut feeling, a visceral instinct. She'd be walking along familiar streets and then feel someone's gaze on her with a tingle of nerves in the back of her neck. Who? Terrified, she'd spin wildly, hoping to catch her stalker in the act. But so far, she'd been completely unsuccessful, unable to locate a single person or even a group of people paying her the slightest bit of untoward attention. Nothing, absolutely nothing, out of the ordinary. Enough to make her wonder if her father's and uncle's murders had made her become overly fearful.

These days, she had to make herself venture out of her home, despite craving the fresh air. Her neighborhood had always been perfectly safe, and she loved her street.

Even now, on a perfect spring day, she swore she could feel someone watching her. Unsettled, she managed to force herself to continue on her walk, though every instinct screamed she should run home as fast as she could. As usual, she resisted the urge.

Paranoid? Maybe. But then she had reason to be on edge considering her father and his brother had been murdered a few months ago. The killer had yet to be caught. Even so, she didn't like feeling uneasy outside her own house in her wonderful Hyde Park neighborhood, the one place she should have felt safe. Until a month and a half ago, despite occasional bouts of bad weather, she'd always enjoyed her early-evening strolls around her block, waving at neighbors and enjoying a bit of fresh air.

Now not so much. In fact, she'd begun to realize

she might need to consider stopping them altogether. Which would be a shame, since she considered walking her main stress reliever after working as a pediatric nurse in the NICU—Neonatal Intensive Care Unit. She hated to lose that one little bit of joy in what could sometimes be long, and often painful, days.

Determined to persevere, she'd continued her walks, heart often racing, always alert, looking for proof that the eyes she felt watching her were real. If she saw anything, any tangible evidence to confirm her fears, she'd stop immediately.

Her family would be worried if they knew. Ever since the devastating death of her fiancé, Micha, two years ago, they had a tendency to treat her as if they believed she might break. Plus, with everyone still raw after her father's and uncle's murders, she hadn't wanted to worry them.

Same with the man she'd been dating, though she'd decided to tell him that evening over dinner. Since Harry Cartwright was a police officer, she figured he just might take her seriously. Maybe he'd even offer to help.

Someone had to. Because instead of going away, it was getting worse.

Carly picked up her pace. Once she'd made it around this next corner, she'd be able to see her house. The sight of her tidy little brick bungalow never failed to lift her spirits. Though she wasn't a runner, if need be she figured she could always sprint for home.

Again, she scanned her surroundings, unease sitting like a lead balloon in the pit of her stomach. She saw nothing out of the ordinary. A man walked his dog on the other side of the street. A woman holding fast to her child's hand moved at a leisurely pace several houses ahead.

Yet she could not shake the feeling of being watched.

Frustrated, she rounded the corner, still at a brisk walk but on the verge of breaking into a jog. And then she saw him, stepping out into her path from a driveway, his dark sunglasses and longish, wavy brown hair doing nothing to disguise his achingly familiar—and ruggedly beautiful—face.

It couldn't be. No freaking way.

Shocked, Carly froze. Now she knew she'd officially ventured into the land of needing professional help. Because the man standing less than ten feet in front of her had died two years ago. How could she be looking at a ghost?

He took a step toward her, disturbingly solid. No apparition, but muscle and bone and skin. Real.

"Micha?" she heard herself ask, as if from a distance. Because it couldn't be and yet… "Micha Harrison, is that really you?"

Of course, this man, whoever he was, with his striking features and stylishly shaggy hair, would now speak and tell her no, she'd made a terrible mistake. Because people just don't come back from the dead.

"It's me," he said instead, his words and the familiar husky voice making her stagger. "Carly, we really need to talk."

She couldn't catch her breath. Heart pounding, she stared.

Talk? She wanted to scream, push past him, but she couldn't seem to make her legs move. How could he be there, this beautiful, rugged, beloved man who'd destroyed her by his absence. Which had all apparently been one huge pack of lies.

"Have you been following me?" she asked, still numb, struggling to make sense of how she was supposed to feel. The man she'd loved, whose ring she just stopped wearing on a chain around her neck, had died. She'd never forget the day she'd opened her front door to find a uniformed soldier standing on her porch with the gut-wrenching news that Micha had been killed.

Had that been fake? Clearly, it must have been. But why? Why would the man who'd promised to love her forever do such a thing to her? How dare they? How dare he?

Suddenly furious, she wrenched herself away from him and broke into a run. Despite her lack of expertise, her anger fueled her and she raced down her street and into her driveway.

To her immense relief, Micha didn't chase after her.

Once she'd made it safely inside her house, dead bolt locked, she doubled over. Out of breath, in pain, her rage warring with a stunned sense of disbelief. And the grief, oddly enough, resurrected from the dark place she'd shoved it, as surely as the man she'd had to let go.

Micha wasn't dead. She wasn't sure how to process this. Dimly aware of the tears streaming down her face, she angrily swiped at them with the back of her hand.

A moment later, the sorry bastard had the nerve to knock on her front door.

She froze, then squared her shoulders, took a deep breath and wiped her eyes once more. On the one hand, she wanted to fling open the door and tell him to get the hell off her porch. On the other, she wanted to throw herself into his arms and hold him tight, as she'd dreamed of doing so many times while aching from his loss.

Alive. The love of her life. He'd ruined her for anyone else. She'd hung on to the memory of him, of their love shining bright and incandescent. She'd *mourned* him, damn it. He hadn't died. Alive. And he didn't bother to show up until two freaking years later.

Pain, fresh and as new as the day she'd learned of his death, slammed into her gut, almost sending her to her knees.

Carly had never been an indecisive person, but she honestly didn't know what to do.

Micha knocked again. "We need to talk," he said, the solid wood door muffling his raspy voice. "Please, Carly. Let me in. I promise you I can explain."

She wanted to. Oh, how much she wanted to. Right now, she warred between a furious need to pummel him with her fists and to haul him up against her and kiss him senseless.

Micha had destroyed her. And now he wanted to tell her how and why.

In the end it was this, curiosity over the explanation, wondering how anyone, anywhere, could possibly rationalize what he'd done, that made her unlock the door and invite him inside.

Stepping back, she said nothing as he moved past her, his shoulders every bit as wide as she remembered. Still silent as she secured the dead bolt and turned to face him in the entryway of the house they'd chosen together. She'd gone ahead and purchased it after his death.

He still wore his sunglasses. The better to hide from her, she supposed, her chest twisting. "Take them off," she demanded, pointing.

He did, revealing his dark brown eyes and something else she hadn't expected. Scars. Numerous ones, a network of them around his forehead and right cheek.

Unable to help herself, she moved closer, reached out and traced her finger over the lines. Her touch made him shudder, which brought her back to reality. Shaking her head, she took a hasty step back.

"What happened to you?" she asked softly, trying to infuse a bit of steel in her voice. "I thought you were dead."

Her question made him swallow hard. She couldn't keep from following the movement in his damn-him-for-still-being-so-sexy throat.

"Could we sit somewhere and talk?" he rasped. "Please?"

Talk. She struggled to process the word. As if this was an ordinary situation, easily solved with a rational conversation. Except right now, she thought viciously, he should be groveling on his hands and knees, full of abject apologies and recrimination over what he'd done. He'd let her believe him dead for two freaking years. She should show him the door, toss him out on his rear.

Except…she really wanted to know what had happened. His reasons. What would make a man destroy the woman he'd supposedly loved. Just like that, the flare of anger dissipated, leaving her weak.

Usually when stressed, Carly talked. Chattered actually. But this time, she didn't feel the need to fill the silence with words. No. Not now. That would have to be Micha's job.

"Sure," she said, leading the way down the hall into the living room. At the last moment, she reconsidered and veered into the kitchen, indicating her red-and-chrome retro dinette set. "Can I get you something to drink?"

Her polite and distant tone made him flinch. She wanted to shrug and tell him to take what he could get. Civility, no matter how remote, was a far better response than giving in to her tangled emotions.

"No, thank you." Dropping into a chair, Micha dragged his hands through his shaggy hair. He'd never worn his hair so long, she thought absently. When they'd been together, he'd kept it closely cropped in a military-type cut, fitting since he'd been a soldier.

Still Micha didn't speak. She waited, but he simply watched her, his achingly familiar features a study in emotion.

Fine. Then she'd start. She had so many questions. She deserved answers.

"You've been stalking me," she said. "Why?"

"I wanted to make sure you were all right," he admitted. "I hadn't planned on letting you see me, but…" He shook his head, letting the words trail off.

"It's been two years, Micha." The anger came roaring back, though she managed to keep her voice steady. "Not only did you let me believe you were dead, but after all this time, you couldn't be bothered to get in touch with me and let me know you were all right. Why now?"

She took a step toward him, still trying to rein in her

emotions, not entirely sure she was succeeding. Once, the big man sitting at her kitchen table had known her well enough to see right through to the heart that beat erratically inside her chest. If he still could, then he'd understand the complicated mixture of raw pain and sadness, anger and, oddly, defeat.

Since he hadn't responded, she took a deep breath and continued, as ruthless as she knew she had to be. "I've moved on, Micha. I'm finally getting on with my life. I'm dating a very nice guy, Harry, and—"

Micha pushed to his feet, towering over her. "I know, Carly," he said, his voice rough. "And believe me, I'm well aware I have no right to show up and disrupt your life. I just couldn't stay away." His gaze blazed with heat. "I tried, Carly. Believe me, I tried."

Something—maybe his palpable anguish or the way the heat in his eyes brought back memories of his big hands on her skin—had her taking a half step toward him. Pushing to his feet, he met her halfway, sweeping her up against his broad chest, slanting his mouth over hers in a kiss that was everything it shouldn't have been.

Two years vanished in a flash. For weeks, months, she'd dreamed of this, yearning for him, aching for his loss, so how could she possibly let him go? She might be full of regrets later, but for now she chose to give in and ride this wave of welcome passion. For the first time since learning of his death, Carly Colton came alive.

She denied him nothing. Greedily, she clung to him, allowing herself to touch his muscular, still-familiar body. Despite the velvet warmth of his tongue alongside hers, part of her still couldn't help but wonder if she might wake up to learn that this turned out to be yet just another dream.

But the force of his arousal pressing against her had to be real, her own body heavy and warm in response. Her skin tingled and she couldn't shed her clothes fast enough. Gaze locked on hers, he did the same.

More scars crisscrossed his chest, his stomach, and wound a horrific path down his arm. She noted these, knew she'd ask about them later, but all she cared about now was the man inside his skin.

Unbearable, this craving. She was weak, yet on fire, her heartbeat throbbing in her ears, ecstasy spiraling with each stroke of his tongue against hers.

Naked finally, skin to skin, her flesh on fire. He called her name, a guttural moan, as his lips seared a path to the hollow of her throat.

She arched her back, giving herself over to him even as she tugged him closer, wanting him inside her. Needing him inside her with the heat of a thousand suns.

"Wait," he managed, grabbing his discarded jeans and removing a condom from his wallet. Watching as he tugged it over his magnificent arousal, her mouth went dry.

Dizzy with desire, she reached for him again the instant he'd finished sheathing himself. His dark eyes smoldered as he swept his gaze over her, even as he murmured her name like it was a prayer.

Somehow, they made it to her bed, falling onto the sheets, their bodies still tangled together.

He took her then, sweeping her beneath him with one simple motion, both familiar and thrillingly new. The engorged tip of him pressed against her. Ready, warm and wet, she opened herself to him. Micha had finally come home.

"I never forgot," she gasped as he entered her, filling her completely. The feel of his hard body, both familiar and foreign, electrified her, sending her into a kind of pleasure overdrive. Micha. She writhed beneath him, urging him to move, but maddeningly he held himself completely still, tension running through every muscle in his body.

"Hold still," he managed to order. "Please. If you don't, this just might be over before it even begins."

This statement, coming from a man who'd always been able to take his time leisurely bringing her to pleasure, drove her wild. She could scarcely catch her breath, but with her heart pounding, she managed to do as he'd asked and not move. Though she could do nothing to stop the little pulses her body gave at him so deep inside her.

And then he began to move.

Pure and explosive pleasure, sweet agony of the kind she'd never thought she'd experience again. She saw colors, heard music, felt her heart expand even as her body melted. She could no longer control her cries of pleasure, matching his thrusts with wild abandon.

As she gave herself over to her release, she felt him catch his breath as he did the same. This at least hadn't changed.

They held each other as their shuddering subsided, she clinging to him as if he might vanish in the space of the next gulp of air she allowed into her lungs. And he…he held on to her with a similar sort of desperate possessiveness. She traced her fingers over him, exploring while no longer in the throes of passion. His muscular body bore more scars, a tangled web of jagged lines that surely had something to do with his disappearance. She'd hear the story behind them soon, though not now, not yet. She wasn't ready.

Neither spoke. She, because she didn't want to ruin the fragile peace of the moment with reality. He, most likely because if he did he might have to explain. And right now, she really didn't want to hear it.

Her phone chimed, the calendar alert reminding her she'd agreed to meet Harry for dinner in less than an hour. Just like that, her insides twisted into a knot.

"You should go," she told Micha, trying not to look at him in all his naked, masculine splendor. "I have plans tonight."

"With him?" No inflection in his voice, just the question, asked so quietly.

Miserable now, she nodded. "Yes."

With a sinfully languid movement reminiscent of a big cat stretching in the sun, he got up from her bed and sauntered toward her bathroom, detouring into the hall to scoop up his clothes on the way. "I'll be out of your hair in a minute."

Despite everything, she couldn't tear her gaze away from his naked rear. She'd always loved his body, surprisingly graceful despite his sheer size. Now his skin looked like something she was familiar with from her work as a nurse. She'd spent a few of her clinical rotations in the burn unit. She'd seen skin grafts that looked like this, and horrific burns that had eventually healed, leaving their mark behind.

She ached to run her fingers over those scars, to kiss

them to show she still found him beautiful and sexy, and always would.

No. She couldn't even let her thoughts go there. She needed to shower and get ready to meet Harry.

And probably ruin forever what had been a burgeoning relationship.

Micha emerged from her bathroom a moment later, fully dressed. His shaggy hair even appeared to have fallen back into its former artful disarray. He looked, she thought grimly, both the same and completely different.

She followed him down the hall toward the front door. He reached for the knob to let himself out, but at the last moment he turned.

"Don't go to meet Harry tonight," he said, letting her see the naked emotion in his eyes. "Stay here with me and talk. We've got a lot of catching up to do."

Heaven help her, she caught herself swaying toward him. At the last moment, she caught herself and shook her head. "Like I said earlier, I've moved on. I've started over, made a life for myself. His name is Harry," she pointed out. "We bonded over our shared grief. He lost his wife and daughter in a car accident around the same time I lost you. I'm not going to bail on him when he's been there for me all this time."

A flash of something—jealousy, maybe—crossed his face. "Are you planning to tell him about this? About…" He swallowed. "What just happened between us?"

She lifted her chin, letting him see some of the bitterness she felt. "I am. I'm not going to lie to him, Micha. All I can do is admit to my mistake and hope he forgives me."

"Mistake." Expression anguished, he stared at her. Spotting a pad of paper and a pen on the table near the door, he jotted down his number. "Call me if you change your mind or just want to talk."

Slowly, she nodded. Then he let himself out the door without another word.

The instant it closed behind him, she instinctively locked the dead bolt. Devastated, she fought the urge to double over and cry. Refusing to allow herself to think, she spun around and marched toward the shower. She needed to wash every last bit of Micha off her body before she told Harry what she had done.

Somehow, she managed to make herself look presentable by the time Harry arrived to pick her up. When he rang the bell, she let him inside. He wore his usual faded jeans and cotton button-down shirt, with a baseball cap on his head. He looked familiar and comfortable and she didn't know how on earth she could break his heart.

With her own heart hammering, she struggled to make small talk. She knew she should tell him now, instead of in a crowded restaurant, but struggled to find the right words.

"What's wrong?" Harry finally asked, his sharp gray-green gaze missing nothing.

"Micha's alive," she blurted, inwardly wincing as she braced for Harry's reaction. He simply stared at her for a moment, clearly trying to assess the situation.

"Could you, er, elaborate?" he asked in what she'd come to think of as his professional police officer tone.

She nodded. "Maybe you'd better sit down?"

"Sure." With a wry smile, he walked into her living room and took a seat on the couch. "Go ahead," he said, once he'd gotten settled. Gaze watchful, he appeared calm and merely curious. His rock-steadiness had always been one of the things she'd liked about him. Harry would never abandon her and pretend to be dead for two years.

She told him everything, starting with the constant feeling of being watched all the way through ending up in bed with Micha. "He had no explanation for where he's been these past twenty-four months," she finished weakly, even though she guessed that detail wouldn't be what Harry would be focused on.

Instead of the hurt or even anger that she'd expected, Harry continued to regard her soberly. "During the time we've been together, we've talked a lot about the people we've lost," he said. "I know how much you loved Micha and how deeply you grieved his passing."

Confused, she frowned. "Yes, but he wasn't really dead."

Harry pushed to his feet. "You've been given a great gift, Carly. A second chance."

"What are you saying? That you think I should get back together with him?" Which defied comprehension. "After what he did?"

"Yes." Expression fierce, Harry swallowed hard. "Do you know what I'd give if Marie and Emily could walk back in my front door?" Anguish twisted his handsome features. "I'd give anything, forgive everything, if I could have a second chance like the one you've been given. Give Micha a shot."

"But—"

"I wish you nothing but the best, Carly." He kissed

her cheek. "I hope the two of you can work things out. You deserve that kind of happiness."

On that note, Harry left, leaving Carly to stare after him, more bewildered than before.

Harry's easy acquiescence, while surprising, told her one thing she hadn't expected. She hadn't lost him. She'd never had him to begin with.

Micha coming back to life might seem like a miracle, but after two years she wasn't the same trusting woman she'd been before. Despite her overwhelming physical reaction to him, she couldn't simply pick up where they'd left off, pretending he hadn't done something so unquestionably horrible. If only he had been able to see her, doubled over with the pain of his loss. How long she had grieved, how changed her life had become. While he'd done what? Gotten the military to deliver a fake death notice? Or had they, too, actually believed him to be deceased, which seemed much more likely?

Either way, clearly Micha hadn't been the ordinary soldier he'd pretended to be.

So how many lies had there been? How could she take back a man she couldn't trust?

Her head began to hurt, almost as much as her heart. While part of what Harry had said rang true, she wasn't sure she could ever get past what Micha had done. Heck, she wasn't even sure she wanted to. Because, honestly, if Micha could do something like that to her, she very much doubted he'd ever loved her. At least, not the way she'd loved him.

But then why had he returned? Why now, when she'd thought she might finally be able to settle into some sort of normal existence? Sure, Harry hadn't made her feel even one tenth of the joy, pleasure and fulfillment she'd experienced with Micha. Music had seemed sweeter, colors brighter, and even food had tasted better. Life had been vibrant then and she'd honestly thought she'd found that once-in-a-lifetime kind of love. Clearly, she'd been wrong.

Now she just needed to figure out how to deal with Micha's presence back in her life.

Chapter 2

Micha Harrison had made love with his Carly. Still reeling, he tried to process a real-life scenario where his former fiancée not only welcomed him back with open arms but kissed him and touched him as if she'd been as starved for him as he'd been for her. He hadn't let himself think, only feel. And he had to admit, sex with Carly felt better than damn good.

Then, once they'd slaked their passion, she'd done an immediate about-face.

In his military training as intelligence gatherer—aka spy—Micha Harrison had learned how to not react to just about any scenario. He'd developed a hell of a poker face, a skill that had served him well in every single situation he'd found himself in while serving his country. In addition, he'd taught himself to clamp down on his emotions, to never give in to impulse or panic and, most important, not to be swayed by pain. The latter had been what had almost cost him his life. Most men, when captured by the enemy, eventually gave in to the agony of torture. Micha had not. Because of that, they'd almost killed him.

Micha was good, damn good. He could retreat inside himself to an untouchable place, no matter what hell rained down upon him.

Yet despite all of his training, all of his skills, Carly proved to be the exception. *His* Carly.

He hadn't meant to let her see him. Now healed and finally healthy, though scarred, he'd returned to Chicago with the intention of simply checking on her. With all of his heart, he'd hoped to find her happy and well, having fully moved on with her life.

At least that's what he'd told himself. All of that went out the window at the first glimpse of her, which had hit him like a punch in the stomach. Her long blond hair still looked soft as silk and her bright blue eyes were as lovely as ever.

Two years and the loss of him had done little to dim her light. That light had been the first thing he'd noticed about her when he'd met her. Carly freaking *glowed*. He'd never been one to believe in auras or any of that sort of nonsense, but Carly nearly changed his mind. She radiated an appealing mixture of goodness and compassion and humor, qualities a man as broken as him had been unable to resist.

Her sensuous beauty had been a bonus, though she'd never been able to see herself the way he saw her. Larger than life, everything he loved about Chicago exemplified in one person. He hadn't been looking for love, but it had found him. Until meeting her, he'd believed his military career would be his life; that he'd need nothing more.

Growing up on a small dairy farm in rural Ohio, all Micha had dreamed about was escaping an existence of livestock and drudgery. With no money for college—like his brother, Brian, before him—Micha had enlisted in the army right after graduation from high school.

To his surprise, he'd thrived. He'd actually found his niche in the military. He'd always done more than his best, giving it his everything. His higher-ups had noticed, singling him out for specialized training.

And then one day on leave in a city he loved, his life had completely changed for the better. He'd finally, at the ripe age of thirty-one, understood love songs and romantic movies, things he'd semi-scoffed at before. All because of Carly and her love.

Until he'd met her, his life had been the military. In the army, he'd finally found the one thing that had been missing all his life—a sense of belonging. The military had become his family, especially when his older brother had been killed while on tour in Syria. His parents had been devastated, and when Micha had taken leave to go home for the funeral, they'd demanded that he return home and take over the dairy farm since Brian wouldn't be able to now. They'd known Micha had only wanted to escape that life and now they expected him to step into his brother's shoes. Incredulous and grieving himself, he'd refused.

That's when his father, both broken and stern, had declared if he remained in the army he would no longer consider Micha his son. Reeling from a now-double loss, Micha had packed his bags and returned to base without even attending his brother's funeral. From that moment on, he'd been determined to dedicate the rest of his life to the service of his country.

Life had clicked along. Over time, the ache of losing his parents had begun to fade. His mother occasionally secretly wrote him, though she asked him not to write back. He'd given her his cell number, but she'd never called. As years passed, he'd been satisfied with his lot and mostly fulfilled.

When he went stateside on extended leave after the successful conclusion of an extremely dangerous mission, he didn't visit the farm or the family that no longer wanted him. Instead, he'd decided to visit the city that had always fascinated him growing up, the place where he could see himself living one day. Chicago. The Windy City.

And as fate would have it, that was where he met Carly. Being in special ops, he'd known better than to go and fall in love. But some things were inescapable. The instant he'd seen her, something had clicked inside him, as if a puzzle piece that had been long missing had finally been fit into place. They'd started out meeting up for coffee and then had gone on a few dates. They'd both fallen fast and furious. For the first time in his adult life, he'd experienced pure, unadulterated happiness. He'd realized there could be more to life than his military career.

Before he'd allowed himself to consider the repercussions, realizing he wanted to spend the rest of his life with her, he'd proposed. She'd joyfully accepted, and they'd planned a wedding for when he'd wrapped up his latest mission, which happened to coincide with the end of his enlistment. Luckily, he hadn't yet re-upped. Of course, she hadn't the faintest idea what he did for the army. He hadn't been allowed to tell her. But he'd vowed as soon as he completed this mission and his military service came to an end, he'd tell her everything. He'd leave his military career so he and Carly could marry and start a family here in Chicago. He'd figure out a civilian job soon enough.

Except life had something else in store for him: capture and torture, rescue and numerous horrendous injuries that would have ended his career. With burns over 60 percent of his body, the pain had been excruciating. Skin grafts and a medically induced coma had been part of what had saved him, but once he'd finally been allowed to regain consciousness, he'd almost wished he had died, as the army had at first believed. Scarred, disfigured, he'd believed Carly wouldn't want him now. Even if she had, he'd convinced himself he was no longer worthy.

Water under the bridge, or so he'd told himself. So great was his disfigurement and so much time had passed, he'd known he could never return to that happy, perfect time of his life. But he'd never stopped thinking about Carly, missing her with every fiber of his being.

Two years later, finally healed, he'd done a bit of internet searching. Carly appeared to have gotten over his loss and had moved on. She'd even recently changed her social media status to *In a Relationship.* Micha had also been surprised to learn she'd purchased the historic brick bungalow they'd longingly talked about owning once they were married. He'd recognized it from some of the photos she'd posted. Carly had gotten on with her life, as people do, while Micha felt as if he was treading water in the same place. With his military career over, he hadn't found a new direction for his life yet. All of his energy had been used to survive and heal, battling the twin demons of self-doubt and depression while missing Carly.

They should have had a life together, damn it. Instead, he'd lost two entire years. He told himself he just had to see her, one last time, and then maybe he could finally move on. Part of him suspected he'd known that was a lie even before he'd hopped a plane to Chicago.

She hadn't been difficult to find. He'd gone first to the hospital, hoping to see her arrive for work. He'd actually watched her from the parking lot, while sitting in his rental car, feeling like a creeper yet unable to help himself.

The first sight of her, striding across the pavement in her nurse's scrubs, had stolen the breath from his lungs. Carly, his Carly. Seeing her, he felt alive for the first time in two damn years.

He must have told himself a hundred times that he needed to go, get back on that plane and fly to Denver or LA, somewhere far enough that he wouldn't be tempted to disrupt her life. As far as she knew, he'd died in Baghdad two years ago. Maybe it was best to let things stay the way they were.

Except his heart, that traitorous thing that still beat strong and sure inside his chest, wouldn't let him. Somehow, he'd managed to stay away from her for three entire days, revisiting all their old haunts, hoping he'd run into her. To his utter disappointment, he hadn't.

Instead, he'd started watching her house. He told himself he just wanted to be certain she really was happy and, most important, safe. He'd learned about her father's and uncle's murders—in fact, that had been one of the major factors in his decision to check on her in person. If anything happened to Carly, Micha knew he'd lose his mind.

And then he'd been standing on the sidewalk down the street from her house, trying to decide whether or not to knock on her door, and she'd come out, clearly taking a walk and enjoying the beautiful spring day. Unable to resist, he'd begun trailing after her, taking care to keep himself hidden.

Until he'd given in to impulse and stepped out of the shadows and into the sunlight. And if that wasn't a metaphor for the part she played in his life, he didn't know what was.

Now, moments after making love, she'd looked him in the eye and told him she was meeting her boyfriend. He'd swallowed his pride and asked her not to go, partly because he had a lot to tell her, but mostly because he couldn't stand the thought of her with another man.

Whatever he'd expected when he'd found her again, it hadn't been this. And while he knew he really had no right to feel betrayed, he did, anyway. The only thing that tempered those feelings was imagining how Carly must feel, believing him dead these past two years, only to find out he wasn't. Talk about hurt and betrayal.

Back at his hotel, he took a shower and got dressed, trying to decide where to go for dinner. Lou Malnati's

Pizzeria sounded perfect, even though it, too, had been one of the places he and Carly used to go back in the day.

His cell phone rang just as he got into his car. Carly. His heart skipped a beat. He'd imagined by now she'd be having a meal with her boyfriend.

"Do you have any time this evening to talk?" she asked, defeat tingeing her voice. "It turns out my date tonight was canceled."

While it might be wrong, Micha allowed himself to feel relieved satisfaction. "Sure," he replied. "In fact, I was just about to drive up to Lou Malnati's. Do you want me to pick you up?"

She went silent while she considered his invitation. In his mind, he could see her, no doubt pacing while she tried to decide if their talk should be in public or not. In the end, the lure of deep-dish won out.

"I haven't been there in forever," she said. "And since I haven't eaten, pizza sounds great."

"I'll be there in fifteen minutes," he told her. He couldn't help but feel optimistic, not only because she was open to sharing a meal with him, but because she was also willing to hear him out.

He pulled up in front of her bungalow and parked. Carly came out before he even had time to kill the engine. Though it had only been a couple of hours since he'd seen her last, just the sight of her had his heart beating faster.

"Hi." She got into his rental car, glancing sideways at him. "I have to say, it still feels really weird to see you."

"Really weird isn't the reaction I'd hoped for," he countered.

Though she smiled faintly at that, she didn't reply.

Navigating Chicago's traffic felt comfortable, almost as if he'd never left. Staring out the window, appearing lost in thought, Carly didn't talk for the rest of the drive.

He knew better than to prod her. He'd let her go at her own pace.

She waited until they'd mostly demolished a large pie before sitting back and crossing her arms. "Explain," she demanded. "All of it, especially how you could allow me to believe you were dead."

Taking a deep breath, he nodded. "In the military, I worked in special ops. My job was to gather intelligence."

"Like a spy?"

"Sort of." He tried to keep his voice expressionless, to recount the story as if it had happened to someone else. "When I left you to go on that last mission, I was captured by a terrorist cell. They imprisoned me for six months." He decided not to mention the torture. Even now, he could hardly stand to even *think* about the things they'd done to him.

"Six months." She winced. "That's a long time. Did you escape or were you rescued?"

"They sent in a team to get me out, at the risk of their own lives." If he closed his eyes, he could still hear the gunfire, smell the smoke, hear the urgency in the man's voice who'd cut him free. There'd been shouting and smoke, ducking and dodging, as he'd tried to run on legs that could barely stand.

With his rescuer's help, they'd made it to the waiting chopper, which took off the second he'd been shoved inside.

They began to climb, amid heavy gunfire. Micha was in bad shape. He already knew that, but the expressions on the faces of the medics who began tending to him told him it might be worse than he'd thought.

And then they were hit.

Somehow, the chopper pilot had kept them aloft, taking them out of enemy territory. When they'd finally gone down, initial reports had indicated no survivors.

"I was badly burned and my back was broken. Some locals found me, unconscious, and got me to a hospital. I didn't have my dog tags and couldn't speak, so no one notified my commanding officer." He met her gaze, his own unflinching. "That's why you were notified of my death. I'd listed you as kin along with my parents."

Expression troubled, she nodded. The compassion in her bright blue eyes warmed his heart. "How long were you in that hospital before you were able to tell someone that you were an American?"

"I'm not sure. Months, I know. I was in and out of consciousness, they said. They did surgery and tried to patch me up as best they could, but no one believed I'd ever walk again."

Carly reached across the table and covered his hand with hers. "But you proved them wrong."

"I did. But not until I'd recovered enough to insist they notify the US base that I was there." In all this dark retelling, he could now offer the one bright spot in those terrible times. "Turns out I wasn't the only survivor of that chopper crash," he said. "Andy Shackleford, one of the team who'd rescued me, made it, though he lost his leg. And the medic who'd been taking care of me was also found alive. He had burns, too, and some broken bones, but all in all, he was in much better shape. Of course, he hadn't been held captive for six months, either."

Across from him, he could see Carly struggling to come to terms with what for her seemed like a complete rewrite of history. He ached to take her in his arms and hold her, not just to comfort her, but for himself, as well. He rarely spoke about what had happened to him, mainly because doing so brought it all back. The pain, the frustration, the urgent need to get back to the life he'd had before.

"Once the army finally got me stateside, I had multiple surgeries. I still wasn't given very optimistic odds as to whether I'd walk again, but I was determined." He took a deep breath and locked his gaze on hers. "Because of you, Carly."

Those words had her stiffening, her gaze gone cold as she removed her hand from over his. "You didn't even try to contact me, Micha. Not even once. You let me continue to think you were dead." She shook her head, the sheen of unshed tears in her eyes. "I grieved. Every single day. For weeks, for months, for *years*. Why, once you were able, didn't you reach out and let me know you were still alive?"

He considered his next words carefully, not sure he could explain properly. But he knew he had to try and, hopefully, by sharing honestly, he could gain her understanding. One thing these two years had given him was the ability to look back objectively.

"This was a low point in my life," he said haltingly. "I couldn't see past the darkness." Ashamed, he admitted the truth, something he'd never said out loud. "For a really awful period, I honestly considered taking my own life. My career—to which I dedicated everything—was over. I had scars, both physically and mentally. I didn't think you'd want me. I wasn't the same man at all."

"But you didn't even give me a choice." Carly pushed to her feet, refusing to meet his gaze. "I'd like you to take me home now," she said. "Thank you for explaining. Clearly I have a lot to think about."

Try as he might, he couldn't detect any lingering bit of sympathy in her expression. He'd given her nothing but the truth, so he'd done all he could.

He left enough cash on the table to pay the bill plus a tip, and did as she asked. When he pulled up in front of her house, she turned to eye him.

"You gave me quite a scare," she said. "Following me around these past six weeks." She got out of the car and he followed her.

"Six weeks?" Confused, he shook his head. "I've only been back a week. What are you talking about?"

She stared at him, her eyes wide. "I've had the sense that someone has been watching me for the last month and a half," she said slowly. "It had gotten to the point where I'd decided I might have to stop taking walks."

Immediately, he thought of her father's and uncle's murders. "Have you told someone? Your family? The police? Isn't your boyfriend Chicago PD?"

"Former boyfriend," she corrected. "And no, I haven't said anything about this to anyone. I'd planned to mention it to Harry tonight."

This time, he didn't even allow himself to react to the other man's name. "I've got some friends who can do some checking for me," he said. "Contacts in both the military special ops and the FBI. We'll see what they can dig up."

"Knock yourself out," Carly said, turning and walking back into her house.

Micha sat in his rental car until she'd made it inside and closed the front door. He'd start making phone calls immediately once he got back to his hotel room. And he'd be back to see her again tomorrow, and the day after that, every day for as long as she'd let him.

Just like before, being around Carly made him toss all his careful plans out the window. Except this time, finished with the military, he actually could follow through and do what he should have done before—court Carly properly and finally make her his wife.

But first, he needed to concentrate on keeping her safe.

Unsettled, Carly had felt like a jittery mess all through dinner. Despite being a big fan of Lou Malnati's, she'd had to force herself to eat. The deep-dish was delicious, as always, but it would have been far too easy to allow herself to fall back into what had once been a comfortable sort of old habit with Micha.

Except two long years had gone by. She didn't know this man anymore. And he didn't know her. She was no longer the same wide-eyed innocent she'd been before. After losing Micha, she'd resigned herself to living a life without finding the same kind of passionate love. Harry had confided in her that he felt the same, and if this easy companionable friendship they shared was the best they could do, so be it.

In retrospect, she understood why he had found it so easy to let her go.

Micha was another story. When she got out of his rental car, it had taken every ounce of self-restraint she possessed to keep from inviting him inside. Too easily, she could imagine what would happen if she let him kiss her again. What she *wanted*, she admitted. But she kept her spine straight and marched up her sidewalk, letting herself into her house and locking him out.

When Micha had informed her that he'd only been in town a week, her first reaction had been a shiver of fear snaking up her spine. How could that be, when the feeling of being watched had started over a month ago?

Then, as usual, she began to question herself. Maybe she'd only imagined it. Perhaps it had been paranoia, brought on by her father's and uncle's murders.

As if Micha knew her thoughts, her phone rang and his number came up on caller ID. Her heart began to pound as she answered. "Are you calling from out front?" she asked, her resolve rapidly weakening. If he was, she suspected she'd go open the front door and invite him in.

"No, I'm driving back to the hotel," he responded. "But I have a few more questions if you don't mind."

She closed her eyes, full of both thankfulness and regret. "Go ahead. What do you need to know?"

"Do the police have any leads on your father's killer?"

"No," she answered. "And I doubt one has anything to do with the other. I wasn't involved in my father and uncle's business. They were shot outside their offices. My cousin January is engaged to one of the police detectives, named Sean Stafford. He'd tell us if there'd been any new leads."

"Good to know. I'll touch base with him, too. Since I'm going to be around awhile, I might as well do some digging."

Surprised, she gripped the phone tightly. "Are you? Going to be around awhile, that is?"

"Yes, I am."

"Why?" She couldn't resist asking. If he had expectations, she might as well level with him.

"You know why." The slow smile in his voice lit a simmer deep inside her. "But I'll spell it out, anyway. We were meant to be together, Carly Colton. I won't be going anywhere again. Not this time."

"Slow your roll," she replied. "It seems to me like you're taking a lot for granted." She held up her ringless hand, even though he couldn't see the gesture. "We're no longer engaged." She saw no need to tell him his ring no longer hung on a chain nestled between her breasts, close to her heart. In fact, she'd only made the decision to take it off last week.

"I understand," he said softly. "But I'd like to ask you to give me another chance."

"I'll have to think about that," she said. "Do you have any other questions?"

"Not right now," he said, sounding far too cheerful. "I'll talk to you later." And he ended the call.

Putting her phone down, she strode into her kitchen, her hands shaking as she fumbled to get a drink out of the fridge.

So much had happened in the span of one day. Her head ached nearly as much as her heart.

Micha was alive. She'd always believed she'd buried most of her heart with him. Now he, instead of Harry, would be looking into the possibility that she might have a stalker.

It felt good, she acknowledged, giving over some of her fear to someone else. Normally, such a thing would make an independent woman like her bristle. But ever since her father and his twin had been brutally murdered, she and the rest of her family had been on edge. Being a Colton meant their family was well known and easily identified. Like any prominent family, they had enemies as well as friends.

Since she had to work an early shift tomorrow, she knew she'd need to turn in early. But with everything that had happened, she was way too keyed up to go to sleep any time soon.

In just one day, her reality had completely changed. Everything she'd believed to be true for the last two years had been completely upended. The weirdest part of discovering that Micha hadn't died was that the discovery did nothing to dispel that small knot of grief she carried around with her. Now, instead of mourning his loss, she supposed she grieved what might have been.

Seeing him had been a shock. In fact, she still hadn't processed or sorted through all the tangled emotions that his resurrection had caused. Making love with him had been a huge mistake, a kind of knee-jerk reaction to the shocking sight and touch and feel of him. Her visceral reaction had come without thought, without reason. Now, after the fact, she understood it had been something she should never have allowed to happen.

She'd need to make sure it didn't occur again. Because she knew if she let it, she'd be risking her heart.

She'd finally gotten over losing him. Not completely—she'd begun to see such a thing only faded in small doses, with waves of grief overwhelming her unexpectedly. She'd gone from a period of being unable to function, to attending grief counseling. There, she'd learned how to claw her way out of the dark pit of despair and begun making plans to be able to face her new reality.

Now her new reality had been blown to rubble. She wasn't sure she was emotionally equipped to deal with that kind of fallout again.

Micha seemed to think they could pick up right where they'd left off. As if he hadn't broken her heart. She wasn't certain she could risk feeling that way again. She didn't think she'd survive.

Sitting at her kitchen table sipping on her drink, she tried to adjust to her new reality. It sure wasn't easy.

A rattle and a thud outside made her go still. It seemed to have come from her backyard. Was someone trying to break into her house?

Heart pounding, she hurried into the kitchen. She double-checked the dead bolt, making sure it was locked. Staying away from the window, she stood still and listened, praying the sound didn't come again. She'd been meaning to get a lock for that back gate and now she seriously wished she had.

Outside, the wind had picked up. Maybe that had caused the noise. She'd left her phone in the living room. She ran back and grabbed it, trying to decide whether to call 911 or Micha.

Micha? Thoroughly annoyed with herself, she had to admit having him around made her feel safe.

Another thud, louder this time. Deciding not to mess around, she dialed 911. Feeling slightly foolish, she told the dispatcher she thought someone might be trying to break into her house. They promised to send someone as soon as they could. Carly hung up, nerves still on edge. She had to fight the urge to call Micha, which annoyed her to no end. The man had barely been back in her life for half a day. She'd survived on her own for the last two years. She'd managed by herself, thank you very much. And she'd continue to do so now.

A squad car pulled up fifteen minutes later. Carly stayed inside, nervously waiting to see if they found anything. She could hear them moving around in her backyard and saw their flashlights.

Finally, they knocked on her back door. She opened it to find two of Chicago PD's finest standing on her back stoop.

"We did a complete search of the premises, ma'am," one of the officers said. "No intruder turned up, but we think we located the source of the noises you were hearing. We found a stray dog trying to get under your storage shed. She's pretty emaciated. Since Animal Control is closed, we'll send them around to pick her up in the morning, if that's okay."

"A stray dog?" Lately, she'd been thinking a lot about getting a dog. She'd intended to go up to the pound and pick out an older pup but wasn't sure if her occasional twelve-hour shifts were conducive to having a pet. "Is she friendly?"

"She is," the other officer chimed in, grinning. "I

had a sandwich I'd picked up for lunch and didn't get a chance to eat. She gulped that thing down. Maybe put some water out for her?"

"Can I see her?" Carly asked instead. Maybe this dog, a homeless stray, was meant to be hers.

"There." The second guy pointed with his flashlight. "She's standing right there, watching us."

Peering into the darkness, Carly spotted a thin, black dog watching them intently, her eyes gleaming in the flashlight beam. Crouching down, acting on instinct, Carly spoke softly, attempting to call the animal over. "Come here, pretty girl," she crooned. "Would you like to come inside out of the cold?"

To her surprise, the dog inched closer.

"I don't have any dog food." Distressed, Carly continued to crouch in what she hoped was a nonthreatening way. "Is it okay if I give her chicken or beef?" As the dog slunk closer, Carly could see all of the canine's ribs and backbone. "It looks like it's been a really long time since she had a good meal."

"Sure. Anything healthy will help fill up her belly. Are you planning on keeping her?"

Startled, Carly look up. "I… I've been thinking about getting a dog, so I guess I am. Would that be allowed?"

"You'll need to have her scanned for a microchip," Officer One said. "You can do that at any veterinary office or you can bring her by the shelter when it opens. If there's no chip, talk to the shelter about them letting her serve out her stray hold with you instead of there."

"Stray hold?"

Officer Two shrugged. "Just in case someone might be looking for her. You never know."

That made sense.

"I want to do everything by the book," Carly said. "Thank you so much for checking everything out for me."

"No problem." Officer One touched his hat. "We were all sorry to hear about your father and uncle."

Carly murmured a thank-you. Even to this day, she often found herself startled by how many people had known the two elder Coltons.

"We'll close the gate behind us," Officer One said. "It was open, which is how the dog got in."

She thanked them again, standing on her back stoop while they walked away. The dog, she noticed, turned her head to watch them go, but made no move to follow. Carly crouched down again. "Come here, baby girl," she crooned. "Let's get you inside where it's warm. I'll find something you can eat, I promise."

To her shock, the dog slunk closer, posture wary, but nonthreatening. As the skeletal creature climbed the back-stoop steps, Carly almost cried. Taking care not to make any sudden moves, Carly opened the back door and stepped inside, still calling the dog to her. A full tummy and a warm bath might go wonders to helping the poor animal feel better.

Chapter 3

Micha checked the time to make sure it wasn't too late, and then called the cell phone number of one of his former combat buddies, Charlie Crenshaw, now working stateside for the Chicago PD.

"Hey, man," Charlie said once Micha identified himself. "It's great to hear from you. Last I heard, you were laid up in the hospital over at Walter Reed. Are you all better now?"

"I am. Actually, I'm back in Chicago." He took a deep breath. "As a matter of fact, I wanted to check and see what kind of progress has been made on the Colton murders. Since you're the only Chicago cop I know, I figured you'd be a good place to start."

"Why?" Charlie asked, sounding more confused than suspicious.

"I used to be engaged to Ernest Colton's daughter, Carly. She's had the feeling that someone's been following her for the past six weeks and is worried it might be related to the murder."

"Okay, I get it." Charlie cleared his throat. "I trust you, Micha, so what I'm about to tell you can't go any further. All right?"

"Agreed," Micha responded immediately. "I'll keep my mouth shut until you give me the go-ahead."

"Good, because the chief wants to talk to the Colton family before the news gets out to the general public. There's been a second set of killings, with the same MO as the twin Colton men, though they weren't twins. Right now, the theory is serial killers, and the FBI has been called in to help investigate."

"Damn." Micha whistled. "Now I'm even more worried about Carly being followed."

"Give her my number and tell her to call me tomorrow. Once I've received an official complaint from her, I can request a protective detail."

Relieved, Micha thanked him. "I'll pass the info along to her. Is it okay if I let her know about the new murders?"

"We'd prefer to notify the family first, but if you think she can keep it to herself, go for it. Just remember, you didn't hear it from me."

"Got it," Micha replied. "Thanks again, man."

"No problem. Let me know when you want to grab a beer and catch up. I work days, so I'm off most nights."

Micha promised to touch base again soon and ended the call. He sat for a moment, staring at his phone, and ultimately decided to wait until the morning to talk to

Carly. He didn't want to worry her and possibly cause her to lose sleep.

He wondered if she had to work tomorrow. Since he had no idea of her schedule and hadn't thought to ask, he figured he'd simply show up at her house with coffee in the morning. They could talk and he'd tell her what he'd learned from his friend. Then, if she was open to it, they could make plans to meet up later.

That night, he slept better than he had in years. He'd come back to the vibrant place his soul had always recognized was his true home, and the woman he'd known from the moment he met her was meant to be his.

He was up bright and early the next morning. On his way to her place, he stopped at her favorite coffee shop and got them both lattes, hers with extra whip. He texted her as soon as he got into his car, letting her know he had coffee and asking if it was okay if he gave it to her personally.

A few seconds later, she texted back. Sure, but I have to leave for work in fifteen minutes. I don't have a lot of time.

He made it to her house in five and rang her doorbell with his elbow, a coffee in each hand. She answered a moment later, her blond hair up in a ponytail and wearing pale blue scrubs.

"Good morning," he said, handing her the coffee and drinking her in with his eyes.

Accepting it with a half smile, she thanked him.

"How about I drive you to work this morning?" he asked, going on impulse. "That would give us more time to talk."

She regarded him silently. "But then I wouldn't have a way to get home when my shift is over."

The fact that she didn't decline outright gave him hope.

"I'll pick you up," he offered. "Maybe we can go get a bite to eat or something."

"I can't. I have to come home and take a stray dog to the vet. I'm having her scanned for a microchip, and if she doesn't have one, I'm having her checked out."

A dog. His heart squeezed. Back when they were engaged, he'd hoped to get a dog together as soon as they were married, though he'd never brought it up. "Can I meet her?" he asked, a little too much emotion in his voice.

Carly glanced at her watch. "I don't have time. I've got her a spot all fixed up in my kitchen."

He nodded. "Okay. Maybe later. Now how about that ride to work?"

"I don't know." She regarded him dubiously. "There's been a lot of water under the bridge in two years, Micha. We can't simply pick up where we left off before."

Trying to hide his disappointment, he nodded. "That makes sense. How about we start out as friends instead?"

"Friends?"

Her skeptical tone made him grin. "Sure. And as your friend, how about I drive you to work and pick you up later? I'd love to meet your new dog."

"As long as you understand that what happened between us yesterday can't happen again."

Though this took him by surprise, he realized it wasn't entirely unexpected. If Carly wanted to take things slow, then that's what they'd do. "I understand," he told her. "Now if you're ready, let's go. I have something important I want to tell you."

"Give me just a minute." Turning, she let herself back into her house, leaving him standing on the front porch. He sipped his coffee while he waited, wondering how he could still feel so strongly for her while she apparently did not feel the same way. It figured, because time had basically stood still for him. He'd been completely disconnected from the regular world for a long time, both while being held captive and then while in the hospital recovering. Despite the aching certainty that he'd finally landed right back where he belonged, he knew he'd need to give Carly time.

She reappeared a moment later, letting herself out and locking the door behind her. "I'm a little worried about Bridget," she mused as she walked with him to his rental car. "She's been a stray for a while and I'm guessing she's not housebroken. I made an area near the back door with newspaper, so I'm hoping she'll use that. If not, then I'll just clean it up."

"How long are you working today?" he asked.

"Unless something happens, I'm only working eight to five," she replied, getting into his car. "The vet is open until six, so I have to rush home and get Bridget." She eyed him. "I don't have a collar or leash or even proper dog bowls. Oh, and I need dog food. Would you mind picking some up for me and I'll reimburse you?"

"Of course I don't mind. What about a dog bed? What size dog is she?"

"Maybe forty or fifty pounds, I'm guessing." Swallowing, she buckled herself in. "Thank you. I really appreciate your help."

He noticed the way she glanced around her neighborhood, an unmistakable hint of apprehension in the stiff set of her shoulders.

"Are you okay?" he asked.

Her sideways glance and rueful smile told him she wasn't sure. "I don't know," she admitted. "It's been so weird lately. I'm actually glad you offered to take me to work."

"Do you see anything out of the ordinary?" Curious, he started the engine and pulled away.

"No, not really. I just can't shake the feeling that someone is watching me."

"Then they would have seen me on your front porch," he pointed out. "Maybe if they realize I'm going to be showing up a lot, they'll move on to something else and leave you alone."

She sighed, but didn't argue with his statement, which he found encouraging.

"I called one of my buddies who works for Chicago PD," he said. "I wanted to know if they'd had any leads in your father's and uncle's murders."

This made her sit up straighter. "Oh, yeah? What did he say?"

"Well, Chicago PD wants to notify your family first. I think they're planning on doing that today." He shrugged. "I feel you should be told because this might have some bearing on your own safety, especially since you've been feeling as if someone is watching you."

He took a deep breath. "Are you okay with knowing before but not saying anything until your mother and aunt are told? Because my friend will have my head on a platter if it gets out that he told me."

"Yes, I am. I have to work, anyway. Why so much secrecy?"

"There's been another double murder, done in a similar manner to your dad and uncle. Now they're thinking serial killer, and they've called in the FBI to assist."

She stared at him, her mouth slightly open. "A serial killer?" she asked. "For real?"

"That's the working theory right now."

"What's the common thread?" Arms crossed, she eyed him. "Don't serial killers usually have a type they kill? Is it because my dad and uncle Alfred were twins?"

"I don't know. My contact didn't elaborate. I'm guessing you'll find out more info once the police department informs your family."

Slowly, she shook her head. "They're going to flip. I hope they tell Heath first, so he can break the news to my mother and aunt."

"There's more. I told my friend how you felt someone might be following you." He handed her a slip of paper with Charlie's number. "He needs you to call him and make an official report. Once they have that, they can start protecting you."

Accepting the paper, she frowned. "What do you mean by that? Are you talking about a bodyguard or something?"

"No. You have me for that." He smiled. "More like they can send a patrol car around your neighborhood more often. Maybe have someone parked out in front of your house to keep an eye on things. I doubt they have the resources to do that 24/7, but because of your connection to the murders, it's better to be safe than sorry."

He saw the moment she realized. "You think the killer might be targeting me." A statement rather than a question, but he knew to tread carefully.

"I think we don't need to take any chances." A reasonable response. "No need to panic, but just continue to be careful."

They pulled up to the hospital. He parked at the curb to let her out. "I'll pick you up here at five."

Gaze locked on his, she slowly nodded. "Okay. If I can get off earlier, I'll text you. I really need to check Bridget for a microchip."

He watched her walk away, her sweet round behind swaying in her scrubs. Unsurprisingly, he had to push away a surge of raw lust. Though he regretted the way things had gotten out of hand between them the day before, if anything the way they'd combusted so quickly told him he still had a chance of making things right with her. He'd just need to be careful to take it slow. The last thing he wanted was for Carly to cut and run.

Now he just needed to find out if someone was stalking her and why. He hoped it had no ties whatsoever to her father's murder and the two latest killings, but no way in hell was he taking a chance. Not when Carly's life might depend on it.

Carly called Micha's police friend as soon as she got inside. She knew if she waited until she started her shift, she probably wouldn't have a chance.

The officer picked up on the second ring. "Charlie Crenshaw."

As soon as she identified herself, his casual tone became more professional. When she told him she'd had the feeling someone had been watching her for the last six weeks, he asked her several pointed questions.

"No, I haven't actually seen anyone. No, no one has sent me weird emails or written messages. No vandalism or anything like that." She thought of last night, calling 911 because of the strange noises she'd heard, but figured that would already be on record. And after all, the sound had turned out to be a stray dog.

Listening to herself, even she began to have doubts.

To his credit, when she'd started to feel like she might have been imagining the feeling of being watched, Officer Crenshaw promised to file a report.

"What does that mean?" she asked. "Where do we go from here?"

"We'll start by having officers patrol your street more often," he replied. "More frequent drive-bys might help."

"Thank you." Relieved that he hadn't said she'd be put under constant surveillance, she ended the call. Since she wasn't even positive about being watched, she would have been extremely uncomfortable losing that much privacy. Hearing about the two new murders gave her pause, though. She wondered who would be notifying her and when. Most likely, her eldest brother, Heath, would be tasked with that chore. As president of Colton Connections, he'd become unofficial head of the family with the two eldest Coltons' deaths.

Expecting his call, she debated whether or not to give him the news about Micha over the phone. It might be easier to do that in person.

Instead of a call, Heath sent her a text. Sunday, cookout in Oak Park at one. Can you make it?

Since she was always off Sundays unless she switched shifts with someone, she texted back in the affirmative. Apparently, Heath wanted to give his news in person, as well.

Things were pretty quiet in the NICU, relatively speaking. Carly loved working with infants and had a soft spot for the vulnerable preemies. She was grateful for days like this, when she could take care of her charges without rushing from one incident to another. She even had time to chat with a few of the parents, many of whom she'd gotten to know well.

When her lunchtime arrived, she smiled at the nurse who'd come to relieve her so she could eat. They all knew better than to comment on the calm day—to do so practically guaranteed it would end.

She headed down to the cafeteria, planning to grab a salad and her personal weakness, a diet ginger ale. The cafeteria always made sure to keep some in stock for her. As she rounded the corner, she stopped short, stunned at the sight of Micha sitting on a bench just outside the cafeteria entrance.

After the first initial rush of seeing him, she frowned. "Now I'm really beginning to feel like you're stalking me," she said. "What are you doing here?"

He stood. "I thought you might want to have lunch." He held up a bag. Fontano's Subs. Her favorite.

"You remembered." Touched, despite herself, she let her gaze search his face.

"Yep. Homemade meatball with red sauce." He grinned. "And corned beef for me."

For just an instant, the force of his smile took her back. Micha had used to meet her for lunch all the time when they'd first gotten engaged. Sometimes he'd bring her a treat, sometimes they'd eat cafeteria food. What had been important was spending the time together. She'd missed their lunches a lot once he'd gone back to active duty.

Now, though, two years had passed. She'd grown used to eating her lunch alone. She wasn't sure her heart could withstand taking a giant step back into the past.

Noticing her hesitation, his warm smile dimmed. "I can go," he said. "If you want me to."

Eyeing the paper sack, she relented. "I'm sorry. You can stay. You just caught me off guard. Let me go get us a couple of drinks and we'll grab a table."

"In the courtyard?" He nodded toward the outside eating area. With the warm weather, a lot of people took advantage of the chance to get out.

She shrugged. "Sure, if you can find a table. If not, inside's fine."

Inside, she grabbed her diet ginger ale and a cola for him. After paying, she made her way outside, spotting Micha at a two-seat table under a small umbrella.

"Wow," she commented, handing him his drink and taking a seat. "You really lucked out."

Smiling again, he opened the paper bag. She inhaled deeply, her mouth beginning to water at the wonderful scents that escaped. Around them, she saw a couple of her coworkers giving her curious looks, but she ignored them.

As soon as he handed her the meatball sub, she unwrapped it and took a huge bite. The flavor had her humming low in her throat with pleasure. She looked up to find him staring at her, his warm gaze making her face heat.

"I haven't had one of these in a long time," she said, going for a second bite. "So good." She rolled her eyes.

Laughing, he unwrapped his own sub. "I love your gusto," he murmured, before digging into his corned beef.

Love. She pretended not to notice his choice of words. "I talked to Officer Crenshaw," she told him. "He's promised to make sure there are extra patrols on my street."

He nodded. "Any word from your family? I'm assuming by now someone will have notified them about the new set of murders."

"Heath has called a family meeting on Sunday," she replied. "I'm guessing he wants to let us know in person."

"Are you going to tell them about me?" he asked softly.

She finished her sandwich, wadding up the wrapper, and then took a deep sip of her ginger ale. "Yes. That's another thing best done face-to-face, I think. I'll tell them Sunday."

Now that they'd both finished eating, she checked her watch. "I don't want to hog this table," she said, pushing to her feet. "I've only got a few minutes before I need to get back to work. Thank you for bringing me lunch."

"You're welcome." He followed her back into the hall. "When's your next day off?"

"Sunday."

"May I see you?" he asked.

"I'm going up to Oak Park, remember?" she replied.

"After? How about dinner?"

Shaking her head, she considered. "I'll let you know."

"Fair enough," he replied. "I'll pick you up after you get off." And then he walked away without a backward glance.

She watched him go, her emotions conflicted. Once, he would have kissed her goodbye. Though she certainly knew she couldn't return to that past, to that place in time, she missed that kiss with a sudden aching yearning.

The rest of her shift passed uneventfully, a blessing and a respite in a nurse's day. Carly had chosen pediatric nursing early in her career, though she had to do a required stint as an ER nurse before moving to the children's floor. She'd gravitated toward the NICU, where the most seriously ill or premature babies were cared for.

She loved her job, despite getting her heart broken on those awful days when they lost a patient. She always cried, as did most of the other nurses and doctors on her team.

Shaking her head to clear away those dark thoughts, Carly finished up her charts and got ready to hand everything over to the night nurse who'd be arriving soon. She had to admit the thought of seeing Micha again made her heart beat a little faster. Though she knew it might be foolish, she couldn't contain the quick rush of joy she felt seeing him pull up in front of the hospital entrance and wave to her.

Getting in the car also brought back an odd combination of nostalgia and uncertainty. To cover, she checked her watch. "We've got to hurry. I don't want to be late for the vet appointment."

"Okay. All your supplies are in bags in the back seat."

She turned to look. "Thank you. I'll write you a check later." Locating the collar and leash, she removed the price tags. "I'm going to need these."

Once they reached her house, she jumped out of the car. "I'll be right back." As she unlocked her door, she wondered how much damage the stray dog might have done. She'd barricaded her in the kitchen with an old comforter to sleep on, food and water in old plastic bowls, and she'd also laid out newspaper near the back door in case of accidents.

When she stepped inside, her house seemed quiet. A bit apprehensive, she walked back to the kitchen, moving away the old baby gate she'd pulled from the garage.

Bridget sat on the old comforter where she'd made a nest. She eyed Carly warily, though her ears remained up and her tail wagged. She'd eaten all the boiled chicken, but as far as Carly could tell, there'd been no potty accidents.

Moving slowly, Carly crouched down and reached to put on the collar. To her surprise, the dog lowered her head and allowed this. Since Carly had already attached the leash, she stood and gave a little tug to see if Bridget would follow her.

The dog slowly got to her feet and did.

Carly led her outside, locking the door behind her. Signaling to Micha to wait, she took Bridget to the side grass, waiting while the dog relieved herself.

"How about cars, girl?" Carly asked, leading the

dog over to the back door. When she opened it, Bridget promptly jumped inside.

"She's been someone's pet," Carly mused, climbing into the front passenger seat. "She's clearly used to walking on a leash and riding in cars. I don't know how long she's been on her own or why, but if someone is missing her, I hope we can find them."

"Hopefully, she's chipped," Micha said. "If not, you can check with shelters. Plus there are usually lost-dog groups on social media."

Though Carly nodded, she couldn't help but feel a twinge of disappointment. Truly, she felt as if Bridget was meant to be her dog. She guessed she'd just have to wait and see.

Inside the vet clinic, despite two other clients and their dogs waiting, Bridget stayed close to Carly, sitting with her side pressed against Carly's leg and her head down. She ignored Micha and the other two dogs.

Once they were taken back to an examination room, Carly explained how she'd come to be there with Bridget. The vet tech, a young woman with purple hair and a broad smile, went and got a microchip scanner and waved it over the dog's neck and shoulder areas. The device beeped.

"We have a chip," the tech announced. "We'll contact the chip company and get information on the dog's owner."

Heaven help her, Carly thought she might cry. She managed to nod, all the while continuing to stroke Bridget's soft fur. "Thank you," she said. Micha squeezed her shoulder, as if he understood her inner turmoil.

"There's no sense in doing any vaccinations or exam yet," the young woman continued. "You should wait until we hear back from the dog's owner. There's no charge for today."

"Okay." Deflated, Carly took Bridget's leash and headed outside, blinking back tears. Silently, she loaded the dog into the back seat of Micha's rental car, before climbing in the front and buckling herself in.

"It's going to be all right," Micha said as he got in on the driver's side. "You did a good thing. Gave the dog shelter and now she's on her way to being reunited with her owner."

Carly nodded, keeping her face averted while she struggled to get her emotions under control.

"You really wanted to keep her, didn't you?" Micha asked, touching her lightly on the arm.

"I did." Squaring her shoulders, Carly turned to eye Bridget, now curled up on the back seat. "But I'm glad she has a home. With me."

Back when they'd been together, they'd never discussed having or not having a pet. They'd talked about dreams and values and how many children they'd like to have, but not about cats versus dogs versus pet-free. In fact, until recently, the closest thing Carly had to a pet had been a squirrel that lived in the large oak tree outside her kitchen window.

Curious, she eyed Micha. "What about you? Do you have any pets?"

He shook his head. "No. Up until now, it's been military and then hospitals. But I grew up with dogs." Glancing at Bridget in the back seat, he smiled. "I like yours."

"Thanks," she replied. "I like her, too."

As they pulled up in front of her house, Micha didn't say anything but she could tell from the hopeful look in his eyes that he wanted her to ask him in.

"I appreciate the ride," she said instead. "It was good to see you. But it's been a long day and I want to give Bridget a bath and feed her, plus start taking her out on the leash to see how she does."

He nodded. "Okay." Hesitating, he glanced up and down the street. "Stay safe."

"You, too."

Puttering around her house, Carly found herself constantly reaching to pet her dog. Bridget seemed reluctant to leave her side. She suffered through her bath with a kind of quiet dignity, ate her bowl of kibble with gusto and curled up on the couch with her head resting on Carly's lap while they watched TV. After, Carly took Bridget outside on the leash to relieve herself. Once she had, they came inside and Carly gave her a treat as a reward.

"Ready to go to bed, girl?" Carly asked. Bridget immediately began wagging her tail as if she understood. Heart lighter than it had been in days, Carly led the way back to her bedroom.

Carly had placed the brand-new dog bed on the floor near her nightstand and when the time came to turn in for the night, she showed Bridget where she should sleep. To her surprise, the pup seemed to understand immediately and curled up there with a soft grunt. Closing her eyes, she promptly went to sleep.

After taking a couple of pictures with her phone, Carly resisted the urge to text them to Micha. Instead, she washed her face, brushed her teeth and got into bed. Turning out the light, she drifted off to sleep.

The vet clinic called early the next morning. "I'm afraid I have some bad news on the owner of the stray dog you found," the caller said. "We've located the previous owner and learned he is deceased. His daughter stated she does not want the dog."

Somehow, Carly managed to restrain herself. "I'm sorry to hear that," she said. "That means I can keep her, right?"

"Yes, you can. Or you can drop her off at the shelter if you prefer."

Glancing at Bridget, sleeping in a stray patch of sunlight, Carly grinned. "That's not happening. She's mine now. I guess I need to make another appointment to get her vetting done."

They settled on a date and time and Carly ended the call. She walked over to her new dog and bent down, crooning softly as she reached out to pet her. "You're not going anywhere, baby girl."

Bridget eyed her, yawned and then went back to sleep.

Carly got up and started dancing around her kitchen. While she found it sad that Bridget's owner had died and unbelievable that his daughter hadn't wanted the dog, Carly couldn't help but rejoice in the knowledge that she got to keep her.

Impulsively, Carly grabbed her phone and punched in Micha's number. He answered immediately, his kind, husky-voiced greeting generating a warmth deep inside her. Talking quickly, she told him the news. "So now I really have a dog," she concluded. "I made another vet appointment to get her checked out."

"Congratulations. I wish I was there to celebrate with you."

She caught her breath, her heart skipping, any words she might have said caught in her throat.

"Too fast?" he asked.

"Kind of. Yes."

Quickly, he changed the subject. "Are we still on for dinner Sunday night?"

Again, she hesitated. "I'll probably be eating a huge meal over at the cookout, so I doubt I'll be hungry."

"I get that. Maybe we can just grab a cup of coffee."

"Micha…"

She could picture him steeling himself. "Yes?"

"I know we agreed we'd try to be friends for now, but I think maybe this is moving way too fast."

"Hey, it's just coffee." His quiet laugh sounded forced. "Actually, I just want to see you."

His words and the husky tone to his voice had warmth unfurling inside her. Was she really that weak?

While resistant, she considered the idea. "We really should give each other a few days' space," she replied.

"Please. We can do whatever you want. Even if you just want to sit outside in your backyard and watch your dog play."

The quiet plea in his husky voice made her relent. Once, she'd never been able to deny him anything. "Look, I've got to head in to work. I'll call you when I'm on my way home from Oak Park tomorrow," she said. "We can figure out something."

Murmuring assent, he ended the call. Staring at her

phone, Carly wondered how it was possible to miss someone so badly when her emotions were all over the place. Losing him had shattered her. She wasn't sure she wanted to set herself up to be destroyed again.

Chapter 4

After ending the call, Micha rejoiced—just a little—at the fact that Carly had actually relented and decided to see him Sunday after her family get-together. Even talking to her on the phone affected him. Listening to the unabashed joy and excitement in Carly's voice as she'd told him about her new dog, his heart had squeezed. He ached for her. Hearing her sweet, sexy voice over the phone wasn't enough. He wanted to be there to share in her happiness, to take her in his arms and dance around her kitchen the way she always did when she was happy. He could see it as clearly as if he was there.

Beautiful, sexy, sweet and smart Carly. The back of his throat stung with emotion. Whatever emotion she experienced, she did with gusto. Her joy was infectious, infusing him with hope for a brighter world. He had no idea how she did it, but merely by her existence, Carly made him want to be a better person. Worthy of someone as special as her.

At this very moment, there were two things Micha craved in this world. The first was to keep Carly safe. After that, the second would be for her to finally understand that they were truly meant to be together.

She belonged with him and he belonged with her. No terrorists or helicopter crash, burns or long convalescence could take that away from them. He felt it deep in his soul. Once, Carly had felt it, too. Their connection had been instant and deep, searing them forever.

Two years and a huge miscommunication had separated them, driven a wedge in between them. Yet when he'd first seen her, every emotion had come rushing back, filling him with love and desire. And Carly had felt the same things, too. They'd devoured each other, fallen into each other's arms as if no time had passed since they'd been apart.

Imprisonment, horrific injuries and learning she'd been wrongfully notified of his death had conspired to keep them apart. He'd almost let those things and two years apart change him, letting himself believe that he could continue in life without her. Until he'd actually caught sight of her once more and realized how wrong he'd been.

Micha had never been a poetic man. He considered himself a realist, pragmatic and grounded. Except when it came to her. Carly changed everything. He had no doubt that they were each half of the same soul, destined to be together for as long as they drew breath.

He knew she would realize this eventually, he just

didn't know when. He knew he had to go slowly, cautiously, so he didn't scare her away. She held the pain and grief she'd been through wrapped around her like a shield. Regaining her trust would only be accomplished slowly. He knew he'd have to resist every impulse to rush things.

As for keeping her safe, at least Chicago PD had gotten involved. While a start, that wasn't nearly enough, so Micha had decided he would become her personal bodyguard and do his best to keep her safe. Considering that he didn't want to freak her out, he planned to do much of that as quietly as possible in the background.

Since he knew he'd be staying in Chicago, he needed to look for a place to rent. His only real criteria would be the location—he wanted to live near Carly. In Hyde Park, if possible.

He figured he'd ask her if she'd mind going with him to look. After all, she'd lived in the city and knew all the good areas as well as places to avoid. He'd bring that up Sunday night when he saw her.

Saturday had a completely different traffic pattern than the days of the week.

With little to do while Carly was at work, Micha drove by her house, with the idea of searching the neighborhood looking for For Rent signs.

He slowed as he approached her place. A white, windowless van was parked at the curb in front. Other than that, the neighborhood appeared quiet.

Telling himself a vehicle like this was nothing out of the ordinary, nevertheless he reduced speed even more. That was when he saw the guy coming out from Carly's backyard. He wore a dark hoodie, too warm for such a nice day, black jeans and a baseball cap pulled low. His furtive movements combined with his odd attire set off all sorts of alarm bells.

Was this the guy who had been stalking Carly? Did he have something to do with the murders of Carly's father and uncle?

Pulling up behind the van, Micha jumped out. He intercepted the intruder halfway between the fence and the sidewalk. "Can I help you?" he asked, as if he actually owned the place.

The guy looked up, clearly startled. Micha caught a glimpse of a short, reddish brown beard.

Instead of responding, the man took off running. Not for the van, but down the sidewalk. Micha ran after him, wondering if he might actually be one of Carly's neighbors. That would definitely explain her feeling of being watched for a good while.

But no, instead of dashing into one of the other houses, the guy kept running. Micha heard the sound of a vehicle starting. He glanced over his shoulder, realizing too late that there had been someone else at the wheel inside the parked vehicle. The runner had an accomplice, who was driving the white van.

And it was headed directly toward Micha.

Turning, Micha faced the van and waited. If it swerved up onto the sidewalk, he planned to jump left, behind the wide trunk of an old oak tree.

Instead, it barreled past him, screeching to a halt long enough for the man Micha had been pursuing to jump in. Once he had, it roared off, running a stop sign before disappearing around the corner.

"Damn." Micha grabbed his phone and called Charlie Crenshaw. His friend picked up immediately. Once Micha relayed what had happened, Charlie promised to send two officers to Carly's house right away.

Jogging back down the street, Micha waited by his rental car. He dialed Carly's number, aware she probably couldn't take the call while working. As he'd suspected, his call went directly to voice mail. Not wanting to unduly alarm her, he simply left a message asking her to call him.

Dragging his hand through his hair, Micha couldn't shake the feeling that he'd failed. He should have tackled that guy, taken him down and held him until the police arrived.

A moment later, a squad car pulled up. Micha told the officers everything he knew. "No, I didn't think to get the license plate number," he said. "Everything happened really fast."

"All right," one of the uniformed men said. "Please wait here while we check out the house."

Micha nodded. Another thing he should have done, except he hadn't wanted to take the chance of missing the police when they pulled up, or worse, being taken for an intruder.

Debating whether or not to follow them, he stopped when his phone rang. "Carly," he said. "I'm at your house with the police." Explaining what he'd witnessed, he finished with letting her know the police were making sure she hadn't been broken into.

"Bridget's in the kitchen," she said, her voice shaky. "I have to make sure she's all right and didn't get out. Can you please check on her for me?"

"Of course." He spotted the two policemen returning. "Let me call you back."

Moving to meet the officers, Micha tried to get a quick read from their expressions but couldn't.

"Everything looks fine," the first one told him. "No broken windows, back door is still locked. No idea what the guy might have been doing, but it doesn't appear he gained entry into the house."

"Well, the dog barking inside might have scared him away," the second one said. "Listen, we've got this street on our daily patrol. We'll keep a close eye on things."

Thanking them, Micha stood by his car and watched as they drove away.

What had the intruder been doing in Carly's backyard? If he hadn't been trying to break in, and clearly he hadn't since he'd emerged before Micha had a chance to confront him, then why had he been back there?"

Immediately, Micha wondered if he'd installed a camera or some sort of listening device. It would have to be hidden, and protected from the weather, but still have a good view of the house. Again, though, he had to ask himself why.

Either way, he needed to check it out.

Letting himself in through the gate, which the policemen had left open, he made a mental note to ask Carly to get a lock. Double-checking everything, he made sure the back door was still secure. The instant he checked the knob, Carly's new dog began to bark. Micha grinned. At least he could tell Carly that Bridget was all right.

Next he moved on to the windows. They all were secure, locked up tight. The back shed door sat slightly ajar. Inside, Micha found an ancient push lawn mower and some old paint cans. He realized the small pile of leaves had likely been where Carly's new dog had made her bed. Nothing appeared to have been disturbed, so Micha went back outside. He stood in front of the shed, facing the house, trying to ascertain where someone might place a hidden camera so they could keep an eye on things 24/7.

He searched every place that made sense and some that didn't, finding nothing. Maybe he was being too paranoid. After all, a camera out here would only have an extremely limited view of Carly when she came outside.

But what if… What if the man had placed something up against a window with the intent of capturing activity inside the house? Unless Carly kept her back blinds or curtains closed, a camera like that would do an excellent job of monitoring her every movement.

Trying to remember the home's layout, he checked the master bedroom's windows first. Nothing. Moving on to the back door, he found that also clear. The last window was in the kitchen, over the sink. And that's where he located the tiny camera, aimed inside. Which made sense, because Carly left those blinds raised a few inches so her plants could get light.

Micha debated, but left the camera in place for now. He also debated calling the police back out but decided to notify Carly instead. It would be her decision how to proceed from there.

Once he'd made his way back to his rental car, he called Carly. "First up, Bridget is fine," he told her. "I can hear her inside the house, barking."

"Thank goodness." Carly sounded so relieved. "What about my house?"

"No break-in or damage. All the windows and doors are intact. The police checked everything out and left."

"Really?" With an audible exhale, Carly sighed. Micha could picture her at that very moment, rolling her shoulders and practicing deep breathing exercises to try to get rid of her tension. "Then what was that guy doing in my backyard?" she asked. "Or do you suppose you surprised him before he could do anything?"

"He was leaving when I pulled up," Micha reminded her. "After the police left, I went in your backyard to take another look. I found something. A tiny video camera installed on your kitchen window, looking inside."

Carly went quiet before letting out a murmured curse word. "Did you call the police back out?"

"No, not yet. I wanted you to see it for yourself first. You've got to pretend like you don't know it's there until the police can check it out. They might have a way to trace the feed all the way back to the source," he said.

"Which would mean we could catch the guy," Carly finished. "Okay, that makes sense. But I've got to tell you, it seriously creeps me out."

"Understandable."

She made a sound, somewhere between a strangled laugh and an exasperated cry. "I guess they can watch videos of Bridget for the rest of the day. Talk about an invasion of privacy."

"I'm sorry," he said.

"I have a favor to ask you. Would you mind being there when I get home from work? I really don't want to deal with that alone."

With that, his day became a hundred times better. "Of course I'll be here. What time do you get off?"

"I'm working a short shift today. I'll be home around three."

After ending the call, he got into his car, his heart lighter. Carly needed him, which made his heart sing. Meanwhile, he could get the ball rolling with Chicago PD.

He called his buddy Charlie again, detailing what he'd seen. "But I want Carly to see it before you send anyone to check it out. She'll be home sometime around three."

"Sounds good. We'll probably ask the FBI to help on this one. They can probably trace it. Though I might just stop by and take a look at it myself tonight, along with whatever agent the Bureau assigns. I won't have an ETA until I speak with them, but I'll let you know."

"I'll be there tonight with Carly for a bit," Micha said. "Keep me posted."

More shaken than she'd let on when talking to Micha, Carly struggled to get through the rest of her shift. With her focus off, she found herself double-checking everything she did. She felt so *violated*. Not only had a stranger been in her private backyard, but he had attached a video camera to her window. She supposed she should consider herself lucky that he hadn't broken in, but right now she didn't feel that way.

Finally, the hands on the huge wall clock at the nurses' station inched toward two-thirty. Hugely relieved as she completed the last of her charts and handed them off to the nurse coming on, Carly grabbed her purse and headed outside.

As usual, she kept a keen eye on her surroundings, but she was so flustered by the idea of having a video camera watching her every move that she couldn't reach inside and access that gut instinct or sixth sense.

Pulling up into her drive, she could have cried with relief as she caught sight of Micha sitting on her front porch stoop. He stood as soon as she opened her car door, meeting her halfway and wrapping his muscular arms around her. She held on tight, breathing in his familiar scent, wondering again how she'd made it two entire years without him.

That thought right there had her stepping back, out of his reassuring embrace. For a second, she couldn't meet his gaze as she struggled to gather herself back into a cohesive whole instead of scattered pieces. Her defenses had crumbled, however briefly. She'd managed to build them back up, but until then, she'd need to be careful.

"Show me the camera," she ordered.

"Sure. Let's go around back. That way whoever is monitoring it won't know we've seen it. My friend Charlie and someone from the FBI will be here shortly."

Surprised, she glanced at him. "That's fast."

His grin made her melt, damn it. "It helps when you have connections. Come on."

She followed him around the side of her house and threw open the gate. "Maybe I should get a lock for this," she said, closing it behind her.

"Definitely," Micha agreed, glancing back over his shoulder at her. He stopped at her kitchen window, pointing at a tiny metal square situated in the bottom right corner of the window. "That's it. I'm thinking they positioned it there since you leave the bottom of your blinds up a few inches for your plants."

Staring at the miniscule camera, she swallowed hard, willing away a flash of anger. "It's kind of interesting, though. If I moved one of the plants, it would totally block their view. I guess they were counting on everything staying where it is."

"True." He hesitated. "I think if you'd moved a plant, they'd have sent someone out to move the camera."

Frustrated, she turned to face him. "I don't understand. Why would someone do this? My life isn't that interesting, I promise you. And if they're hoping to see me naked, I'd think they'd have tried my bedroom rather than the kitchen."

"If you have a stalker—" he began, interrupted by a noise out front.

"Hello?" a male voice called. "Chicago PD and FBI."

"We're back here," Micha replied. A moment later, two men came around the side of the house. They both were dressed casually, though one wore a police badge on his belt and the other had on a jacket with FBI emblazoned across the back.

"Hi," the shorter man said, offering Carly a handshake. "I'm Detective Charlie Crenshaw with Chicago PD." He glanced at Micha and grinned. "And this here's Special Agent Brad Howard with the FBI."

After handshakes were exchanged all around, Brad asked to see the camera. Micha pointed it out and the two men talked quietly while they studied it.

Inside, Bridget barked several times. Carly jumped,

feeling like the worst dog parent ever. "Oh. Excuse me. I need to let my dog out."

She went around to the front door, not wanting to take a chance of Bridget bolting out the back if she went in that way.

Letting herself into her house, she couldn't help but feel a sense of foreboding. Walking down the hallway to her kitchen, she carefully kept her gaze away from the window and the camera, though it seriously creeped her out that someone might be watching her right this very instant.

Catching sight of Carly, Bridget jumped to her feet, wiggling her entire body in joy. The sight of this made Carly laugh and forget momentarily about the camera. "Hey, baby girl," Carly crooned, climbing over the baby gate and crouching on the floor. Bridget rushed over, licking and wagging her tail and contorting her little black body in all kinds of expressive and happy moves.

After a moment or two of cuddling, Carly stood, grabbed a leash and clipped it to Bridget's collar. "Ready to go outside and go potty?" she asked, grinning to herself at the way she talked to her dog as if she were human and understood every word.

Bridget barked, just once, almost as if responding "Yes!"

Still smiling, Carly led her to the back door. She was curious to see Bridget's reaction to the three men in the backyard.

As soon as they stepped outside, Bridget froze. She let out a low woof, the hair rising on her back.

"It's okay," Carly said, petting her gently. "They're friends."

Bridget glanced up at her, as if seeking reassurance.

Which Carly gave her. "It's all right. Come on, let's go over here and go potty." She led the dog over to the back corner of her yard, near the shed where Bridget had been living before. Once Bridget had taken care of business, Carly walked her back over to the others.

"Hey, girl, remember me?" Micha crouched down, holding out his hand. To Carly's surprise, Bridget sniffed him and immediately wagged her tail.

"Look at that, she knows me!" Clearly delighted, Micha grinned up at Carly.

"Smart dog," Charlie the detective said. At the sound of his voice, Bridget froze. She looked from him to the FBI agent, then to Micha and Carly.

"Too many new people," Micha commented. Moving slowly, he got to his feet and backed away from the clearly terrified dog.

"She's shaking." Carly's heart broke. "Bridget, it's okay. I'm right here."

Despite the reassuring tone and words, Bridget wasn't having it. She pressed her too-thin body against Carly's leg as if she wished she could disappear behind it.

"Ms. Colton?" Brad Howard asked. "We're about to get out of your hair for now. We'd like to ask you to leave this camera in place and try to pretend like you don't know it exists. I'm going to ask for one of our best IT specialists and see if he can trace it. But it's got to be transmitting for him to do that. Will that be all right with you?"

"How long will it have to be there?" Eyeing the tiny

camera, she shuddered at the thought of someone watching her while she went about her everyday life.

"I'm thinking a day or two," the FBI agent responded. "Maybe three at the most. It all depends on how long it takes to get the video feed tracked."

Slowly, Carly nodded, all the while absently stroking her new dog's head.

The two men thanked her and let themselves out of her backyard. Once they were gone, Bridget relaxed.

"That was weird," Carly told Micha. "I'd hoped they would just take the video camera with them."

"What the FBI agent said makes sense. It's got to be transmitting to be tracked. If they'd pulled it, whoever is monitoring the thing would have just shut it down. That's why it's important that you pretend it's not there."

She grimaced. "Easier said than done, but I'll try."

With the other men gone, Bridget had finally gotten brave enough to venture a few feet away from Carly so she could sniff the grass. Once the dog had finished, she tugged on the leash as if letting Carly know she was ready to go inside.

Carly glanced at Micha, standing several feet away with his hands in his pockets. "Would you like to come in?" she invited. "I really don't want to be alone with that camera just yet. It's going to take me a little bit to get used to the idea."

"I'd love to," he replied, the warmth of his smile going straight to her core. She had to take a deep breath to gather her suddenly scattered thoughts.

Letting them in the back door, Carly did her best not to glance in the direction of the camera. This proved more difficult than she'd imagined. She bent over, released Bridget from the leash and busied herself pouring dog kibble in a bowl.

"Are you hungry, girl?" she asked, setting the bowl on the floor. Bridget immediately began chowing down.

Carly smiled, though she still felt unsettled. As if he sensed this, Micha came up behind her and gently pulled her into his arms from behind. Mouth against her ear, he nuzzled her neck. "If they're watching right now, I want them to understand that you're mine," he murmured.

She should have protested that statement. She wasn't his, not any longer, but her brain appeared to have short-circuited. Instead of moving away, she allowed herself to go limp in his arms and relax into his embrace.

Bridget briefly glanced up at them but continued eating.

Carly turned. He kissed her then. A slow, leisurely exploration of his lips on hers, his tongue inside her. Despite her every resolve to the contrary, she kissed him back, a slow burn unfurling through her cells and making her knees go weak.

Just when she thought she'd collapse in a puddle of desire on the floor, he broke away, kissing first the tip of her nose before moving on to her shoulders and neck.

"I need your help with something," he asked, still nibbling on her ears, which sent little shivers of lightning through her. At that very moment, she doubted she could deny him anything, so she nodded. He traced the hollow of her throat with his lips, making her again weak with longing. She knew she could move away, tell him to stop, but she didn't want to. No one had ever been able to make her feel the things Micha did, not before him or after him, and she'd missed this.

"What?" she finally asked, breathless.

"After I turn in the rental car, I'll need a ride to the dealership so I can buy something of my own. After that, I want to look for a place to live. Living in a motel is getting old and expensive."

Somehow, he managed to make even that sound sexy. "Mmm-hmm."

"And I need your expertise," he continued. "You know the area. Will you go with me?"

"I will." Taking a half step back, she finally managed to put some air between the two of them so she could think. "Are you looking to rent or buy?"

"Rent," he replied, the heat in his gaze almost as intoxicating as his kisses had been. "I'd like to find something low maintenance, like maybe a condo or a town house."

"I have a Realtor friend I can check with," she managed, taking another step back when all she really wanted to do was lose herself in his arms.

Bridget, apparently having had enough of being ignored, chose that moment to give a single, loud bark. Eyeing Carly mournfully, she managed to make herself look both pitiful and expectant.

Both Carly and Micha laughed.

"I'm sorry, girl." Carly dropped to the floor and beckoned the dog over. "Come here and I'll love on you, too."

Micha went still at her words, but Bridget immediately sidled over, tail wagging ninety to nothing. Carly began petting her.

"Is that what you were doing?" Micha asked quietly. "Loving on me?"

Unable to meet his gaze, she concentrated on her dog and tried for a flippant response. "Right now, Bridget is the only one around here who gets loved on."

Then, feeling guilty, she glanced up just in time to see the hurt flash across Micha's expression. "I'm sorry," she said quietly. "I'm not trying to be mean, just real."

"Real?" He shook his head. "Real is returning my kisses. That connection we have between us is real. I don't understand how you can pretend it doesn't exist."

"I'm not," she replied. "But, Micha, everything with you is intense. Too quick, too fast and too deep. You need to slow your roll."

"I'm trying." Still, he smiled at her choice of words, which relieved her much more than it should have. "You know how you affect me."

She ducked her head, unwilling to respond. He didn't need to know the inner battle raging inside her. She craved his touch, his kisses, his body inside her, while also aware she had to protect her heart. She wasn't sure she could have both.

Chapter 5

Micha's initial intention had been to show the sick bastard who was spying on Carly that she was his and no one else's. Frustrated, he'd struggled to come up with a way to convey the fact that he'd lay down his life to defend her, but other than speaking directly to the camera and giving everything away, he couldn't conceive of one.

Instead, he'd done what he'd been aching to do from the moment she'd arrived home. He kissed her.

Like always, the passion simmering just beneath the surface had erupted. He'd struggled against the urge to take that kiss a step further, aware she wanted him to as well, which was the most powerful aphrodisiac possible.

Yet he hadn't. One, because he didn't want the voyeur to see this over the video camera, and two, because

Carly had told him it couldn't happen again. She'd practically made him promise and the one thing he couldn't go back on with her was his word.

"Did you want me to go get something to eat?" he asked, aware he'd need the time to get his composure back.

Glancing up at him, he saw a flash of panic in her eyes at the thought of being alone. He hated the fact that she now felt that way in her own home.

"How about I order us some Chinese takeout?" she said instead. "Do you still like sweet and sour chicken?"

"Sweet and Sour Saturday." He grinned. "I haven't had it in years, but yes." Once, they'd not only done Taco Tuesday, but Sweet and Sour Saturday, and even the occasional Meatball Monday. Though the first time they'd had Chinese takeout together would always be special. He wondered if she remembered and then wondered how she could forget. Was her food choice for tonight intentional, some sort of hint, or was she simply in the mood for sweet and sour chicken? Briefly, he considered asking her, but decided to do so would be unwise.

Though her tentative smile dimmed at his unintentional reminder of the time they'd spent apart, she nodded. "Let me call it in. They usually can get it here in thirty minutes or less."

While she placed the order, he got up and wandered over to the kitchen window—and the camera—pretending to study her plants. One of them, a good-size aloe vera plant, jogged his memory.

"I gave you this," he said, once she'd finished with her phone call.

"You did," she agreed, coming to stand beside him. "It was a lot smaller. I've transplanted it twice since then."

They both eyed the plant, neither glancing at the camera. He wondered if she also struggled with the urge to slide the plant over to block the camera's view. Of course they couldn't.

What they could do was move out of the area the video camera could see.

"How about we go catch up on the evening news while we wait for our food?" he asked her, casually holding out his hand.

After a moment's hesitation, she took it, her slim fingers intertwined with his. "Come on, Bridget," she called. "Let's go snuggle on the couch."

Though he knew he had to stop reacting to her every word choice, *snuggle on the couch* had him aching to do exactly that. But she'd been speaking to her dog, and the instant she sat down, she patted the seat cushion next to her as a signal to Bridget to jump up.

Ignoring Micha completely, Bridget did, curling into Carly's side and effectively preventing Micha from getting close. Which probably had been Carly's plan all along, Micha thought with a wry grimace.

Carly got out her phone and typed a text. A second later, his phone pinged.

Can the camera still hear us? she'd asked.

I don't know, he texted back. "It's unlikely since it's having to record through the window." He spoke those words out loud. "Relax. Since the guy who planted it didn't get into the house, it's unlikely there are listening devices or other cameras in here. Unless…"

"Unless what?"

"Have you had any break-ins?" he asked. "Recently, that is."

"No," she replied. Bridget placed her head on Carly's leg, nudging her for attention. When Carly resumed rubbing the dog's tummy, Bridget groaned with happiness. For the first time in his life, Micha found himself envying a dog.

"No one's come inside to do any kind of repairs or installations?"

She frowned. "No."

Relieved, he nodded. "If no one's been inside, then you should be safe from any internal monitoring devices."

"Good." Carly used the remote and turned on the television. "I DVR the evening news," she said. "That way I don't miss any of it."

For the next few minutes they caught up on the headlines of the day.

The doorbell rang, signaling the arrival of their food. Micha jumped up, motioning to Carly to stay seated, and went to get it. He gave the delivery driver a ten-dollar tip and brought the bags back into the living room.

"Let's eat in front of the TV," Carly suggested, sending an aggrieved glance toward her kitchen. "That used to be my favorite room in this house."

"It will be soon again," he reassured her. "Hopefully, that camera won't be there too much longer."

Clearing off the coffee table, she nodded. "We'll just spread everything out here."

Bridget, who had been eyeing the bag of food, licked her lips.

"I think your dog will like that," he teased.

Carly cracked a smile at that, then reached into the bag and began unloading the containers. "Here you go," she said. "I forgot how much they give you."

He hadn't. Everything about the first time they'd had this meal would forever remain etched in his soul.

The first bite—sweet and sour chicken, delicately breaded and seasoned with something that tasted like flowers—brought back so many memories that he stopped chewing and allowed himself to let the flavor wash over him. For the rest of his life, he knew he'd always associate mind-blowing, passionate sex with this meal.

"Do you remember…?" they both asked at the same time. Carly's color seemed high, her breathing jagged.

"The very first time we made love," she said softly.

He managed to nod, reaching for a second bite. After a moment, she did the same. They continued to eat in a kind of supercharged silence, he unable to help but wonder if she'd invite him to her bed after the meal.

"I didn't do this on purpose," she finally muttered, clearly able to discern his thoughts. "I just thought Chinese food sounded good. It wasn't until I placed the order that I realized I might be sending you the wrong message."

Struggling to conceal his disappointment, he simply nodded and cracked open his fortune cookie. The message inside made him laugh. "'Better times are ahead,'" he said, reading it out loud. "Good to know." Taking a bite of the cookie, he eyed her. "I can't wait to see yours."

She pushed her container away and reached for her cookie. When she read the little slip of paper inside, she shook her head, the tiniest hint of a smile tugging at one corner of her mouth. "Here," she said, passing it over to him.

Reading it, he grinned. "'Passion awaits you.' That's perfect."

"Is it?" She leaned back in her chair, her expression once again serious. "If I'd invited you to dinner with the intention of luring you into my bed with sweet and sour chicken, it would be. But since we've already settled on the fact that's not going to happen, it almost feels like…" She shrugged.

"Like I got the restaurant to put that particular message into your cookie?" Still grinning, he shook his head. "You know I didn't."

"I know," she groused, her color still high. "But you have to admit it's an odd fortune to receive. Why couldn't it have said something like 'You'll win an all-expenses-paid trip to Cancun'?"

"I'd be happy to take you to Cancun." The words slipped out before he'd had time to consider them. "If you really want to go, that is."

"Figure of speech, Micha. That's all." Getting to her feet, she started to gather up the empty containers. "I can't believe we managed to eat all that."

He got up and helped her. Together, they took everything to her kitchen trash can. Both studiously avoided glancing at the camera. Bridget, having abandoned her sleeping place on the couch, followed them, nose twitching as she sniffed the floor.

"I didn't drop anything, girl," Carly said, ruffling the dog's fur. "Chinese food wouldn't be good for you, anyway."

Micha couldn't help but find the way she spoke to Bridget as if she was human charming. He checked his watch. "I guess I'd better be going."

Again, that brief flare of panic in her eyes. But this time, she simply nodded. "I'll walk you to the door."

Until the actual moment he stepped out onto her front stoop, he'd harbored a wild and fervent hope that she'd change her mind, kiss him and invite him into her bed. Instead, she put on a brave smile that broke his heart and waved goodbye.

Halfway down the sidewalk, he pivoted, about to tell her he couldn't stand to leave her alone with that camera mounted in her kitchen window. But she'd already quietly closed her front door, so he got in his car and drove back to his lonely hotel room, where he knew he'd spend the rest of the night dreaming about her.

Leaning against the back side of her front door, Carly listened until Micha started up his car and drove off. The awful sense of loss she felt at his absence both stunned and worried her. The video camera on her kitchen window freaked her out, and she wasn't sure she'd manage to sleep a wink tonight.

Bridget slipped up next to her, nudging Carly's hand with her wet nose. "You'd alert me if anyone tried to break in, wouldn't you?" she asked. Though she knew the dog most likely didn't understand her question, having her there made Carly feel slightly more secure.

"I've got a big day tomorrow," she said, continuing her habit of speaking to Bridget as if she was a person. "I'd take you with me, but I'm not sure how my family would react. So you'll have to stay here. At least I won't be gone as long as I am when I work all day."

She took Bridget out once more before getting ready for bed, glad of the way the back porch light illuminated most of her backyard.

As soon as she got into her bed, Bridget came and sat by her side, looking up at her as if asking for permission. "Come on up, girl." Carly patted the comforter.

Bridget needed no second invitation. Gracefully, she leaped up, turned two full circles and settled into her place next to Carly's leg. Carly fell asleep with the comforting weight of her new dog pressed against her.

In the morning, she had her usual cup of coffee in the living room rather than at the kitchen table. Today, she'd have to break the startling news of Micha being alive to her entire family. Knowing how much they'd all loved him, she felt pretty certain they'd be ecstatic, but she didn't want to have to share her own conflicted emotions. She loved her family, but her personal life needed to stay just that—personal.

She tried to make the drive out to Oak Park on a regular basis, more often these days after losing her father and uncle. Her brothers, Heath and Jones, did the same. Since the two families lived next door to each other, they'd begun having combined dinners on a regular basis, attended by all the cousins. They used to have those all the time growing up, so everyone felt a faint hint of nostalgia, which made them miss the two elder Colton men even more. Their loss created a huge hole in all of their lives.

After spending the morning puttering around her house, enjoying her dog and avoiding the kitchen, that afternoon Carly got in her car to make the trek northwest to the suburb. Though no one knew yet that Micha was alive, she had still debated inviting him, but knew doing so would make more of a statement than she was prepared to handle right now, so she went alone. She couldn't decide whether to break the news before Heath dropped his bombshell about the new murders or after. She guessed she'd just play it by ear.

Since the day was unseasonably warm for April, they'd decided to move the get-together outside and have a backyard cookout in their shared backyard. Grandma Jones had been positively gleeful at the prospect. She'd assigned everyone a different dish to bring, but everyone knew they'd all be purchasing theirs from Tatum's restaurant True.

Since Carly had brought Harry to the last family dinner, she knew everyone would question his absence. That would be as good a time as any to tell them Micha wasn't dead, after all, though she dreaded the assumptions that were sure to follow.

Carly's brothers, Heath and Jones, were in charge of manning the massive stainless-steel grill. Two other men, Sean Stafford and Cruz Medina, stood with them, shooting the breeze. Carly's three cousins—Simone, Tatum and January—were already outside, chatting with Heath's fiancée, Kylie.

As Carly walked over, she noticed that January

couldn't seem to tear her gaze away from her fiancé, Sean. Ditto for Tatum, who was making googly eyes at her new man, Cruz. Since Tatum was a renowned chef who owned True, a restaurant downtown, she was in charge of the food. Everyone just purchased whatever sides they'd been assigned from her, which basically meant she was catering the luncheon, right down to providing seasoned and marinated cuts of meat for the guys to grill.

None of the cousins had inherited Tatum's cooking skills. Simone worked as a professor at the University of Chicago, January was a social worker as well as a busy volunteer, and Carly a nurse; they all preferred to eat Tatum's wonderful cooking over their own. Grandma Jones often chided them, but she, too, dug in with gusto to whatever Tatum brought, so Carly knew she didn't really mind.

Until the double murder, they'd been a loud, boisterous, close and joyful family. Over time, and slowly, Carly hoped they'd all manage to make their way back to where they'd once been.

Walking into the spacious backyard, Carly immediately headed over to her mother, who sat in a brightly painted Adirondack chair next to her aunt. Both women, identical twins who took great pains to wear their hair differently, looked up at her approach.

"Carly!" Aunt Farrah stood, somehow managing to look both warm and regal at the same time. She enveloped Carly in a perfumed hug, before releasing her and sitting back down.

Carly's mother, Fallon, also pushed to her feet. She crushed Carly to her, holding on so tightly that Carly struggled to breathe. When Fallon finally released her, Carly stepped back and studied her mom. Fallon's short, curly hair looked as stylish as ever, and she'd clearly taken pains with her makeup, outfit and jewelry. This had to be a good sign, Carly thought.

"What's new, sweetheart?" her mother asked, her intent gaze sweeping over Carly. Ever since losing her husband, the older woman had become subdued, her former vibrant personality dimmed. While Aunt Farrah Colton had always been loud, in an outgoing, charming way, Fallon had always been more reserved, yet warm and caring. Carly actually missed her aunt's occasional yelling. At least she had her twin, Fallon, living next door to grieve with. Since both women had lost their husbands at the same time, they leaned heavily on each other.

They all mourned differently, Carly reflected. Carly had thrown herself into her work, picking up extra shifts and keeping as busy as possible so she didn't have time to think. Of course, ever since losing Micha, she'd been a bit of a workaholic. The loss of her father had just intensified those tendencies again.

"I got a dog," Carly said, figuring she'd start with that and work up to the really big news. After all, at some point Heath had to make his announcement about the new double murder. No doubt he planned to wait until after they'd all eaten, so the news wouldn't put a huge damper on everyone's mood.

"You what?" Fallon's perfectly arched brows rose. "I wouldn't think you have time to deal with a puppy."

"Bridget isn't a puppy, Mom. I rescued a dog. The vet says she's about two years old and has likely had at least one litter of puppies. She's got an appointment tomorrow to get spayed."

The twin sisters shared a glance. "What kind of dog, dear?" Aunt Farrah asked.

"The vet thinks she's a lab mix." Carly pulled out her phone, ready to show pictures. She certainly had a lot of them.

Her trio of cousins ambled over, clearly curious. Everyone dutifully oohed over Bridget's pictures.

"She's really thin," January said, expression concerned. She'd always been tenderhearted, which was part of the reason she'd gone into social work and did so much volunteer work. "Are you feeding her several small meals a day?"

"I am," Carly replied, which made her cousin beam.

"Where's Harry?" Simone asked, glancing around as if she expected him to appear at any second.

"We're taking a break," Carly replied, bracing herself for the comments that were sure to follow. Her cousins exchanged quick glances. Simone frowned, while January appeared confused. Since she'd been the one to set Harry and Carly up, Carly knew she owed her an explanation. "He's a great guy and I appreciate you introducing us. We just weren't right for each other. He's good with it, though, much more so than I thought he'd be. Maybe you can work your magic and fix him up with someone else."

Still frowning slightly, January nodded.

Tatum hugged her. "I'm sorry. Are you okay?"

"Mostly," Carly allowed. She figured she might as well get this over with now, though she wanted her brothers to hear, too. "Heath, Jones. Do you have a minute?"

Since they hadn't actually started cooking anything, they came over.

Jones slung a casual arm across her shoulders. "Looking good, Carly." She smiled up at him, while inside she couldn't help but wonder how they all were going to take her news.

"What's up?" Heath asked, his shaggy dark blond hair blowing in the slight breeze.

"Micha is alive," she blurted, inwardly wincing at her bluntness. "He showed up at my house a couple of days ago."

Everyone started talking at once, asking questions. Heath cleared his throat loudly and held up his hand. "Quiet," he ordered. "Let Carly explain."

Carly told them everything, all except the part where she'd fallen into bed with Micha. When she finished relaying Micha's story, Simone shook her head. "That explains Harry's absence."

Which meant that Carly had to tell them Harry's reaction. Part of her still couldn't digest the fact that he'd let her go so easily.

"Proof he wasn't the right guy for you," Jones drawled supportively, hugging her again. "I hope you're not losing any sleep over him."

"I'm not," she said, surprised to realize the only thing stung had been her pride. Looking up, she realized both her mother and aunt had tears in their eyes.

Carly eyed January. "Thank you for fixing me and Harry up. He's a great guy. I promise you, I never wanted to hurt him in any way."

"It sounds like you didn't," January admitted. "He'll be okay. But poor Micha," she said, sighing. "It sounds like he's been through so much."

Carly nodded, not sure how to react to that. While Micha had suffered a horrible ordeal, that didn't excuse the fact he hadn't reached out to her in two damn years. "All this time," she said out loud, "I thought he was dead."

"I'm so happy for you," Fallon said, sniffing. "You get to have a second chance. I wish your father could have been here to see that. He always was fond of Micha."

Carly's stomach twisted. She didn't have the heart to tell her mother that she wasn't sure she wanted a second chance with Micha. Especially not now, when she knew her mother would have given anything to have her husband back. As would Aunt Farrah.

"When's the wedding taking place?" Simone asked softly. "Or haven't you had time to start planning it yet?"

"I want to cater it," Tatum interjected. "Or maybe you could just have the reception at True."

Overwhelmed, all Carly could do was slowly shake her head.

Standing across from her, Heath narrowed his eyes, something in the tightness of his expression letting her know he understood at least some of the tangled emotions inside her.

"Give Carly a break," he ordered. "I imagine all of this came as quite the shock."

"It did," Carly managed. She checked her watch. "Shouldn't you two start grilling? I'm hungry."

Grinning, Jones touched his finger to his forehead in a mock salute. "We'll get right on that. Come on, Heath."

Carly exhaled as her two brothers sauntered away. For a moment there, she'd seen a flash of anger in Heath's steely gaze. She'd been really glad he wouldn't be confronting Micha yet. She had a lot of her own upset feelings to deal with first without her older brother bringing his own into the mix.

"Why didn't you bring Micha today?" Tatum asked, one brow raised. "It would have been great to see him after all this time."

"I agree," Simone said. "I always liked him."

Carly shrugged. "Can we change the subject, please?"

All three of her cousins laughed. January hugged her this time. "Sure we can."

A quick glance at her mother revealed she and her sister were in a deep, whispered conversation. Which was fine. Carly knew the two women could use a distraction. Since she didn't want to worry anyone, Carly decided not to mention her feeling of being watched for the last six weeks. At least not yet. The police knew, Micha knew, and that would have to be enough for now.

Once the meat—tender, delectable cuts of beef, chicken and pork that Tatum had marinated, seasoned and prepared—had been grilled, all the sides were carried out and placed on a long table. It would be a feast. Carly, unable to keep from wondering what Micha would make of it, hung back a little while the others lined up to fill their plates.

Heath joined her, his expression troubled. Since she'd promised she wouldn't, she couldn't reveal that she already knew about the recent double murders. No doubt her older brother was worrying about how to tell the family without causing a mass panic.

Meanwhile, Heath apparently took her preoccupation for worry about Micha. "It's going to be all right, Carly." He patted her shoulder. "Right now it must feel overwhelming, but things will sort themselves out."

She managed to summon a smile. "I know they will," she replied, even though she knew no such thing. "Life sure can be complicated."

"It can," he agreed. "If you need to talk through anything, or just feel like some company, you know you can contact me or Jones anytime."

"That's right," Jones chimed in, balancing a very full plate as he passed them on his way toward a seat. "Or if you want to come by the brewery and drown your sorrows, I'm up for that, too." He winked. "I brought some of our newest beer for everyone to sample today if they want."

Once everyone had gotten their food and sat down to eat, Carly allowed herself to simply be in the moment, pushing her worries away for later. A delicious meal with her family, lots of laughter, bright sunshine and spring warmth would lighten anyone's mood.

Heath and Jones went back for seconds. Carly almost followed their lead, but Tatum reminded everyone to leave room for dessert. Since whatever Tatum had chosen to concoct was bound to be spectacular, Carly stayed in her seat.

Grinning, Heath returned to his chair with a second heaping plate. Jones did the same. "I'll always have room for any of your delicious desserts," Heath said, before digging in.

Tatum waited until both men had cleaned their plates before getting up and disappearing inside the house to retrieve her concoction. Everyone took wild guesses on what she might have made since she'd refused to say, claiming she wanted it to be a surprise.

"I'm hoping cheesecake." Carly sighed. "Or cobbler."

"Or tiramisu," January interjected. Simone nodded her agreement. "Tatum makes the best tiramisu."

"I vote chocolate," Jones chimed in.

A moment later, Tatum reappeared. She carried a large covered metal pan. "Something new," she said with a mysterious smile. "Bourbon bread pudding."

Everyone collectively sighed.

"My mouth is already watering," Heath said.

Rapt, everyone watched while Tatum dished up portions into bowls. Next to them, she'd placed a carton of French vanilla ice cream with a metal scoop on top. "Come and get it," she announced, stepping back. "Mom and Aunt Fallon first."

Simone stood, fetching the two older women's portions before grabbing her own. One by one, the rest of them got their dessert.

As usual with anything Tatum made, it tasted amazing, managing to be both light and filling, the flavors both simple and complex. Carly ate it slowly, so she could savor every bite.

By the time everyone had finished, a contented silence fell over the group. Carly glanced at her big brother, figuring now would be the time he broke his bit of news.

Heath looked around and then slowly stood. He took a deep breath before tapping his spoon on the side of his water glass to get their attention. "Everyone, I'm afraid I have a bit of bad news," he said. "Chicago PD has notified me that there was another double murder, with a similar MO to Dad and Uncle Alfred. The FBI has been called in. They're thinking we might have a serial killer on our hands."

After a moment of stunned silence, everyone started talking at once. Carly stayed quiet and listened while everyone expressed worry, shock and concern.

Heath let them go on for a moment or two before raising his hand and clearing his throat. "The police have promised to keep us posted. They've asked everyone to be careful and let them know if you see or hear anything unusual. If it is a serial killer, they aren't sure what attracts him to his victims."

"How do you know it's a male?" Fallon asked.

"Most serial killers are."

"Were the victims also twins?" Jones asked, shooting his brother a dark look, no doubt upset that Heath hadn't filled him in first.

"No." Heath looked from one family member to the other. "Despite that, or maybe because of it, I'm still worried. I want you all to promise me you'll report anything unusual."

Everyone murmured their assent. Carly kept her mouth closed, though she figured she'd probably better tell her brothers about her stalker. But if she did, she knew Heath would sweep in and take over, like he always did. Being the head of the family and the family business had given him more than enough responsibilities and things to worry about. She decided to keep it quiet for now. After all, Chicago PD and the FBI were already involved. And she had Micha to help keep her safe.

Chapter 6

Since Micha had no way of knowing what time Carly would return from her family get-together out in Oak Park, he spent the afternoon looking at For Rent listings online. He found several that looked promising and bookmarked them to revisit later with Carly. Once he'd finished with that, he started studying sales prices of vehicles he liked. He figured out a strategy, decided how much he was willing to spend in cash and then he drove north to a Jeep, Chrysler and Dodge dealer and took a look at the new Jeep Wranglers. The dealership was closed on Sunday, so Micha parked outside the gate and walked around the lot looking at vehicles.

He found a fully loaded black one he liked, jotted down the information and resolved to come back Monday when the sales office was open.

On the way back to his hotel, he realized he needed fresh air, so he took a detour and drove to Burnham Park, where he could walk along the lakeshore and see the water. Everyone, it seemed, had come out on such a beautiful spring afternoon. The tennis courts were full, the path crowded with joggers, cyclists and people out for a walk.

Here, in the midst of nature, with Lake Michigan glittering in the sunlight, he missed Carly so much he ached. To him, she represented everything he loved about his city of choice. Walking in this beautiful green space might be nice, but he needed Carly with him to fully experience it.

He found an empty bench and sat. Once, he and Carly had huddled together in this very spot, bundled in their winter coats, hats, scarves and gloves. They'd been giddy with love, braving the icy chill of winter to marvel at the beauty of the frozen lake. He wondered if she'd ever come here by herself, after his supposed death. Maybe she'd sat on this same bench, mourning him.

It couldn't have been easy for her. If the situation had been reversed, and he'd lost her, the devastation would have surely taken him under. Instead, he'd spent a good chunk of time unconscious, even more in physical therapy relearning basic skills, all the while yearning for someone his fuzzy brain couldn't remember. Then when he'd clawed his way to some sort of normalcy and realized what he'd lost, so much time had passed that he'd understood he could never have her back.

Still, unable to let her go, he'd traveled to his favorite city to see her one last time. As if. He'd hashed the scenario out over and over, unable to rationalize simply letting her go.

And now he knew he never could. If she sent him away, he'd end up living the rest of his life as half a person.

His phone rang. When Carly's name flashed up on the screen, his heart skipped a beat. *Here's to second chances*, he thought, and answered.

"I'm on my way back to the house," she said. "If you want to come over in about thirty minutes, that'd be great."

"I'm at Burnham Park," he told her. "So not far from your place at all. Maybe we could take Bridget for a walk here sometime."

"She'd love that," she promptly said. "But not until I've made sure she's up to date on her vaccines first."

"You're already an awesome pet parent," he said. "I'll see you in a half hour."

After ending the call, he remained on the park bench a few more minutes, soaking up the atmosphere and feeling like the luckiest man alive.

Then he got up and made his way to his rental car to make the short drive over to Carly's house.

Despite taking his time, he still arrived before her. He parked at the curb in front of her house and went to sit on her front porch steps. When she pulled into her driveway a few minutes later, he got up and went to meet her. Bridget, apparently recognizing the sound of Carly's car, began barking inside the house.

The sound made Carly grin. "I love having a dog," she said.

"It sounds like she's glad you're home." He slung a

casual arm across her shoulders. Though she tensed at first, she actually allowed herself to lean into him a little. When she reached her front door, she stepped away from him and unlocked it. She barely had it open wide enough for her to step through when a blur of black fur came barreling at her, barking in what Micha could only describe as a happy sound. Happy, hell. The dog sounded ecstatic.

Carly crouched down, grinning broadly while her new pet welcomed her home. "Come on, girl," she finally said, getting to her feet. "Let's get you outside."

Micha waited in her kitchen while she took her dog out back. Ever conscious of the camera, he avoided glancing at the window at all.

A moment later, Carly and Bridget returned. "It's gone," Carly announced, slightly breathless. "The video camera is no longer attached to my window. I even checked the ground below, just in case it fell. There's no sign of it anywhere."

Naturally, he had to go look for himself. As she'd said, the camera had disappeared as if it had never been there.

"What does that mean?" Carly asked, frowning.

"I'm not sure," he admitted. "It's possible whoever installed it figured out we were on to them."

"Do you think maybe the FBI took it?" she asked, turning to grab the dog food bowl so she could feed Bridget.

"Let me see if I can find out." He sent a quick text to Charlie's cell phone. A moment later, Charlie called him.

"What do you mean the camera is gone?" Charlie

asked, getting directly to the point. "The FBI hasn't had a chance to get their analyst out to look at it. They're having to fly someone out from New York. I think he's arriving here tomorrow."

"He'll be too late."

Charlie cursed.

"I'm just glad it's gone," Micha admitted. "But for the record, both Carly and myself were careful not to do anything to alert anyone that we knew the camera was there."

"I'd better notify the Bureau." Charlie sounded resigned. "There's no reason for them to send their specialist out here now."

"Thanks, man. I'll let you know if anything changes." After ending the call, Micha turned to find Carly watching him.

"I take it he didn't remove it?" she asked.

"Nope. The FBI didn't, either." He decided to try for a little humor. "Maybe the guy realized he had the wrong house."

Though this earned him a smile from her, she shook her head. She put the dog bowl full of food down, where Bridget immediately began devouring it.

Watching the shadows in her eyes as she gazed at her dog, Micha fiercely wished he could protect her always. He vowed he would, no matter the cost.

"You have an awfully intent look on your face," she commented. "What are you thinking about?"

Not wanting to worry her even more, he shrugged. "Nothing in particular. How'd your family get-together go?"

Her smile told him she didn't believe him. "It went

well. I told them about you being alive. And here in Chicago."

"How'd they take it?"

"Well. You know how much they liked you. Several people asked why I didn't bring you with me."

"What did you say?" he asked, needing to know.

She sighed. "I changed the subject. Honestly, Micha. I'm still not sure how I feel about all this. Having you back and here with me is wonderful, but it's also scary as hell."

"Scary?" Her choice of words made him consider. "How so?"

Now she wouldn't look at him. "Losing you hurt, Micha. It took me a long time to pick myself up and climb out of that deep, dark place."

The pain in his heart made him rub his chest. "Would you rather I hadn't come back? Would you…" He had to swallow hard to keep his voice from breaking. "Would you rather you still thought I was dead?"

"Of course not."

Her instant denial made him feel slightly better. "I'm glad," he began.

She shook her head and held up her hand, interrupting him. "I'm still struggling with the fact that you waited two entire years before even attempting to contact me. I know you have your reasons, you've been pretty clear on that. But what you don't seem to understand is this. I can't go through that again. I wouldn't survive losing you a second time."

So much pain. And yet, so much love. He could fix this, he thought, given enough time. For now, all he could do was simply show her he wouldn't be leaving her again.

Needing that skin-to-skin contact, he gently tugged her close and brushed his mouth across hers. "I'm sorry," he murmured. Though he immediately released her, his body stirred. Wide-eyed, she stared at him, her lips slightly parted, almost as if she wanted him to kiss her again.

Instead, he turned away. "I found a few places I might be interested in looking at renting," he told her, grabbing his laptop. "If you don't mind, I'd like you to tell me what you think."

"You've got to stop doing that," she said, though she smiled as she spoke.

"Kissing you?"

"Stopping," she replied, laughing a little. The naked vulnerability in her eyes told him how much it had cost her to say that.

With his laptop forgotten, he crossed the space between them. She met him halfway. This time, he kissed her properly.

Bridget barked, running back and forth from the kitchen to the front door. Carly immediately stepped back, her color high. "Is someone out there?" she asked her dog. "What is it, girl?"

Though his arousal made it difficult to walk, Micha headed for the entry. Carly followed close behind. "Let me grab Bridget," she said. "She seems pretty upset. I don't want her running out."

Waiting until she had her dog's collar, he opened the front door. Outside, the late-afternoon sunshine seemed mellow. A car or two drove by and he could hear kids down the street playing. Just a typical spring afternoon in Chicago.

A squirrel dashed across the front lawn. Watching it climb up a tree, he wondered if Bridget had somehow sensed its presence. He'd bet she'd chased a few squirrels for food when she'd been living on the streets.

Returning to Carly, he shrugged. "No idea what she might have been barking at. I saw a squirrel, but nothing out of the ordinary."

"Okay, good," she replied, clearly relieved. She let Bridget go, and the dog heaved a huge sigh before making a beeline to her dog bed. Turning several circles, she finally settled down and closed her eyes.

Since the previous mood had been destroyed, he went to get his laptop so he could show her the places he thought he liked.

"Wait," she said. "Did you write down the addresses?"

"I actually printed out the info sheet on each. I brought my top five."

His comment made her grin. "Wow, you're organized."

He smiled back. "I kind of have to be. It's not easy living out of a hotel room."

"How about we take a drive and look at a couple of those properties?" she asked. "While we'll only be able to check out the outside, at least you can get a feel for the neighborhood. That way, you'll know if you want to make an appointment to see the interior."

Surprised and gratified, he looked at her and nodded. "I'd like that," he said. "Do you want to do that now?"

"Sure, why not? We can bring Bridget with us since she enjoys car rides."

"Sounds good. Let's take the rental car since I'm hoping to turn it in tomorrow. I went and looked at cars today, too, even though the dealerships are closed."

Finally, after taking Bridget out back once more, she asked if he was ready to go.

"Sure. I'll drive." He waited while she put the leash on her dog. They went out the front since he'd parked at the curb.

Since the rental car had remote start, he decided he might as well use it at least once, so he pressed the button on the key fob. Instead of instantly starting, he heard a familiar catch in the ignition. Acting on instinct, he spun and launched himself at Carly, knocking her to the ground just as the car exploded.

Ears ringing, head throbbing, Carly tried to process what had just happened. Her elbow hurt, knee, too, and she was pretty sure she'd torn her jeans in the fall. Micha lay on top of her, so still she worried he'd been seriously injured, and she couldn't see her dog anywhere.

"Micha?" she croaked. "Bridget?"

Instead of responding, Micha groaned.

Meanwhile, she could hear the roar of the fire consuming his rental car. Squirming, she tried to move him. Her futile efforts appeared to rouse him. He groaned again, and pushed himself off her, rolling away before collapsing on his back on the front lawn.

"We've called 911," someone said.

Her neighbor, she realized. Without Micha's weight

crushing her, Carly managed to rise up on her knees. A small group of people had begun to gather near her yard. "My dog," she said. "Have you seen my dog?"

No one responded. She blinked and decided she wanted to stand. Her pounding head thought otherwise, but she had to make sure Micha was all right and also find Bridget.

Sirens sounded in the distance. Fire truck and ambulance, most likely.

"Are you okay?" Micha asked, his deep voice full of gravel and rasp. He'd managed to sit up. A cut on his arms dripped blood onto his jeans.

"I think so," she replied. "How about you?" Without waiting for him to answer, she slowly got to her feet. Shaky, but standing. "What the hell just happened?"

"Someone set up the car to blow." He shook his head, then winced. "If I hadn't used the remote start, we would have been in that car."

With dawning horror, the truth of his words hit her. They wouldn't have had a chance for escape since the bomb had detonated the instant the engine started. They would have been killed. Even her dog.

Her dog.

"Bridget is missing," she said. "The explosion must have terrified her."

"I don't blame her." Moving with deliberate caution, Micha got up. Other than a tear in the shoulder of his T-shirt, he appeared all right. The cut on his arm appeared to be superficial and the bleeding had slowed to a trickle. "My ears are still ringing," he commented.

"Mine, too."

The sirens got louder. A moment later a fire truck

and an ambulance turned onto her street, lights flashing. The small crowd of neighbors clustered closer together as the emergency vehicles pulled up and parked.

Micha swayed, looking for a moment as if he might lose his balance. Carly went to him, slipping her shoulder under his arm to offer support. Shooting her a grateful look, he allowed himself to lean on her.

While the fire department began working on getting the car fire put out, the EMTs came over to check on Carly and Micha. Though Micha tried to wave them away, it was clear he'd been hurt. Carly thought she was okay, even her ears weren't ringing as badly, but also agreed to an exam. The EMTs led both of them over to their ambulance. By now the police had arrived and two uniformed officers were taking statements from neighbors.

"I need to find my dog," Carly announced. "She was with us when the car exploded. I've got to make sure she's okay."

"In a minute, ma'am," the EMT said. "Let me make sure you're all right."

Nodding, she allowed him to check her out, taking her temperature, shining a light into her eyes and asking numerous questions. No, she had no joint pain. No, she didn't think any bones were broken. Thanks to Micha shielding her with his body, she had no cuts or burns, other than the scrapes on her elbows and knees. Yes, she knew she was lucky, but she really had to go look for her dog. It killed her to think Bridget was hiding somewhere terrified and alone.

"We'd like to take you to the hospital for observation," the other EMT told Micha.

"No." His emphatic reply left no doubt. "I'm fine. I've been banged up far worse in Afghanistan. I'm not leaving Carly alone."

Though they argued, he refused to be swayed. And since they couldn't force him to go to the hospital, they finally ended up passing him over to the police detective who'd arrived to take his statement.

Carly managed to slip away, determined to find Bridget. She went into her backyard, fairly certain she had a good idea where Bridget would have run to hide.

She found her dog exactly where she'd expected, in the shed, cowering in the corner. Immediately, Carly crouched down, speaking in a soothing low voice, determined to remain there as long as she had to until Bridget was willing to approach her.

To her surprise, once Carly started talking, Bridget crawled over to her, low to the ground, almost on her belly. She was panting heavily, but her long tail wagged as if to say she had hope that Carly could help her. Since her leash was still attached to her collar, Carly simply gathered it up, still crooning reassuring words. To her surprise, Bridget pressed right up against her legs, allowing Carly to touch her.

"You must have been terrified, weren't you, girl?" Carly asked, gathering the dog close and holding her tight. "I was, too. Come on, let's get you inside the house."

Once she'd coaxed the still-shivering animal into the kitchen, Carly took a deep breath and hobbled back out front to check on Micha. A police officer, catching sight of her coming down the steps, hurried over to intercept her.

"Ma'am? We've been looking for you," he said, his tone brisk. "Your husband has finished giving his statement and we need yours."

Too exhausted to correct him, she simply nodded. "Lead the way."

As he walked her over toward a small group of police officers, she spotted Micha's friend Charlie. He caught sight of her at the same moment and hurried over.

"There you are," he said, taking her arm. "I've got this, Trevor."

Charlie waited until the other officer had walked away before leaning in close. "We're waiting on the FBI," he said, pitching his voice low. "We suspect a definite tie to whoever placed and removed the camera."

She nodded. "I thought the same thing."

"What we don't know is who the explosive device was targeting. Since it was in Micha's rental car, it most likely was him. But on the other hand…"

"Whoever did it might have hoped I'd go somewhere with him," she finished.

"Yes. But they couldn't have known for certain."

Micha walked up, still moving carefully, but looking much better than he had before. "Hey," he said, putting his arm around her shoulders. "Did you find Bridget?"

"I did." She shifted her weight, aware he probably needed to lean on her for balance. "She'd run into the shed and was hiding there. I've moved her into the house. She doesn't appear to have been hurt."

"Good." He let his gaze sweep over her. "What about you? Everything okay?"

She nodded. Before she could speak, one of the policemen came over with some questions.

By the time EMTs, the fire department and law enforcement left, most of the neighborhood spectators had wandered back home. Dusk had arrived and it would soon be dark. Micha had finally sat down on her bottom porch step, clearly too tired or hurt to stand any longer. Carly could definitely relate. She felt weird—a mixture of amped-up restlessness and exhaustion.

"Let's go inside," she told Micha, putting her hand out for him to use to help him get up.

He managed a grateful smile and allowed her to pull him to his feet.

They made it inside with him leaning heavily on her. She helped him to the couch, where he lowered himself with a grunt. Bridget came running up, sniffing his legs, though she didn't jump up on the couch near him.

"Where are you hurt?" Carly asked. "Maybe you should have let them take you to the hospital for tests."

Shaking his head, he eyed her. "No way am I leaving you alone after someone just tried to kill us. No way in hell."

Touched, she wanted to hug him but knew better. "Us? Do you think they targeted your rental car hoping I'd get in it with you?"

"No." He grimaced. "Both Chicago PD and the FBI believe I was the target this time. They can't rule out it was somehow tied to the video camera, and the fact that it happened in front of your house is suspicious to me, but they feel strongly you would have just been collateral damage."

"Collateral damage," she repeated. The coldness of the term made her shiver. "But why, Micha? Why would anyone want you dead?"

"That's just it. I don't know."

"It's just too much of a coincidence," she said. "I've been feeling as if someone's been watching me for weeks, which is even more frightening since someone murdered my father and uncle. You magically reappear, back from the dead." She sighed. "After that, someone puts a video camera on my kitchen window, I learn there's been another murder with a similar MO to my father's, and then someone blows up the car you and I were about to get into. Does that about cover it?"

"Come here." He patted the couch next to him. "We're alive, and unhurt for the most part. Sit. Try to relax. We'll deal with the rest later."

But she felt too jumpy to just sit. Restless and conflicted, an almost sexual energy buzzed through her. She had no idea how to deal with herself except to try to keep busy as a distraction.

Meanwhile, Micha watched her, almost as if he knew the way she felt. She eyed him back, wondering how badly he'd been hurt. Since she needed some way to occupy herself, checking him out would be a start.

"Let me take a look at you," she ordered. "Let's get your shirt off."

This made him laugh, though he immediately winced in pain. "This definitely isn't how I pictured you asking me to take off my clothes."

"Off with it." She refused to rise to his baiting. "I'm sure the EMTs checked you out thoroughly, but I want to see for myself. I take it you don't have any broken bones?"

"No, ma'am," he drawled, struggling to get his torn T-shirt off.

Moving carefully, she helped him, pretending her fingers weren't trembling. Once the shirt came off, she gasped at the huge, angry purple bruise on his shoulder. He had another, even larger one lower on his rib cage. There were a few scratches and scrapes, but overall it didn't appear he'd been seriously injured.

Thank goodness. But her relief did nothing to ease her tension. She needed something else. She needed… him.

Impulsively, she placed a gentle kiss on his shoulder. "I'm glad you're all right," she said.

"Me, too." His gaze had darkened, but he kept still, clearly letting her make her own choice.

"Thank you for protecting me." She kissed him again. A low thrum of desire had settled low in her belly. They'd survived a horrible attack—together— and she felt an almost overwhelming need to reaffirm their survival.

"How much do you hurt?" she asked softly, wanting to be sure.

Turning his head, he met her mouth with his own. "Not that badly," he murmured, kissing her deeply.

She kept her gaze on him as she removed her torn clothing, piece by piece, matter-of-factly with no attempt to shield herself from his heated gaze. Though he struggled, he watched her while he did the same, leaving on only his boxers. She straddled him, closing her eyes as she allowed the desire coursing through her veins to overtake her.

Pushing down his boxers, she freed him, allowing herself to marvel at the sheer force of his erection before she lowered herself over him, taking him deep inside her.

He made a sound, arching his back and driving himself into her. Laughing and wild, she pushed him down, pushing away her inhibitions, her worries and fears, everything but her desire for him.

Letting go. And holding on. As her climax slammed into her, she called his name. An instant later, he joined her. It wasn't until she'd collapsed on top of him that she started to cry.

He held her while she let the tears fall, asking no questions, saying nothing. She wasn't sure exactly of the reason for the waterworks, but her life had changed with her father's and uncle's murders and had continued to change up until this very moment.

Finally, she'd cried herself out. Sniffing, she wiped at her eyes with the back of her hand and sat back. "Sorry about that," she said.

"No need to apologize." Reaching up, he used his fingers to tuck a wayward strand of her hair behind her ear. "That was intense. I get it."

"Intense." She tested out the word. Not terrifying, or even frightening, but intense. "You're right," she said. "It was. All of it."

"I didn't use protection," he murmured, his gaze locked on hers. "But I can assure you I haven't been with anyone else and I was tested for everything before I left the hospital."

She nodded. The last thing she wanted to do was bring up another man right now. "I've made sure I was always protected, as well," she said, hoping that would suffice. "And I take birth control pills, too."

Before he could respond, she got up and grabbed her discarded clothing, hurrying to the bathroom to get cleaned up.

Inside, she eyed her wild-haired, flushed self in the mirror, refusing to allow even the tiniest bit of regret. She stepped into the shower, rinsing herself off.

"Mind if I join you?" Micha's voice, just outside the door.

Startled, she found herself grinning. "Come on in," she said. "I'll wash your back if you'll wash mine."

"Agreed," he replied.

The intimacy of soaping each other off, wet bodies pressed so close together, aroused her again, to her stunned disbelief. When she felt Micha's arousal pressing against her, she laughed out loud. "Again?" she asked, breathless with anticipation.

"Again," he replied, his hands silky on her slick body.

They made love under the warm spray of water, this time taking their time, lingering over exploring each other, which drove Carly over the edge more quickly than she would have liked. Micha immediately followed, giving a primal cry of release.

Later, clean and dry and feeling human again, Carly opened a bottle of red wine she'd been saving for a special occasion. She figured being alive after narrowly missing being blown up in a car explosion qualified. Micha ordered a pizza, her favorite comfort food. Though she shouldn't have been hungry, considering how much she'd eaten earlier, she managed to devour three slices. "I guess I worked up an appetite," she said, smiling. Bridget lay curled at her feet, staring longingly at the remains of the pizza.

"Me, too." Micha got up, moving restlessly around the room. He appeared distracted and unsettled, the opposite of a man who'd just made love to her twice.

"What's wrong?" Carly finally asked, slipping Bridget a small bit of crust.

Micha stopped moving long enough to meet her gaze. "I'm worried that by trying to protect you, I've put you in danger. The more I think about it, the more likely that car explosion was meant for me. You could have been killed. Because of me."

"I get that," she replied. "But since we don't know who might have been the target, it's pointless to blame yourself. Besides that, do you have any enemies? Someone who hates you enough to want to kill you?"

"Not that I know of." Voice as grim as his gaze, Micha shook his head. "But I'm thinking whoever rigged that car to blow had to be handy with explosives. I knew people like that over in Afghanistan. For whatever reason, I was the intended victim."

"But what about that video camera?" she asked, genuinely perplexed.

"Maybe someone was watching you hoping I'd show up," he told her. "No more secrets, Carly. What happened in the war seriously messed up people. While I was rescued, others lost their lives. I need to do some checking with some of my military contacts."

Moving closer, he put his hands lightly on her shoulders. "I'll keep watch over you, I promise. If there is someone after you, I'll keep you safe. If there's someone after me…" He paused. "I'll deal with them. We need to be extra vigilant."

Carly scratched Bridget's head, right behind the ears.

"I wonder if she was trying to warn us when she barked earlier," she said. "We looked outside, but no one was there."

"She probably was," he replied. "Whoever rigged that car worked quickly and efficiently, which means highly skilled."

She shuddered. "What if they do that to my car while I'm at work? I'm not sure what to do."

"Let me use your car tomorrow," he told her. "I'll drop you at work and park it. I'll stand guard. Maybe we can catch this person red-handed."

Though his plan sounded dangerous, she agreed. She could see no other choice.

Chapter 7

Either way, Micha figured he had a good chance of catching the person who'd blown up his rental car. If the bomber was actually after Carly, Micha would watch out for her no matter what. He'd give his life for her if need be. And if Micha himself was the target, well, he'd already been to hell and back. Somehow, he'd survived. After that, nothing shook him. He'd actually welcome putting a rapid end to this craziness. Bring it on.

In the meantime, if any bright spot emerged from all of this, it was that the near-death experience had clearly caused Carly to push away her lingering misgivings about Micha. To his delight, for the first time since his return into her life, she invited him to spend the night with her, in her bed. His heart had leaped at the warmth in her bright blue eyes when she'd asked him to stay.

Not wanting to appear overly eager, he'd pretended to have to consider her offer, when in fact he could hardly contain his joy. For once, she wasn't pushing him away. He hated that it had taken such a horrible event to cause this, but he also understood she'd made a choice. Instead of turning away, she'd leaned in. He'd take it. Hell, when it came to Carly, he'd take whatever she was willing to give. Somehow, he suspected she knew this.

That night he'd held her close while she slept. His heart was full.

In the morning, they made love again, this time with the comfortable ease of longtime lovers. Micha took his time pleasuring her, holding off on his own release until she'd had hers. After, she clung to him without talking, almost drifting off to sleep until her dog's soft whine reminded Carly she had to get up and take care of Bridget.

As Carly stirred, Micha propped himself up on his elbow to watch her. He wasn't sure what to expect—would she have regrets? To his relief, she glanced at him and grinned, her gaze bright and unabashed. "I've got to let Bridget out and feed her. Don't you dare try to leave while I'm gone," she said.

Astounded, he shook his head. "Carly, you know better. I'd never treat you—treat *us*—as a one-night stand. I'm not going anywhere except to take a quick shower."

"Good," she replied, calling her dog. "There are spare towels in the bathroom cabinet. Make yourself at home."

Make yourself at home. Her choice of words humbled him. Profoundly grateful for his good fortune in the midst of this turmoil, Micha had a quick shower while Carly took care of Bridget. Then, while she showered, he puttered around her small kitchen, deciding to surprise her with breakfast.

By the time she emerged, hair still damp, he'd put together a skillet of scrambled eggs, made toast and fried up some turkey bacon.

"Wow!" she exclaimed, taking a seat as he poured her a glass of orange juice. "This all looks awesome. When did you learn to cook?"

Pleased, he lifted one shoulder. "I picked it up a little bit here and there over time."

Making little sounds of pleasure, she devoured her breakfast, her dog lying under the table, gazing up at her hopefully. Micha ate quickly, too, unable to keep from watching her eat, wondering if she knew there was something sensual in the unabashed pleasure she took from the food.

When she finally pushed away her plate, he eyed her. More than anything he wanted to take her back to her bed and coax a response from her body. He couldn't believe he was once again turned on, even after making love this morning and the night before.

She picked up on the heat in his gaze and shook her head. "I know what you're thinking and I can't. I've got to be on time for work."

He didn't try to hide his regret. "Too bad. Is there any way you can take a day off?"

"Just so we can go back to bed?" She laughed. "I'm flattered, but…"

"More than that." He spread his hands, still hopeful. "I'm hoping to buy a new Jeep today, plus I've got to get to the car rental place and file an insurance claim.

All of that would be a lot more enjoyable if you came with me."

"A new Jeep?" she asked. "Let me guess. Jeep Wrangler?"

Her response made him grin. "Yep. How'd you know?"

Now her expression stilled. Her gaze skittered away before she raised her chin and looked at him again. "When I used to dream about our life together once we were married, I always pictured you driving a Jeep Wrangler. Silly, I know. But it just seemed to suit you."

Touched, he nodded, unsure if he should try to force words past the lump in his throat.

Luckily, Carly didn't seem to notice. "Anyway, I'd love to take a day off," she told him, drinking the last of her juice. "But I can't. I'd have to find someone to cover my shift and it's too short of a notice. Working with the littles in the NICU, it's imperative to have enough nurses on the floor."

Though disappointed, her response made him love her even more, if such a thing was possible. Carly had been born to be a pediatric nurse. Her caring, nurturing nature guaranteed she'd been good at it. "I understand. Is it all right if I use your car to take care of everything?"

"Ahh, now we get to the real reason you wanted me to take off." Her teasing tone let him know she didn't mean it. "But yes, you can use my car. Just don't let it—and you—get blown up." Though she smiled as she spoke, he could tell she was serious.

"I won't take my eyes off it," he promised. "I'll run

my errands after I stand guard outside the hospital for a bit."

"Guard outside?"

"Yes. I want to see if anyone tries to mess with your car. If so, I can catch them red-handed."

With a sigh, she grimaced. "Be careful, okay?"

Touched by her concern, he promised he would.

He had her drive to work while he sat in the passenger seat, making no effort to hide. She parked in the covered parking garage. After turning off the ignition, she sat for a moment. "Now what?" she asked, checking her watch. "I can't be late."

He leaned over and kissed her cheek, inhaling the lightly floral scent of her. "Give me the keys. Then we'll both go inside."

"You will? I thought you were going to watch my car. How are you planning to do that?"

"Because after I go inside with you, I'll stand just inside the entrance. If someone is watching with the idea of planting another bomb, I'll see them."

She shivered. "I don't like that," she said, dropping the keys into his hands. "Do you really think that same person will do that again?"

"You never know," he replied. "It depends on how determined they are to get their target. Either me or you. You should be safe inside at work. And if anyone tries to mess with your vehicle, I'll catch them red-handed. I'll give it a few minutes. If nothing happens, I'll go talk to the police and the car rental agency, and maybe swing by the dealership. I'll be back in time to pick you up when your shift is over. Just don't go outside until I come get you."

Though she agreed, she grimaced, her expression troubled. "I don't like not feeling safe," she said. "And I hate having to worry about you, too."

He kissed her again, this time a gentle press of his lips on hers. "We'll all be fine," he promised with an assurance he didn't have to fake. "We've got Chicago PD, the FBI and my friends in special forces working on this. It won't be long until this guy is caught."

Appearing unconvinced, she nodded and then got out of the car. "I've got to go. I don't want to be late."

He walked just inside the automatic doors with her, watching until she entered an elevator. From inside here, he had a clear view of her car and anyone who went near it.

Though he watched and waited for thirty minutes, nothing happened. Finally, he walked back outside and got into her vehicle. He couldn't help but brace himself as he started the ignition, half expecting to hear that familiar click before being blown to bits.

Instead, the engine started just fine. Glancing around him, he saw nothing out of the ordinary so he backed out of the parking spot and headed toward the car dealership he'd visited yesterday when they'd been closed.

Once he arrived, he parked and walked inside, pretending to inspect the vehicles on display in the showroom. Immediately, several salesmen appeared, talking quietly among themselves, their suits nearly identical in color and style. Finally, one man detached himself from the group and strolled over, smiling broadly. "Can I help you?" he asked. "I'm Johnnie."

"As a matter of fact, you can," Micha replied. "I'm

interested in a Jeep Wrangler out on the lot." He led the man over to the one he'd chosen.

"Would you like to take it for a test drive?" Johnnie asked.

Micha declined. "I've driven them before." Instead, he asked the man to name his best price without doing the usual talk-to-my-manager dance. At first, Johnnie looked a bit startled, but then he grinned. "Give me a minute," he said, jotting down the inventory number and motioning to Micha to come inside with him.

Two hours later, Micha found himself the proud owner of the sweet black Wrangler. Johnnie told him he'd have it cleaned up and ready to go by Tuesday morning, but Micha insisted he needed it now and was willing to wait. He planned to leave Carly's car parked at the dealership until he could pick up Carly from work and swing back to get it. The lot had numerous cameras, so Micha figured that would be the safest option. And he'd be driving a vehicle that no one would associate with him.

"Now, huh?" Johnnie asked.

"Please." Micha grimaced. "I really need it immediately. Or as soon as you can get it to me."

With a shrug, Johnnie pointed toward the waiting area. "I'll put a rush on it. Might be an hour or two. There's coffee and snacks in there."

Micha sat down to wait. He figured he could use this time to handle the car rental agency and the insurance. Just after he got a cup of coffee and took a seat, his cell phone rang. After glancing at it, he went ahead and answered, even though he didn't recognize the number.

"This is Special Agent Brad Howard," the caller said. "Is this Micha Harrison?"

After Micha replied in the affirmative, Brad got down to the reason for his call. "We have more information on the car explosion. It was a highly sophisticated setup, usually practiced by those with military experience. Rigged to detonate the instant the engine came on."

"I suspected as much," Micha said. "I saw a lot of similar bombings when I was stationed in Afghanistan."

"Interesting background," Brad allowed. "Which, of course, we looked into. I'm sure you guessed we'd be checking on you."

"I'd have been disappointed if you hadn't."

"Could you provide us with a list of people who might hold a grudge against you?" Brad asked. "Even if some of the names seem improbable, they might be worth looking into."

Micha thought back to his time in special ops. "Any enemies I made were terrorists or people working against the USA. None of them would have had reason enough to hunt me down two years later. If someone had wanted to take me out, their best bet would have been during my extended hospital stay. I was in a coma for a long time."

"We'd still like you to compile a list," the special agent requested. "It never hurts to check all angles."

"I'll get you something by the end of the day," Micha promised. "Any news on the double homicide? The one that seemed similar to the elder Coltons' murders?"

After a moment of hesitation, Brad replied. "The victims were older males, both shot in the head. We believe their murders were the work of two gunmen with rifles. I've been tasked with investigating a serial killer possibility. So far, I'm still working on that."

Which meant he either had nothing, or he didn't want to tell Micha. Understandable.

"I'll save your number in my phone," Micha said. "Is it okay with you if I text the list? It's probably going to be really short, anyway."

"No problem. Let me know if you think of anything else."

After ending the call, Micha spent a few minutes trying to come up with names of anyone stateside who could hate him enough to want to kill him. He couldn't think of anyone. Maybe that guy Carly had been dating until Micha showed up again? But no, Carly had said her former boyfriend had willingly let her go. Which meant he clearly hadn't cared deeply for her.

Since he wasn't getting anywhere, Micha decided he might as well call the car rental agency and let them know what had happened to their car. The police had promised to email a police report, and since Micha had taken out insurance, he'd need to file a claim.

Dealing with all of that took a little more than an hour. After hanging up, Micha eyed the clock on the waiting room wall and decided to go search for Johnnie to see if he had an estimated wait time.

Just as he approached the salesman, Johnnie looked up and grinned. "We're all set," he proclaimed. "They're bringing around your new vehicle now."

Walking out front with Johnnie, Micha waited patiently while Johnnie went over all of his new vehicle's features. Finally, he accepted the keys and drove off in the Jeep, feeling confident that whoever had blown up the rental car wouldn't recognize him.

For now, he considered himself essentially invisible.

Troubled and restless, Carly got busy immediately after signing on to her shift. For over a month now, she'd gone through her days with a vague sense of unease, starting after her father and uncle had been murdered. At first, she'd attributed all of that to grief. Then, when she'd begun to suspect someone was stalking her, she'd wondered if she'd gotten paranoid. The discovery of a video camera on her kitchen window and a car bomb blowing up Micha's rental car had definitely proved she wasn't, as well as upped the stakes. Another set of double murders, a possible serial killer on the loose in Chicago and the sudden return of a man she'd believed dead was enough to cause anyone to stumble.

Now that Micha had come back into her life, she not only feared for herself, but she also had him to worry about. Not to mention Bridget, her already well-loved dog, who could be hurt simply by being around Carly and Micha.

While she wasn't entirely sure, she'd venture a guess that since the bomb had been placed in his rental vehicle, Micha had been the target. Why, he seemed to have no idea, or so he claimed. Of course, considering the fact he'd kept so many secrets from her, she wouldn't put it past him to have more that he hadn't revealed yet. As in the reason he might have an enemy who wanted him dead.

Micha, handsome, strong Micha. A single look from his velvety brown eyes still made her weak in the knees.

Having him return to her life felt like a blessing—and a curse.

She hated not being able to trust him. And while she'd actually never stopped loving him, she wasn't sure they could ever have a future together without that. That thought made her heart hurt, so she shoved it aside and concentrated on the seriously ill children who needed her help.

By the time she neared the end of her shift, she sat and did the required charting. She texted Micha, letting him know she'd be out in a minute. He responded immediately, letting her know he was waiting by the side entrance, in a black Jeep Wrangler with the engine running.

Grinning despite herself, she hurried down. Outside, she spied Micha, waving from behind the wheel of the shiny new vehicle. Getting in, she breathed in that new-car smell and checked out the red leather interior. "Nice," she told him. "But where's my car?"

"I left it at the dealership," he explained. "They have security and all that. So we need to go collect it. I hope that's okay."

"Sure." Buckling her seat belt, she glanced at him, her heart quickening. "Did you get everything resolved with the car rental place?"

"I gave them all the information I had. Luckily, I took out their insurance policy, so it's fully covered. Someone from there is supposed to contact me soon."

Nodding, she allowed her eyes to drift closed as he drove, letting the cadence of the wheels on the pavement soothe her. For a few minutes, she allowed herself to pretend they were simply a regular couple who lived a normal, quiet life without danger of violence.

Somehow, she must have fallen asleep because the next thing she knew Micha had his hand on her shoulder, gently shaking her awake, and calling her name in a soft voice.

Blinking, she sat up straight, looking around with bleary eyes. "Oh," she said, realizing they were at the Jeep dealership. "I need to get out, stretch my legs and maybe down a cup of that notoriously awful auto dealership coffee before I get behind the wheel."

He followed her into the showroom, pointing her in the direction of the waiting room. She made herself a cup of coffee so thick she thought of it as sludge, managed to choke down three sips before deciding she was ready.

"I'll follow you home," he said.

Relieved, she nodded. Even though she had her new dog to alert her to any intruders, she really wasn't ready to be alone just yet.

As she pulled into the driveway, she noticed Micha had parked his new vehicle at the curb two houses down. Waiting for him as he walked toward her, she admired his athletic build and tried to decide if that was a wise move or foolish.

"I know," he said as he reached her. "I had to weigh the possibility of it being broken into versus the chance of whoever attempted to blow us up wanting to try again. I chose the lesser of two evils. At least if it's parked down there, no one will know it's mine."

She eyed him. "Your logic makes sense, even if I don't like it. This is one of those times that I really need to clean out that old garage behind my house. Maybe I can move some of the stuff that's in there into the storage shed."

He slung a casual arm across her shoulders. "I can help you with that," he said as they walked up the front porch.

As she turned her key in the front lock, Bridget barked a greeting. The instant she had the door open, the dog leaped on her, tail and behind wiggling with joy. Laughing, Carly got down on the floor with Bridget and gathered her close, petting her. When she finally climbed back to her feet, she brushed off the dog hair and grabbed the leash.

"I'll be right back," she told Micha, lurching forward as Bridget pulled her toward the back door.

When they returned, Carly headed straight for the kitchen with Bridget trotting along behind her. "Are you hungry, cutie pie?" she crooned. "Mama will get you your food."

Looking up, she realized Micha had taken a seat at the kitchen table and was grinning at her. With a shrug, she grinned back and filled the dog bowl with kibble. Once she'd placed it on the floor next to the water bowl, she eyed Micha. Damn, he looked good. Even at the end of a long, hard day. Or maybe *especially* at the end of the day.

"You might as well stay here," she said, crossing her arms and striving for casual.

Micha eyed her, his handsome face devoid of expression. "For tonight? Or…"

Amazingly, she felt her entire body heat. Flustered, she shook her head. It wasn't like she'd just invited him to her bed, though she wouldn't deny that was in the back of her mind, too. "How about we play it by ear? At least until you find your own place. I don't see a reason why you should continue paying for the hotel room."

"I see." Gaze warm, he regarded her. "So long-term, then. Why, Carly?"

"I...I don't want to be alone," she admitted. "Plus, I am enjoying your company."

When he didn't respond, for one terrifying moment she thought he might say no. "I enjoy your company, too," he said softly, appearing to be considering his next words.

A loud knock on her door cut him off. They both went still, though Bridget immediately started barking. Carly muted the TV and looked at Micha.

"Should I answer it?" Carly asked, her voice trembling. She absolutely hated that she now felt unsafe in her own home.

"Do you have a peephole?" Micha asked, making his way toward the front entrance ahead of her. Since she did indeed have a peephole, he looked through it.

"Well?" she demanded when Micha simply continued to stare outside silently. "Who is it?"

"I think it might be your brother," he told her, stepping back. "It's been a while since I've seen him, but that guy really looks like Jones."

"Let me see." She took a quick look through her peephole, before unlocking the dead bolt. "Jones! What are you doing here?" She stepped aside, ushering him into the house, locking the door behind him. "Come on in."

After pulling her in for a quick hug, her brother

grinned, his bright blue eyes full of mischief. "I came to make sure you're all right."

Had he heard about the car bomb? She eyed Jones, with his short dark hair and athletic build, deciding to stay quiet about that for now. The last thing she wanted to do was alarm her family.

"I'm fine," she said firmly.

"Good." Eyeing Micha, Jones held out his hand. "And I'm not going to lie. I wanted to see Micha. It's been two years, after all."

Jones had always liked Micha, and vice versa.

The two men shook. "It's been too long," Micha said.

"Yep. We've got a lot of catching up to do, for sure."

Carly motioned them toward the den. "Jones, can I get you something to drink?"

Her brother laughed and lifted up a paper bag. "I brought a few bottles of our newest beer for you both to try. Micha, I remember how much you enjoyed a good IPA."

"Your newest beer?" Micha asked. "What do you mean?"

Straightening, Jones beamed. "I own Lone Wolf Brewery. It's in West Loop. We only serve beer and a few quick bar snacks."

"It's really nice," Carly agreed. "Though the last time I was there, Jones was still working on getting it ready to open. Lots of space, and I'm guessing he's got it all fixed up now."

"I do." Jones beamed. "I purposely kept it small and intimate. We can hold around twenty people at the bar, and thirty more at tables in the general area. So far, it's exceeding my early expectations," Jones said with modest pride. He dropped down onto the couch and gestured at Micha to join him.

"I'd love to see it." Sitting, Micha accepted the beer Jones handed him. "Tell me about how you got started."

Watching the two men banter, Carly felt a warm glow of pleasure. She kept her distance, wanting to give them time to catch up. But Jones glanced up and shook his head. "Don't try to vanish into the kitchen. Come sit with us. Put up your feet and try my newest beer."

Slightly sheepish, Carly did as he asked. Instead of joining them on the couch, she took the armchair. Jones tilted his head but didn't comment as he handed her a can of beer.

Immediately, she jumped back to her feet. "Does anyone else want a glass?" When both men shook their heads, she practically dashed into the kitchen, beer can in hand.

"Do you think she's avoiding us?" she heard Jones ask.

"She's had a horrible few days," Micha replied. And then, to her horror, he told her brother all about the car explosion.

Stomach in knots, Carly poured her beer into a glass, squared her shoulders and made herself march back into her living room.

Jones's eyes narrowed. "Were you going to tell me about this at all, Carly?"

"Eventually." She glanced at Micha. "Now I don't have to."

Glancing from one to the other, Micha frowned. "Why am I getting the feeling I should have kept my mouth shut?"

Carly snorted.

"You shouldn't have," Jones said. "Clearly, someone has to look out for Carly."

"Ouch." Carly clenched her teeth. "Jones, you just got here. I planned to tell you eventually. I just want to ask you not to mention this to Heath or any of the rest of the family."

"You've got to be kidding me." Taking a long drink of his beer, Jones didn't bother to stifle his disbelief. "Carly, everyone has to be told. This is a clear danger. You never know who in the family might be next."

"Except we aren't sure who was the target," Micha pointed out. "The device was installed on my rental car, not Carly's vehicle. That would seem to make it likely that I was the intended victim, not her."

"Is that what the authorities think?" Jones asked.

"I believe so. The FBI asked me to provide a list of any known enemies."

Surprised, Carly eyed him. Again, he'd kept something important hidden from her. "Why didn't you tell me that?" she asked, carefully keeping her tone neutral. She couldn't help but wonder if he'd kept silent because he'd thought she might not need him to stay with her.

Micha shook his head. "I'd planned to get around to it tonight. We'd just started talking when Jones got here."

"Give the guy a break," Jones interjected in typical younger brother fashion. As the middle child in the family, Carly had often been stuck between Heath's first-born bossiness and youngest Jones's teasing. "Come on, sis. Lighten up."

As Jones had known it would, his admonishment annoyed her. Refusing to give him the satisfaction of reacting, Carly shook her head and sent a jab of her own. "You act more and more like Heath every day."

Instead of being infuriated, Jones laughed. "Touché," he said. He looked from Carly to Micha and back again. "I'm having a little family get-together at the Lone Wolf on Friday at eight and I wanted to personally invite you both."

Carly's first instinct was to balk. She still wasn't sure she was ready to bring Micha around her family. Mostly because she knew when she did, her female cousins would immediately start planning the wedding.

Instead of responding, Carly took a sip of her beer. The light, slightly citrusy flavor made her smile. She drank again. "Jones, this is really good."

"Thanks." Expression serious, her brother glanced between her and Micha. "So are you both going to come?"

Micha simply watched her. She appreciated the way he allowed her to decide, rather than jumping in and agreeing to go.

"You know how pushy the cousins are," Carly said. "They already started as soon as I told them Micha was alive." She met Micha's gaze. "Are you prepared to deal with them acting as if we're having a wedding sometime soon?"

"Are *you*?" Micha shot back. "Prepared to deal with them, I mean? They're your family. I've never had a problem holding my own with them."

"Is that a challenge?" Jones teased. "Because it sure sounded like one to me."

"I can deal with them," Carly responded, again refusing to let her brother get under her skin. "What do you think, Micha? Would you like to go?"

Though it wasn't super obvious, the way Micha exhaled told her he'd released tension. "That sounds like fun."

She nodded, facing her brother. "That settles it. So yes, we'll be there."

About to push to his feet, Jones knocked a coaster on the floor. Both he and Micha reached for it at the same time, just as the front window shattered.

"Gunshots!" Micha said. "Everyone down on the floor."

Petrified, at first Carly didn't move.

"Now!" ordered Micha.

Immediately, Carly dropped to the rug. "What's happening?" she asked, shocked to realize Micha had a pistol.

"Someone shot out your front window," Jones muttered. His eyes widened as he caught sight of Micha, crouched low and moving toward the front door with his weapon drawn. "Damn, Micha. What the hell are you doing?"

Micha barely glanced at him. "I'm betting this was a drive-by. But I want to get outside in case the shooter comes back again. I'll take cover behind that huge tree out front."

Carly's first impulse was to argue, to try to dissuade him. But her brother reached out and squeezed her shoulder. "Don't," he murmured. "I have a feeling Micha knows what he's doing."

Reluctantly, she swallowed back her words, stomach

clenched and chest hurting as she watched Micha open the front door and dash outside.

"Don't get up just yet," Jones warned. "If Micha is right, and there's a second drive-by, they'll go for anything that moves."

"But why?" Her anguished question didn't really require an answer.

Jones gave her one, anyway. "I don't know. Maybe whoever blew up the car is trying again. Micha is here, after all." He hugged her. "Carly, I don't like this. I don't think you should stay here any longer. I have room at my place."

Wide-eyed, she couldn't respond. Heck, she couldn't even think. As a matter of fact, delayed reaction had set in and she'd started to shake.

Seeing this, Jones scooted over and put his arm around her shoulders. "It's going to be all right," he said.

The sound of a motor revving had them both tensing up.

"It's coming back," Carly moaned, out of her mind with worry for Micha.

"That's not a car. It's a motorcycle." Still, Jones kept her down with his arm. "Stay still. Micha clearly knows how to defend himself. He was a soldier, for Pete's sake."

"Special forces," she corrected, almost automatically.

"Well, there you go."

They both listened, bracing themselves for more gunshots. The motorcycle revved again, getting louder as it approached.

Again, the sharp crack of gunfire. A few more, as

Micha must have responded. The rest of her front window caved inward, glass shards flying.

Then the motorcycle was gone, roaring off down the street.

In the silence, Carly could barely breathe. Eyes glued to her front door, she counted to three, waiting for Micha to reappear.

When he didn't, she pushed to her feet, shrugging away from her brother.

Jones got up, too, his expression shaken. "What are you doing?" he demanded.

"I've got to find Micha and make sure he's all right." She couldn't lose him again, she just couldn't. In that moment, frozen in terror, how much she cared for him slammed into her.

"You're not going to lose him," Jones replied, making her realize she must have spoken out loud. Grabbing her arm, Jones put his face level with hers. "I'll go," he said. "Mom would never forgive me if I allowed you to get hurt."

Dizzy, all Carly could do was nod. "I can't lose you, either," she said. "Please, Jones. Stay safe."

As her brother started for the foyer, she sank back down to the floor, barely registering the spray of glass all over her carpet and furniture. Bridget whined from somewhere in the kitchen and Carly began to crawl toward her, needing to make sure her pet hadn't been hurt.

Just then the front door opened, and Micha stepped inside. His grim expression revealed nothing. "Call 911," he told Carly.

Chapter 8

Carly froze, all the blood draining from her face as she stared at him. Concerned, Micha started for her. "Are you hurt?" he rasped, his chest tight at the thought of something, anything, having happened to her.

"N-n-no," she stammered, her wide-eyed gaze sweeping over him. "I'm okay. What about you? That looks like blood on your arm."

Glancing at himself, Micha cursed as he realized she was right. Of course, the instant he noticed it, the damn thing started hurting. "Must be a flesh wound," he said. "Do you have a clean rag or something I can use to stop the bleeding?"

Jones rushed into the kitchen, glass crunching underfoot, and returned with a dish towel. "Here you go," he said, handing it to Micha. "I hope you don't mind," he told Carly. "It's all I could find."

Though it wasn't long enough to tie a proper tourniquet, Micha tried to make due. His arm now throbbed like hell and he at least needed to stop the bleeding.

Seeing the problem, Carly hurried into her linen closet, removed an old but clean sheet and tried to tear it. Failing that, she grabbed a pair of scissors and cut a long and wide strip, which she folded over to make it thicker. "Let me," she said, wrapping it around his arm. "Leave the dish towel in place, but this should work until we can get your arm checked out."

"It's just a flesh wound," he started to protest, but then he noticed how her hands shook and held his tongue.

The instant she'd finished, she swayed and stumbled as if she might fall. Instinctively, he reached for her, wincing as he tried to use his injured arm. Jones noticed and rushed over and helped his sister to the sofa. "Sit," he ordered. "Are you all right? You look awfully pale."

She stared up at him and grimaced. "I don't know," she replied. "I feel really weird." Her gaze became unfocused, though she remained conscious and sitting up. Micha dropped down on the couch next to her and put his arm around her while exchanging a worried glance with her brother.

"I think you might be in shock," Jones said. "Let me get you some water."

More glass crunched underfoot as he got a glass of water and brought it to her. Murmuring a thank-you, she accepted it and took a sip. Keeping one arm around her shoulders, Micha reached in his pocket for his phone, but it wasn't there. Which meant it must have fallen out at some point, likely when he'd been crawling toward the door. Damn it. He needed to find it, but not right now. Carly was his main concern.

"We need to call 911," he said. "Chicago PD is supposed to be doing increased patrols, but they clearly missed this. I want to have Carly looked at."

She opened her eyes. "You need to have your arm checked out first," she said, squirming out from under his arm. "I'm fine. Why don't you go ahead and call them?"

"I need to find my phone first." Micha pushed to his feet and started to search. "It has to be somewhere between here and that big oak tree," he said. "I didn't go anywhere else."

Jones began to help him. "Did you get a glimpse of the shooter?" he asked.

"No. He was wearing a helmet. I squeezed off a couple of shots, but he went by really fast and I wasn't entirely prepared. I'm not sure if I hit him or not."

"I'm calling the police now," Carly said. Though still appearing dazed, she dialed 911 and told the dispatcher what had happened. When she ended the call, she informed them in a shaky voice that the woman promised to send a squad car out immediately. Some of the color had returned to her face and she seemed to be breathing better.

Nodding, Micha continued his search for his phone.

"Here it is," Jones said, pulling it out from under a decorative table near the front door. "It must have fallen from your pocket during all that insanity earlier."

Thanking the other man, Micha did a quick inspection to make sure there'd been no damage. Once he'd ascertained everything was fine, he slid the phone back into his pocket.

In the distance, they could all hear the sirens, which meant the police would be here soon.

"Well," Jones said, dusting his hands off on his jeans. "I guess we still can't really tell who the shooter was after."

"He shot up *my* house," Carly protested.

"But Micha was inside," Jones replied. "So he could have been after either one of you."

"What about you?" Carly took another long sip of her water. "Is it possible someone might be after our entire family?"

Jones shrugged, appearing unconcerned. "Anything is possible," he conceded. "But since I haven't had any threats or anything, I think we can rule that out." Eyeing Carly, he frowned. "Speaking of that, I need to call Heath and fill him in."

Outside, the sirens cut off, though the flash of blue and red lights announced the arrival of the police. A sharp knock on the front door had Micha hurrying to answer it.

Bridget barked twice, then took off for the bedroom, tail tucked between her legs, presumably to take shelter under Carly's bed.

Micha opened the door. There were two patrol cars and four officers. Two of them used flashlights to check the outside. The other two came in and inspected the damage, shaking their heads at the broken glass.

"You're the guy whose car exploded, right?" one of the policemen asked. "I wasn't on duty then, but I sure heard about it. That would have been a hell of a way to die."

Thinking back to some of the things he'd seen in Afghanistan, Micha agreed.

Carly, Micha and Jones all gave their statements, which were duly recorded. Once Jones had made certain nothing else was needed from him, he slipped out to his vehicle to call Heath.

After making sure her dog was safe in her bedroom, Carly closed that door to keep her in there and then got out a broom and began sweeping up the broken glass. "I'm glad Bridget didn't cut her feet," she said to no one in particular.

The two outside officers returned, apparently having finished up. "We're going to speak with your neighbors in case anyone had a video camera. If we learn anything, someone will keep you posted."

Micha crossed his arms. "Just like someone was supposed to beef up patrols on this street after the car bomb?"

The older officer stared him down, though the younger one blinked. "We can check into that, if you'd like. Hyde Park patrols are usually pretty routine, so I'm thinking they would be able to swing by here once or twice per shift."

"What about your arm?" Carly asked, pointing to his makeshift bandage. "He needs to have that checked out."

"Were you shot?" Getting out his radio, one of the cops appeared ready to call for an EMT.

"It's okay." Micha held up his hand to forestall him. "A bullet just grazed my arm. No need to call anyone.

Once I clean and bandage it, I'll be fine. It's just a matter of getting the proper supplies."

The youngest officer appeared unconvinced. He blinked and pushed his wire-rimmed glasses higher up his nose. "Maybe we should have someone look at it, just in case."

"No need," Micha insisted. "I had much worse injuries over in Afghanistan. I'm good."

"Oh, you're a veteran. Well, then I guess you'd know." Reluctantly, the cop nodded.

Micha glanced over at Carly, half expecting her to protest, but she didn't. Her gaze had once again gone hazy and unfocused and she appeared lost in her own thoughts. He ached to go to her and hold her, to chase away the shadows in her expression. She didn't deserve this, no one did, but especially not Carly. How anyone could target such a beautiful, gentle soul was beyond him.

Which made the idea of him being the target here instead of her much more plausible. Which meant he needed to seriously try to figure out a short list of his enemies. But he honestly couldn't think of anyone who hated him enough to want him dead.

Once the police had gone, Carly stirred. "I need to clean up this mess," she said. "I don't want Bridget cutting her feet." Moving slowly and stiffly, she retrieved a broom and a dustpan from her laundry room.

Micha took the broom from her as she walked by him. She didn't resist at all, and he considered asking her to sit back down and leave the cleanup to him but figured keeping her busy might help more.

"Let me clear this out," he said, using the broom handle to bust out the remaining pieces of glass from the window frame. Then he swept and she held the dustpan. Working as a team, she dumped the shards into the kitchen trash can. Once they'd finished the floor, she got out her vacuum and went over the entire area to make sure she hadn't missed any. She turned it off and methodically rewound the cord. "I wouldn't want to take the chance of Bridget cutting her feet," she said, repeating herself, her voice devoid of inflection.

"Are you all right?" he asked, concerned.

She looked up, focusing on him, and grimaced. "You know what? I'm not. Not really. I'm trying really hard to get there, though."

Taking the vacuum from her, Micha urged her to sit, either in the armchair or at the kitchen table. The fact that she nodded and shuffled off to do as he'd asked alarmed him. He'd speak to Jones and see if they could get her to agree to get checked out at the hospital.

Quickly, he used the hose to do the couch. He knew for certain more than a few glass shards had made it there. Then he went to check on Carly. Jones still hadn't returned from his outside phone call. He'd been gone so long that Micha began to wonder if the younger man had left.

Micha debated going in search of Jones, but Carly mattered more. He found her sitting at the kitchen table, staring straight ahead, both hands wrapped around her water glass. She glanced up when he entered, her lips parted. "Hey," she said, greeting him softly.

His chest squeezed. "Hey," he responded in kind, going to her and carefully wrapping his arms around her from behind. "It's going to be all right," he promised, breathing in the slightly floral scent of her hair.

"Is it?" she asked, leaning back into him. "I just don't understand how someone can do such horrible things. Or why."

"Agreed." He lightly kissed her cheek, allowing himself to linger. "We have to believe that sooner or later whoever is doing this will make a mistake and be caught."

"Carly?" Jones's voice as he came through the back door into the kitchen, still on his phone. He glanced curiously from one to the other. "Carly, Heath wants to talk to you."

Carly barely managed to stifle a groan. Micha released her and Jones handed her the phone. She took a deep breath, pressed the speaker button and placed the phone on the table in front of her.

"Heath, the last thing I need right now is a lecture," Carly said, apparently having decided to go on attack first. "It's been a crazy few days. I'm exhausted and terrified. And none of this is my fault." She took a deep breath.

"I get all of that," Heath responded, his voice surprisingly gentle. "None of this is your fault, it is crazy and I can imagine how awful you must feel. But I'm your older brother. It's my job to be worried about you. I'm glad Jones was there."

"And Micha," she pointed out, her gaze sliding over to him. While he felt kind of awkward, listening in to the conversation, Carly clearly wanted him to hear. "By the way, I've got you on speaker."

After a second or two of completely awkward silence, Heath cleared his throat. "Why?"

"Because I'm tired," Carly replied. "And I know you have good intentions, but in this situation, there's absolutely nothing you can do to help."

"I can call Chicago PD and demand more patrols."

"Micha's already done that," Carly shot back.

"What about the FBI? I have contacts there since I've been dealing with the agents who are investigating the possible serial killings." Before Carly could respond, Heath sighed. "Let me guess. Micha's already done that."

Micha decided to speak up. "Hey, Heath. How's it going?"

Instead of responding in kind, Heath went quiet again. "Micha, I need to know something. How much of all this is happening due to you hanging around my sister?"

"I don't know." All Micha could do was give Heath the truth. "We still haven't figured out if I'm the target or if it's Carly."

"Maybe you two should consider splitting up for safety's sake." The hard edge to Heath's voice told Micha that he meant business. But the notion—even thinking about going away and not seeing Carly for a protracted period of time—felt like a knife in the gut. Plus, who would protect her if he was gone?

But still, he hesitated. Possibly Heath was right. Perhaps being around Carly wasn't the best thing right now for her safety. Except...what if he left her alone and she turned out to be the actual target? He needed to stay with her, if only to protect her. While he knew

Heath wouldn't understand in a million years, Micha wouldn't even want to live anymore if something happened to Carly.

To Micha's relief, Carly shook her head. "No splitting up. That's not going to happen," she said, her tone firm. "I just got him back, almost from the dead. I can't send him away so soon. Plus, I feel safer with Micha around."

Her words had him going to her and slipping his arm around her shoulders. He could feel her tension as she waited for Heath to argue. Jones wisely stayed out of it, leaning on the door frame silently in the background watching, while sipping on another one of his beers.

"Well, I guess that's your choice," Heath finally said, which made Carly glance up at Micha, her surprise plain on her face. "But, Carly, I wanted to offer you another choice. Come stay with me. Or even Jones. Clearly someone has targeted your home. You can't tell me you believe you could be safe there any longer, not until this person or people are caught."

Jones finally spoke up. "He's right, Carly. You've got to stay somewhere else for a little bit." He eyed Micha. "How about Micha's place?"

"No, that won't work," Carly answered. Micha silently thanked her for not telling her brothers that he'd been living in a hotel. "I have a dog now. And I don't like the idea of someone driving me out of my own home."

"I don't like the idea of someone killing you, either," Heath said, his tone dry.

Micha decided he'd heard enough. "Look, I understand your concern. I'm right there with you. But if Carly wants to stay in her own home, she should. I'll be here with her. I have a gun and I know how to use it. I give you my word that I'll protect her, no matter what. Even with my own life, if it comes to that."

Carly gasped. "Don't talk like that," she admonished Micha before turning her attention back to the phone. "Heath, I'm twenty-nine years old and a responsible adult. I promise you that I'll be careful. I won't go anywhere alone. When I'm not at work, I'll be with Micha."

"Plus, the police are on it," Micha interjected. "And the FBI is also involved. They should catch this guy soon."

"I still don't like it," Heath grumbled. "Though I can see I don't have a choice."

"You don't." Carly spoke firmly. "I'll see you Friday at Lone Wolf, okay?"

"Fine. I assume you're bringing Micha?"

"Of course," she answered.

Of course. Micha allowed himself a second to bask in that phrase.

"Good." An undercurrent of warning colored Heath's voice. "Micha, you and I will talk then." And he ended the call.

"That sounded like a threat," Jones said, strolling into the room. "Proof positive how rattled big brother is."

"I'm rattled, too," Carly said, her tone sharp. "Aren't you?"

"Yes, I am." Jones shook his head. "We need to get some plywood and cover this window. Carly, do you have any?"

"Plywood?" She shrugged. "I doubt it. But who knows? The previous owner never emptied the storage shed, so there might be some there. And my garage is full, too. I've never gotten around to cleaning it out, though I definitely plan to before winter gets here."

"Let's go take a look," Jones suggested.

Carly grabbed her flashlight. "Let me check on Bridget," she said. Despite Carly calling her, Bridget refused to leave the bedroom, clearly still terrified. Micha suspected Carly would have to do quite a bit of coddling before she could coax the dog out.

Finally, with Carly leading the way, all three of them went outside to look for plywood or something they could use to board up the window temporarily.

Inside the shed, they found several full sheets of plywood, though most of them were either warped or had split. Micha and Jones chose the best one out of the stack. "This will be large enough to entirely cover that window," Micha said.

"Agreed." Jones looked at Carly. "Do you have a hammer and some nails?"

"Yes. They're in the garage," she replied.

With the two men carrying the plywood between them, they headed back toward the house. They made a quick pit stop at the garage, where the sheer amount of stuff Carly had crammed in there made Micha wince.

Carly turned on the light, rummaged around for a moment, and then emerged with a hammer and a box of nails. "I knew I had some," she said.

Working together, Micha and Jones made short work of nailing the plywood over the broken window. "That should work until you can call the glass repair company in the morning," Jones said.

"Thanks." Carly sighed. "I'm also going to contact

an alarm company. Besides an alarm, I might look into having cameras installed on the outside of the house."

Jones hugged her. "I think that's an excellent idea. I'm going home now." He glanced at Micha. "Micha, would you mind walking out with me? I'd like to have a word."

When Carly made as if she intended to follow, Jones shook his head. "In private," he said. "Why don't you go work on seeing if you can get your dog to come out? Poor thing is going to need some heavy reassurance."

Carly frowned. "Jones, is this really necessary? Heath has already said enough. I really don't need you to make things worse."

"Please. I'm not Heath," Jones replied, his tone mildly offended. "I have no intention of chewing Micha out. I just want to have a private word with him."

Considering, Carly finally nodded. She turned away without another word, apparently heading toward her bedroom to check on Bridget.

Jones and Micha headed outside. The neighborhood had fallen peaceful once more, everyone tucked safely inside their houses.

When they reached Jones's vehicle, Jones turned. "Do you love my sister?" he asked.

Micha didn't hesitate. "Yes. Of course I do."

As if he'd expected that answer, Jones nodded. "Then I strongly suggest you do what you can to get her to go somewhere safe until this is over. With or without you." Then Jones got into his car and started it, driving away without waiting for Micha's response.

After stopping by the kitchen to grab a handful of dog treats, Carly walked quietly into her bedroom. She could see the shine of Bridget's eyes from her spot under the bed. Carly sat down on the floor, making no move toward the still-terrified animal, and simply began to speak softly to her. She repeated the same words and phrases, even though the dog most likely didn't understand them, telling her over and over again that she was safe, she was loved and everything would be all right.

She placed a dog treat in the space between her and the bed, where Bridget could see it, and continued talking. Eventually, as Carly had expected she might, the dog inched closer, her nose twitching.

Careful not to make any sudden moves, Carly placed another dog treat on the floor, closer to her this time. After Bridget scarfed down the first one, she came all the way out from under the bed, got the second and crawled into Carly's lap.

Carly gathered her close, still crooning, and stroked her silky fur. At first, the dog trembled, but eventually even that stopped.

The front door opened, which meant Micha had returned from his chat with her younger brother. At the sound, Bridget stiffened and raised her head. "It's just Micha," Carly told her, hoping her new pet understood. When the dog gave a quick thump of her tail, Carly thought she might.

When Micha appeared in the doorway, Bridget let out a low woof. More of a greeting than a warning. Micha got down on his haunches and Bridget wiggled her way over to him on her belly. "Such a good girl," he said, scratching Bridget behind the ears. He glanced at Carly over the dog's head. "Still okay?"

She nodded. "Still okay."

"Do you need help getting up?"

"No, I'm good." Though she felt stiff, Carly climbed to her feet. "Is everything all right with you and Jones?"

"Sure." Micha rose, too, beckoning her to follow. "He didn't read me the riot act, if that's what you're asking. He just asked me to try to talk you into staying somewhere else until this mess is figured out. Which you have to admit does make sense."

They'd reached the kitchen. Bridget went immediately for her water bowl. Carly eyed Micha, trying to think. "Both the car exploding and having my house shot at are terrifying," she admitted. "But I hate to let some crazy person drive me out of my own home. Plus, where would I go? I don't want to stay with Heath or Jones. You live in a hotel. And my dog needs an outdoor space like I have here."

"I could rent a place," he offered, dragging his hands through his longish, wavy brown hair. Two years ago, he'd worn it short, in a military cut. She liked it better this way, she thought. The longer cut made him look sexy, almost roguish. More like a pirate than a soldier. Though bad boys had never been her type, Micha made her want to change her mind.

Mouth dry, she tried to force her thoughts back on track. "Rent a place?"

"One of the ones we were going to go look at," he continued. "That way you'd still be close to work."

Leaning against her kitchen counter, she crossed her arms. "And then what happens if this crazy person finds us again? If he's staking out my job, all he has to do is follow us. Once he knows about your new Jeep, that could be a target, too. We'd have to keep moving, which isn't possible right now. I have a job I love, my first dog and family here. This is our home. We can't keep living our lives on the run."

She caught her breath as she realized she'd said *us* and *we* and *our* rather than simply herself. She'd included him in her future, as if she already decided he'd be there. The realization made her stomach do a somersault.

If Micha noticed he gave no sign. "That's a valid point," he agreed. "Still, until they catch this guy, there's got to be something we can do."

"Precautionary measures?" She was good at those, mostly because she had to be as a nurse. "I've already started on some. As I said, I'm planning on hiring an alarm company to put in a monitored alarm with outside video cameras. Tomorrow I'll call a glass company and get that window replaced. And I'll get that garage cleaned out on my next day off, so we can park our vehicles inside."

Gaze serious, he studied her. Her heart skipped a beat at the heat in his eyes. "Are you sure you want me hanging around? What if this person is after me instead of you? My presence here will only endanger your life."

All this back and forth exhausted her. He needed to take a stance and stick with it. "I'll leave that up to you," she finally told him. "If you don't want to face this as a team, I get it. If you go, I can handle it." She lifted her chin. "I'm used to being on my own."

"Ouch." He winced. "I'd never forgive myself if something happened to you because of me."

"Then you have quite the conundrum," she drawled, refusing to give in to the sudden, sharp urge to beg him to stay. Never again, not after he'd disappeared and allowed her to believe him dead. She still couldn't wrap her head around his decision not to make contact. If the situation had been reversed, she would have moved heaven and earth to make her way back to his side.

That was what hurt more than anything.

Some of her thoughts must have shown in her face. He crossed to her, placing his hand gently under her chin. "I'm not leaving you," he declared, right before he kissed her.

More relieved than she cared to admit, even to herself, she kissed him back. By the time they broke apart, she could hardly think straight.

"Come," he said, taking her hand and leading her into the bedroom.

Carly only got up once for the rest of the night—to take Bridget out. She finally fell asleep, wrapped in Micha's strong arms, feeling safe and extremely well loved.

Carly's cousin Simone called early the next morning as Carly had just gotten her first cup of coffee and filled Bridget's bowl with kibble. Taking a deep breath before she answered, Carly wondered if Heath had already notified the entire family about what had been going on with her and Micha. But if Simone knew, she didn't bring it up. Instead, she wanted to talk about finding their fathers' killers.

"Since classes are out for the summer, I'm planning to dedicate all of my time to this," Simone declared. "January is too busy with work, so I thought I'd ask you if you wanted to help."

"Help with what?" Carly asked, resisting the urge to mention that she also had a full-time job. While she might have today off, she always had a lot to do in her limited leisure time. Especially today.

"Well," Simone said. "Clearly the police aren't making the case their top priority. Now that we know it's likely the work of serial killers—"

"The FBI is taking the lead," Carly interrupted. "At least, that's what I've been told."

"Either way, no one but family has as deep of an interest in catching the murderer," Simone continued, unfazed. "I've been doing a lot of research on serial killers. It's a fascinating subject. I had no idea."

Carly made a noncommittal sound, aware Simone didn't really require a response. Among family, Simone had always been the one who loved to research whatever happened to be her interest at the moment. Right now, that appeared to be serial killers.

"Do you want to meet up for coffee in an hour and talk more about it?" Simone asked. How she knew Carly had the day off, Carly wasn't sure.

Glancing at the clock, Carly sighed. "I can't. I have a ton to do today. In fact, I need to let you go so I can finish getting ready."

Micha walked into the kitchen just then, barefoot and shirtless, with his faded jeans riding low on his hips. Carly completely lost her train of thought. Apparently oblivious, Micha strolled over and kissed her cheek. "Good morning," he murmured, his raspy before-coffee voice sexy as hell as he moved past her.

"Who's that?" Simone chirped. "Is that Micha? Did he spend the night at your place?"

"Yes," Carly replied. "Sorry, Simone. I've got to run." Heart pounding, she quickly ended the call.

Admiring Micha's backside while he made himself a cup of coffee, she knew she needed to finish her morning preparations, but she couldn't make her legs move. Usually, she preferred to start her days off enjoying a leisurely coffee on her back patio but all she could think of at this moment was how to lure Micha back to bed.

"Who was that?" Micha asked, turning to face her, holding his mug with both hands. As he raised it to his mouth to take a sip, she caught her breath, unable to tear her gaze away.

"That was Simone," she replied, pushing the words out past her suddenly parched throat. To cover, she drank some of her coffee and picked up Bridget's now-empty food bowl.

"Ah. I'm guessing Heath has already told everyone about the explosion and the gunshots?"

"That's what's so weird," she said. "Simone didn't mention any of that. Instead, she wanted to talk about investigating our fathers' murders. She's really into research and she's been learning about serial killers and what makes them tick."

Bridget scratched at the back door, whining to indicate she needed to go out. Glad of the distraction, Carly took her dog out, bringing her coffee with her. Once outside, she breathed in the fresh morning air while she watched Bridget explore the backyard. She hadn't known she'd love her dog so deeply or so quickly.

How the hell Micha could still affect her so strongly, especially since they'd spent the night wrapped in each other's arms, she didn't understand. She wasn't sure she even wanted to.

The back door squeaked, alerting her to the fact that

he'd joined her outside. "Nice morning," he said, sounding a bit more normal now that he'd had a few sips of coffee.

"It is." She tried hard to sound normal, too, as if her heart wasn't racing and her skin prickling with the awareness of him.

"I'm thinking of giving up my hotel room today," he said. "Assuming you still want me to stay here with you."

"I do," she replied, even though living together was a huge step. Deciding to qualify that, she turned to face him. "At least until the danger is over."

Micha kissed her cheek. "At least until then," he agreed. "Would you mind giving me my own key?"

She hid her smile. "Of course I don't mind. Roomie." Because she was determined that was all they'd ever be—roommates. She couldn't risk having her heart broken by him ever again.

Chapter 9

Micha dressed carefully for the Colton get-together at Lone Wolf Brewery. He figured Carly's entire family would be scrutinizing his every move. Even though she'd tried to play off her asking him to move in with her as strictly a safety thing, they both knew better. She might try to pass him off as just a roommate, but he knew none of the Coltons would look at it that way. He remembered how they'd scrutinized him when he and Carly had gotten engaged. He was pretty sure Heath had even run a background check on him. Actually, Micha couldn't really blame them. Carly was pretty damn special. It made perfect sense they'd want to make sure the person she chose to share her life with was on the up-and-up.

After the two-year absence, despite what had happened to him, he imagined the scrutiny would be even more intense. Eager to prove to them he would be there for her from now on, he was ready for whatever they dished out. He welcomed it even.

Even Jones, who'd always seemed low-key to Micha, had delivered a brotherly warning. Micha expected no less from the rest of the Colton clan.

Beyond that, he really was looking forward to touring the Lone Wolf Brewery. The idea of crafting and distributing beer interested him. He had to give props to Jones for following his passion.

"What do you think?" Carly asked, emerging from the bathroom wearing a formfitting black dress and sky-high heels. She wore her long blond hair down, a silky curtain swirling around her shoulders.

Stunned, he could only stare for a moment, his entire body zinging with desire. "You take my breath away," he told her. "Now all I can think about is how badly I want to get that dress off you."

She grinned, her bright blue eyes dancing. "Thanks. You don't look too bad yourself. I like your jeans. And that button-down shirt looks great on you."

Ridiculously relieved, he thanked her. Though he'd met and interacted with her entire family numerous times in the past, he felt as if he were meeting them for the first time again.

They took his new Jeep to West Loop. To Micha's surprise, Lone Wolf Brewery was housed in quite a large building with ample parking. A large sign proclaimed the establishment was closed that evening for a private party. "Wow," Micha commented. "This is not at all what I expected."

Carly gave him a curious glance. "What did you expect exactly?"

"I don't know. Something smaller. More on the scale of a first-time brew pub owner."

This made her laugh. "Right. We're Coltons. We don't do anything halfway."

She had a point. The family business—Colton Connections—was well-known in the entire Chicago area. It made sense that when any of the Colton offspring decided to start their own ventures, they'd be done with finesse and flair.

As they walked toward the entrance from the parking lot, Heath came out the back door and intercepted them. "Glad I caught you," he said, sparing Micha a single hard glance. "Carly, I haven't said anything to the family about the car bomb or the shooting. Jones hasn't, either. Let's keep that quiet for now. I don't want to worry Mom, okay?"

"Sure." Carly nodded. She squeezed Micha's hand. "She's got enough to stress about, so that's perfectly fine with me."

"Good." Opening the door, Heath motioned them to go past him.

"Where's Kylie?" Carly asked.

For a moment, Heath's hard gaze softened. "She'll be joining us later. She had a few things she wanted to do at work first."

"Kylie is Heath's fiancée," Carly told Micha. "They met at Colton Connections. She's one of the VPs working for Heath." She flashed a mischievous grin. "It was a workplace romance."

Heath rolled his eyes and strode away without responding.

Watching him go, Carly tugged on Micha's arm. "Just ignore him. I'm guessing he's got something else on his mind."

Micha nodded. Inside, he took his time and looked around, pleasantly surprised again. The decor, while rustic, also managed to look hip. There was lots of dark wood and metal, with numerous large beer tanks located behind the bar. On the wall, a large sign hung with the Lone Wolf label—a gray, smiling wolf's head on a bright red background.

"Nice," Micha said, turning a slow circle to take it all in. Not huge, but not overly small, either. And he spotted a red exit sign, indicating the emergency exit, and made a mental note. Always good to know.

"Thanks." Jones appeared, smiling from ear to ear. "Come. Let me give you both a private tour of the place. We'll be doing a beer sampling later and then I have a big announcement for us all to celebrate."

His enthusiasm had Carly grinning, too. "Sounds perfect," she said. "I really like what you've done with the decor."

"I had help with that," Jones replied. "Tatum did most of it. You know how well she's done with her restaurant. She took one look around and knew exactly how to decorate this place."

"You remember my cousin Tatum, don't you?" Carly asked Micha. "She owns a wildly successful restaurant called True. Not only that, but she's also the chef."

"We'll have to go there sometime," Micha said.

"You bet we will." Carly glanced around. "Where's

the rest of the family? We ran into Heath on the way in but haven't seen anyone else."

Jones shrugged. "Heath has been running in and out. You know how he is. And everyone else hasn't arrived yet. You are a bit early, aren't you?"

"You said seven, right?" Carly checked her watch. "It's five after."

"Actually, I said eight." Jones smiled to take the sting from his words. "But that's okay. You two can be the first to have a private tour. I've got my waitstaff setting things up in the kitchen, so let me show you where the main magic happens."

"Main magic?" Carly frowned. "What do you mean?"

"Where we make the beer!" Jones practically jumped up and down with excitement. "It's a detailed process, so I'll have to explain every step of it to you."

"Maybe you should wait for everyone else so you only have to go over it once," Carly pointed out. Though Jones appeared surprised by the notion, Micha had to admit it made sense. Even if he secretly wanted to see it all right now.

Plus, a tour with everyone would definitely keep the rest of the Coltons from focusing so much on him.

"What about you?" Jones asked Micha, clearly disappointed. "Would you like a quick look around before everyone else arrives?"

Micha shrugged. "Sure, why not. I'd really like to. We'll see it again with the others, too."

The door opened just as Jones was about to lead them off. Carly's mom and her aunt strolled in arm in arm. "I see we're not the only early ones," Fallon trilled.

Meanwhile, Carly's mom had stopped short, her gaze locking on Micha.

"So it *is* true," Farrah said. "You *are* alive."

"Yes, ma'am." Micha flashed her a smile. "Luckily so."

She moved closer, a still-beautiful woman who carried herself as if she knew it. She walked right up to Micha, ignoring her daughter. "Where were you?" she demanded. "Two whole years went by with Carly thinking you were dead. If you only knew how much she suffered."

"Not now, Mom," Carly protested. "We can have this discussion later."

"It's all right," Micha reassured her. "I don't mind." Speaking quietly, he explained about being taken prisoner, the rescue mission six months later that had gone wrong, the crash, the injuries, the coma, all of it. By the time he'd finished Farrah Colton had tears in her eyes.

"Oh, you poor man," Farrah said, hugging him. "I'm so sorry all that happened to you. Carly did mention it, but she must have glossed over the details. It sounds much more horrible coming from you."

Not sure how to respond to that, Micha simply nodded. Carly squeezed his arm, commiserating silently with him.

The door opened again. "Everyone must have decided to come early," Carly murmured. January and a man walked in holding hands, with Tatum and another man right behind. "The one with January is Sean," Carly said. "And Tatum's beau is Cruz. The two men have a lot in common since they both work for the Chicago Police Department. Sean is in Homicide and Cruz is in Narcotics."

This info had Micha eyeing the two newcomers with renewed interest. "I wonder if they know my buddy Charlie."

"I guess you can ask them. Though Chicago has a huge police force, you never know."

"Are they working on the murder investigation with the FBI?" he asked.

"I'm not sure," Carly responded. "Heath is the point person on all of that. He just passes the info on to the rest of us. Though now that Simone has gotten obsessed with the case, she probably knows more than even Heath."

"Simone…" Micha tried to remember. "Isn't she the college professor?"

"Yep. Psychology. When she decides to investigate something, she really dives into her research."

Micha looked around, trying to see if he could spot her.

"She's not here yet," Carly said. "She's always punctual, so she should be here closer to eight."

Rolling his shoulders, Micha gave himself a mental order to relax. Before being taken prisoner, he'd enjoyed social gatherings. He'd considered himself outgoing and got along easily with all types of people.

Since then, that part of him had changed. Though he knew he didn't have to, the second he entered a room he made a mental note to locate the exit, as he'd done here. He constantly checked over his shoulder, tried not to let anyone come up unexpectedly behind him and held a lot more of himself in reserve.

Jones moved among his family, pointing out a fantastic spread of appetizers and samples of beer that had been arranged on the bar.

The door opened and a woman who had to be Carly's cousin Simone arrived. Slim, with chin-length brown hair and the same piercing blue eyes as the rest of the Coltons, she carried herself with a kind of quiet dignity.

Her face lit up when she spied Carly and Micha and she made a beeline for them.

Bestowing a quick hug on Micha, she stepped back and studied him. "I'm so sorry for everything you went through," she said quietly. "I'm so glad you found your way back to us."

"Thank you." He could hardly talk past the sudden ache in his throat. "I really appreciate that."

Smiling, she dipped her chin before turning to Carly. "I heard Heath is planning to update us on the investigation into our fathers' murders. I've tried my best to find out what he knows, but he isn't telling." She dug in her oversize tote bag and removed an old-fashioned spiral notebook. "I've made a lot of notes."

Carly nodded. "Maybe we can look at them later," she said. "Right now we all need to focus our attention on Jones and his wonderful establishment."

"Of course." Simone slid her notebook back into her bag. "I'll touch base with you later." And she headed off to greet the rest of the family.

"I just dodged a bullet," Carly murmured. "There's no way I care to learn everything she's discovered about serial killers. Especially not the gory details of their methods."

"I don't know," Micha teased. "It sounds interesting. You might like it."

Shaking her head, she elbowed him in the side. He grinned at her and took another drink of his beer.

Everyone stood around, beers in hand, chatting and sampling the appetizers that Jones had put out. Though Heath moved confidently among the little groups of his family members, Micha noticed Heath spent an inordinate amount of time watching the front door.

When a slender, dark-haired woman walked through, Heath's expression lit up. She'd barely taken a few steps inside when Heath met her halfway, sweeping her up into his arms and kissing her as if he hadn't seen her in days.

"PDA, ugh," Carly commented, though she was smiling. "I've never seen my older brother so happy. It's amazing."

Micha put his arm around her shoulders and drew her close. "Hopefully, they'll be saying the same thing about you," he said, waiting for her to stiffen.

Instead, she relaxed against him. "I know I should say something sarcastic right now," she murmured. "But you know what? I hope so, too."

Admitting her inner hope to Micha had been a lot less scary than she'd thought it might be. Bless him, he hadn't pressed for more. Instead, he'd simply kissed the top of her head and continued to hold her close. She liked the way she felt, sheltered against his muscular body.

Though she caught a few stray curious glances directed her way, most of her family seemed accepting. Now that everyone had arrived, Jones started his behind-the-scenes tour. Carly half listened as he described the process of making beer. Malted barley, mash, boil, cooling, fermentation, straining—it all sounded like a lot of work. Judging by the animation in both his voice and expression, Jones clearly loved every step of it.

As he led them back into the main bar area, he beckoned to Tatum to join him at the front of the room. "And now for the big announcement!" he said. "Tatum is going to be serving Lone Wolf Brewery beer at True. It's going to be wonderful exposure for us, especially since her restaurant is packed every single night."

"Not *every* night," Tatum chimed in, grinning. "But pretty darn close!" She and Cruz locked gazes and she blushed, going doe-eyed. Carly looked on, happy for her cousin.

"Everyone, feel free to sample any of our craft beers," Jones announced. "And let me know if you have any questions."

Everyone clapped and began congratulating Jones.

As people began circulating, January and her fiancé, Sean, made their way over. Carly introduced Micha. The instant the other man heard the name, he frowned. "I swear I heard about you the other night while at the precinct. Aren't you the guy who had someone put an explosive device inside your car?"

Unfortunately, Sean's question rang out just as one of those occasional odd silences fell over the room. Carly tensed up as just about everyone's heads swiveled around to stare.

Micha nodded, making a face. "We're trying to keep

that quiet," he murmured. "Can we talk about something else?"

Too late. Now January looked from Micha to Carly, clearly horrified. "When was this? Were you there when that happened, Carly?" she demanded.

Sean, noticing how everyone had stopped talking to listen in, rapidly tried to change the subject, but January wasn't having it. "Were you?" she persisted.

"Maybe," Carly muttered, wishing she were somewhere else, anywhere else.

"Good grief. Was anyone hurt?" Clearly oblivious to everyone else's interest, January grabbed Carly's arm. "When did this happen? Why didn't you tell any of us?"

The entire family murmured agreement and moved closer, circling Carly and Micha.

"Chicago PD and the FBI are working on it," Carly said. "It's over, no one was hurt, so let's talk about something else, please."

Heath, clearly catching on to Carly's need for a distraction, cleared his throat and tapped his beer glass with a knife. He waited until everyone's heads had swiveled around to face him. "The police have assured me that they are actively working the investigation. They're not sure if Carly was the target or Micha, though I believe they're leaning toward Micha."

He took a deep breath, waiting until everyone had a few seconds to digest his words. "Now, I'd like to talk a little about the serial killer investigation," he said. "Since Sean here works in the homicide division, I've asked him to give us an update."

Though Sean appeared nonplussed for a second, he quickly regained his composure and strode to the front of the room. Meanwhile, January sidled over to Carly and tugged on her arm. "You're not getting out of this so easily," she whispered. "I think everyone is going to want to hear about this."

"Probably," Carly whispered back. "Now hush so I can hear what your fiancé has to say."

Unfortunately, Sean informed them that the investigation had very little new information. He reiterated that Chicago PD was working jointly with the FBI, touched on the recent murders, but was unable to contribute any new information.

"This is very disappointing," Simone said, once Sean had finished speaking. "I've been doing a lot of research on serial killers and I'd be happy to share what I've learned with anyone who is working the case."

"Thank you," Sean replied. "But since the FBI is very knowledgeable in that area, I figure they have already brought in more than one expert. I'll give them your name, just in case."

Simone nodded.

"Now tell us about this car explosion that Micha was involved in," January chimed up, giving Carly a pointed glance. "I want to know if Carly was there. And I want to hear exactly what happened."

Both Farrah and Fallon nodded. Tatum narrowed her eyes and she and Cruz began murmuring to each other. Simone, who until that moment had been lost in reading something she'd written in her notebook, blinked and raised her head. Heath grimaced, one arm still around Kylie. He mouthed, *I tried*, in Carly's general direction.

Now everyone stared at Micha and Carly, even Jones, clearly waiting.

"Sorry," Micha whispered to Carly, though he kept his arm around her shoulders. Keeping his tone level, he relayed the chain of events, ending with the gunshots destroying Carly's window. She noted he left Jones out of it, which was kind of him, though she figured the family would learn about her brother's presence during the shooting sooner or later.

By the time Micha wound down, you could have heard a pin drop in the room. Carly's mother and aunt clung to each other, wearing identical horrified expressions.

"You need to come home," Fallon declared. "Right away. I won't have you staying at that house if you're in danger."

Carly refused to argue with her mother in front of the entire family. "Let's talk about this later," she said. "Right now, we're here to celebrate Jones and his fantastic beer. Let's try to focus on that."

"Agreed." Jones jumped in to save her. Though Fallon's expression made it clear she didn't like it, she dropped the topic, at least temporarily.

Once everyone had started talking again, Carly tugged on Micha's arm. "I'm seriously thinking about trying to sneak out before my mom can get to me."

"You know she'll just catch up to you later." He kissed her neck, making her shiver. "You might as well just go over and talk to her. She's worried, that's all."

"You make sense," Carly grumbled. "Wait here. I'll be right back."

Fallon and Farrah had taken a seat at a little round table in the corner, from where they had a view of the entire room. Jones had made sure they had a platter of assorted appetizers, and since neither women were big on drinking beer, he'd poured them both a glass of wine.

Fallon nodded as Carly approached. "Sit," she ordered. "You and I need to talk."

Stifling a sigh, Carly sat. "Mom, I know you're worried. I am, too. But there's no way I can drive to work from Oak Park every day. It'd be a ridiculous commute, especially with traffic."

Fallon reached across the table and covered Carly's hand with hers. "I can't bear the thought of something happening to you. How about you go stay with one of your brothers?"

"We've talked about that," Carly replied. "But ultimately, I decided against it. I have a dog now plus I refuse to live my life on the run. Especially since I still have no idea who might want to harm me."

Farrah leaned forward. "Do you think they might be after Micha?"

"It's possible." Carly shrugged. "But the police don't seem to think it's connected to the person or people who killed Dad and Uncle Alfred."

"Tell me, what are you doing to stay safe?" Fallon asked.

Now Carly wished Micha had accompanied her. "Micha isn't working right now," she began, and then as she realized how that sounded, she winced. "He's just getting settled back here in Chicago. But since he was in the special forces, he has lots of contacts. Between them and the police, I honestly feel we should be safe."

Her mother and aunt exchanged glances. Carly found herself holding her breath as she waited.

"Well, you are an adult," Fallon finally conceded.

"I don't like this at all, but I'm going to trust you to do what's best."

"Though it would have been fun to have a dog in the house," Aunt Farrah interjected, smiling. "Even if we're not going to be there much after next month, hopefully."

Carly sat up straighter. "What? Where are you going?"

"We've been trying to get back into our old routines," her mother said. "We've resumed running Gemini Interiors, though they managed to continue on just fine without us apparently."

"And we're considering taking a trip together," Farrah added. "Right now we haven't decided anything firm, but we've been looking at going to Dubai."

Pleased, Carly nodded. Before the murders, traveling had been one of her parents' passions. Often, both couples went somewhere together. In fact, right before the two men had been killed, Carly was pretty sure the foursome was planning a trip to Scotland.

"Or do you think it's too soon?" Farrah asked, the anxiety in her voice reflected in her gaze. "To be honest, the grief has been overwhelming and neither of us has felt like doing much of anything."

"But there's only so long one can mope around the house," Fallon interjected. "That's why we're going back to work. Baby steps, you know."

"I do know." Carly glanced back over her shoulder at Micha, who was talking to Sean. "When they told me that Micha had died, I couldn't get out of bed for days. And we had only been together for a fraction of the time you two were married."

"That doesn't make the pain any less," Farrah wisely

said. "You were at a different place in your relationship than we were. You were just starting out, full of hopes and dreams and making plans. We were settled, having raised our children and paid our dues." She wiped away a stray tear. "We had so much living yet to do. It hurts to have that ripped away."

Fallon reached over and gave her sister a firm hug. "We're getting through this," she said, her voice fierce. "One day at a time."

"Yes, we will." Sniffing, Farrah hugged her back. "And knowing our children have found their happiness in life really helps. Whether with their dream careers or finding the love of their life—or both—it warms the heart to see you all turned out so well."

Carly nodded. "Thanks. Now if you don't mind, I'd better get back to Micha."

"No need." Fallon grinned. "He's headed this way right now."

Despite herself, Carly's heart skipped a beat. She glanced up, straight into Micha's warm brown eyes. Awareness shivered through her.

"Evening, ladies." Smiling at the two older women, Micha planted a quick kiss on Carly's head. "Do you mind if I join you?"

"Of course not." Farrah waved her hand at the empty chair. "Sit. We have some questions we want to ask you."

Hearing this, Carly stifled a groan. She shot Micha a look of warning as he lowered himself into a chair. She knew her mother and her aunt. Micha didn't know it, but he was about to be subjected to an intense grilling by the matriarchs of the Colton family.

The questions started off casually. They asked him about his time in the army and thanked him for his service. Carly watched him relax at her mother's and aunt's friendly tones. Though she knew he could take care of himself, she fought the urge to warn him. Instead, she sipped her beer and listened as Farrah took the lead, switching from wanting to know about the past to pointed questions about the future.

"Once you're married to my daughter, how do you intend to make a living?"

Whoa, Nelly. Carly shook her head and held up her hand to forestall Micha's response. "Mom," she chastised. "No one has said anything about us getting married. Please don't make that kind of assumption."

Eyes widening, Farrah looked from her daughter to Micha and then back to her sister. "But why not?" she drawled. "It seems you two have picked up right back where you left off."

Despite feeling her face color, Carly stared right back. "Mother..."

"It's all good, Mrs. Colton," Micha interrupted, smiling. "We're still working through a few things, though."

"What things?" Farrah asked.

"We need to figure them out on our own," Micha said smoothly, his raspy voice firm.

Carly exhaled, smiling gratefully.

The two older women took the hint. "All right, dear," Farrah said, patting the back of Micha's hand. "You can't blame me for being concerned for my daughter's welfare."

"I can't blame you at all," Micha agreed.

Carly's heart squeezed. She blinked when Micha

stood and held out his hand to help her up. "Are you ready to go?" he asked.

Grateful, she slipped her hand in his and got to her feet. Keeping her fingers intertwined with his, she leaned over and kissed first her mother's cheek, then her aunt Fallon's. "We'll talk later," she murmured. "Have a nice night."

Holding hands still, they went in search of Jones so they could tell him goodbye. Carly felt the gazes of every single family member they passed and realized she didn't care if they saw her and Micha holding hands. Though she knew they'd speculate endlessly, let them gossip. Maybe, just maybe, she might have started to believe she and Micha could actually have a future together.

Chapter 10

Back at Carly's house, Micha excused himself and went to the guest bedroom that Carly had given him to use, even though he'd yet to spend a night in that particular bed.

Visiting Jones Colton's brewery had lit a fire inside him. In Carly's family, so many of them had found and pursued their passion. Carly becoming a pediatric nurse, Tatum with her restaurant and Jones opening his own brewery had made Micha realize he needed to give serious consideration to his own future occupation. As had Carly's mother with her questions about what he intended to do for a living. He wanted to do more than simply earn a paycheck.

Besides Carly and the military, Micha had one other passion. Most might consider this a hobby and for a while Micha had, too. Now he thought he might be able to make it become more.

While being held captive in Afghanistan, he'd begun to carve wooden figures, toys, just to pass the time. To his surprise, he'd gotten quite good at it. His captors had taunted and mocked him, but they'd taken the toys home to their children. And they'd begun asking for more. He'd learned to trade his little wood carvings for extra food or more time in the sun. Sometimes, he'd thought his toys had helped keep him alive.

Later, after coming out of the medically induced coma in the burn unit, he'd been unable to get his fingers to work well enough to hold a knife. This had fueled a new determination inside of him. Having received an honorable discharge, he was no longer a soldier, and after two years away he knew he wouldn't be Carly's husband, but damned if he would give up his ability to make the simple wooden toys.

By the time he'd completed his physical therapy, his fingers no longer fumbled with the knife and the wood. He figured he'd regained nearly 90 percent of his previous skill and he vowed to keep on practicing until he had it back 100 percent. The little carvings brought him great joy, especially when he saw the delight shining from the eyes of a child who'd received one.

In the back of his mind, he'd known he wanted to do something with that, but until he'd seen Jones's enthusiasm for his brewery, he hadn't given serious thought to starting his own business.

Now, full of enthusiasm, he pulled out the plastic tub full of carvings that he'd brought with him from the hotel. He'd spent many nights alone in his hotel room, turning pieces of wood into animals and elves, cowboys and dragons. He'd been meaning to take this latest batch down to a women's shelter, as he'd done before coming to Chicago, but hadn't made the time to locate one yet.

Now he thought he might wait. He'd need some inventory, prototypes if you will.

Since he'd managed to save quite a bit of money during his time in the military, he figured he wouldn't even need a loan. He'd just need to do research on how to best market the toys, which he could begin with on the internet, and whether or not he'd have much competition.

Practically dancing around the room, he couldn't wait to show Carly and hear her thoughts. As a matter of fact, he'd even started working on a carving of her dog, Bridget. Fishing it out of the tub, he guessed he had maybe another hour left of work until it was completed. He figured he'd finish that before discussing any of this with her.

He could begin his research and see if his passion might be commercially viable. Would there be an actual market for his simple, carved toys? He closed the plastic container and slid it back under the bed. He'd finish the carving of Bridget when Carly was at work and present it to her as a gift.

For now, he guessed they'd watch a little television before going to bed. The simple cozy domestic things like that made him happy. The knowledge they'd be sharing a bed again ignited the simmering arousal that being in Carly's presence always brought.

Despite his best intentions, he couldn't manage to contain his glee from Carly. She picked up on his inner excitement the instant he walked into the kitchen.

"What's going on?" she asked, her gaze sweeping his face. "Do you have news?"

He realized she thought he'd heard something about the case. "No, nothing like that. Sorry. Your mother's questions made me think a lot about what I was going to do for work. All my adult life, I've been military. It's difficult trying to see myself outside of that box."

"Does that mean you've thought of something?" she asked.

"Yes."

"Let me guess." Arms crossed, she eyed him. "Stop me when I get close. Security guard. Army recruiter. Police officer. Private detective."

He shook his head to all of those, though he had to give her credit. Every single occupation she'd listed was a logical follow-through for a man recently discharged from the military. If in fact his idea didn't work out, then he'd likely consider one of them.

No *if*, he reminded himself. He needed to think positive.

"Then what is it?" she pressed.

"I'm not ready to discuss it yet. I need to do more research to make sure it's a viable option."

Her frown deepened. "Why are you being so secretive? You know me. I'll tell you the truth. What is it?"

Feeling oddly vulnerable, he asked her to wait there, promising he'd be right back. Returning to his room, he retrieved his plastic container from under the bed. Other than his physical therapists and the people who'd accepted the donations at the women's shelter, he'd shown them to no one stateside. Carly would be the first.

Heart racing, he carried the container in his hand carefully to the kitchen, where Carly waited.

"I carve simple, primitive toys for children. And anyone else who wants one," he elaborated. "I started when I was a captive in Afghanistan and was able to use them to bargain with the guards for food or privileges."

Her eyes widened. "And you're wondering if there might be a market for them here in the US."

"Exactly."

"Colton Connections might be able to help with that," she said. "Let me see them."

He hadn't thought of that. Colton Connections developed patents for innovative inventions. He guessed it wouldn't be all that different from starting up his own toy company.

Slowly, he opened the box. Reaching in, he pulled out one of his favorites, a sitting dragon with wings spread that he'd perfected after carving over a hundred of them.

"That's beautiful," Carly breathed, taking it from him and cradling it in the palm of her hand. "I wouldn't call that a toy. It's more like art."

Art. "I was thinking the first thing I'd have to do would be to figure out a way to mass-produce them. Kids seem to love them. My captors took them home to their children and, once word spread, I had a valuable sort of currency to exchange." He shrugged. "I continued to carve them as part of my physical therapy, though I had to relearn to use my scarred and swollen fingers."

He set the box down. "I make a little of everything. These days, I carve them because I enjoy carving."

"May I?" she asked, gesturing toward his collection.

Slowly he nodded, wondering why he felt so raw, so

exposed. He supposed he'd better get used to it if he truly intended to market his work. Still, he anxiously watched as Carly sifted through his carvings, taking out one and then another, running her fingers gently over the silky-smooth wood.

"They're amazing," she told him, the wonder in her voice proving she meant it. "Clean lines, no jagged pieces, though I'm guessing they'd have to be targeted for older children, who won't try to chew on them."

Grinning, he let his relief show. "Exactly. From what I understand, a lot of the preteen age group might want to collect them."

"I love them." Gently setting them back in his container, she crossed to him and planted a big kiss on his mouth. "I'm amazed at the things your talented fingers can do."

The suggestive comment sent a ripple of heat through him. As she kissed him again, her body moving suggestively against his, he forgot all about his carvings.

They barely made it to her bedroom, shedding clothes as they went. Falling onto the bed and each other, they made love with the kind of intense familiarity that felt both comfortable yet passionately heated. As she'd been doing, she ran her fingertips gently over the ridged outlines of his scars and kissed them. Having her do such a thing reminded him of how he'd truly believed he'd been damaged too much to have a woman like her.

Clearly, Carly didn't think so. She made it plain she accepted him as he was, scars and all.

Damn he loved this woman. He forced himself to go slow, to keep his raging arousal under control, until he'd helped her reach her own release twice. Only then did he unleash himself, pounding into her with the kind of mindless abandon that sent them both over the edge at the same time.

After, they cuddled. Eventually, Carly's breathing deepened as she drifted off to sleep. Micha held her, allowing his gaze to memorize every beautiful detail of her, from the stubborn tilt of her chin to her high cheekbones. The feel of her lush body, pressed trustingly into his, was a freaking miracle he'd never take for granted. How he'd managed to get so lucky twice, he didn't know. Despite all that he'd put her through, she'd given him a second chance. Briefly closing his eyes, he thanked the powers that be for allowing him to find her again. He couldn't lose her. Not now, not ever.

Too fired up to sleep, Micha slipped out from under her arm and padded to the bathroom. When he emerged, he scooped up his clothes on the way and pulled on his boxer briefs before heading to the kitchen.

Once there, he poured himself a glass of water, pulled out his knife and the wooden dog he'd started for Carly, and got to work finishing it.

With sunlight warming her face, Carly stretched, her body aching pleasantly. She let her eyes drift open, rolling to her side to look at Micha. He still slept, turned on his side facing her, his unruly hair and morning shadow making him look sexy as hell, even in slumber.

They'd made love, slept and made love once more, before going back to sleep. Now birdsong outside announced the arrival of morning and she somehow, impossibly, wanted him again. How that could be, she didn't want to overanalyze, so she made herself throw back the covers and make her way to the bathroom. After a quick shower and brushing of her teeth, she towel-dried her hair and pulled on a pair of panties and oversize T-shirt before padding to the kitchen to make coffee and, later, breakfast. Bridget followed her, eager to get outside and then have her kibble.

Flicking on the kitchen light, she let her dog out, waiting while Bridget took care of business. As soon as she was done, Bridget galloped back inside, eager for her breakfast.

Pouring a bowl of dog food and setting it on the floor, Carly went to make herself coffee. The sight of the wooden carving on the kitchen counter made her stop short. Micha had carved Bridget, capturing not only the boundless joy with which the dog faced each day, but the adoration that shone from her big brown eyes.

Reverently, Carly reached out and picked up the piece. She smoothed her fingers over the highly polished wood. Her throat stung and tears pricked at her eyes. Micha might believe his carving to be only a hobby, but the soul of an artist came through. Older children might collect these pieces, but she'd bet adults would, too.

Carrying the figurine with her, she made her coffee and took it and Bridget outside to the backyard. Though she had to be at work in a few hours, she'd gotten up early enough that she had a little bit of time before she had to get ready.

Micha joined her before she'd made it halfway through her first cup. The back-door hinges squeaked as he slipped up behind her, putting his arms around her and holding her close. As always when he touched her, her entire body melted.

"Thanks for the figurine. It's beautiful," she said.

"My pleasure."

She fought the urge to turn around and convince him to go back to bed with her. Instead, she decided to finally ask about one of the things that had been bothering her since he'd showed up alive rather than dead. From what he'd told her in the past, she knew it would be a sore subject. Maybe that, too, had changed during the time he'd been in the hospital. Nearly dying had a way of changing perspective sometimes.

"Do your parents know?" she asked softly. "That you're alive and in Chicago?"

He stiffened, though he didn't move away. "I don't know," he finally replied. "I didn't contact them, if that's what you mean. My father made it very clear that he no longer considers me his son."

While Carly had never met Micha's parents, she had to assume that they, too, had grieved greatly upon being informed of his death. Suffering and grief had a way of changing things, especially words said in anger.

But she wouldn't push, not now, not yet. She'd give Micha time to consider on his own.

So instead of responding, she slowly turned around and gave him a deep, lingering kiss. As she'd known it would, heat instantly erupted between them. Wrapped in each other's arms, they made out as if they'd been apart for days instead of just having climbed out of the same bed that morning.

Finally, Carly came up for air. She glanced around

her backyard and went still. Something was wrong. Her yard appeared empty.

"Where's Bridget?" she asked, trying to quell the rising panic. "Bridget!" she called, adding a whistle. "Bridget, come."

But her dog didn't reappear. A lightning bolt of sheer terror stabbed Carly in the heart. Somehow, Bridget had escaped the yard. She was gone.

For a second, Carly froze, unable to think or move. Then she ran down the steps, refusing to believe what her own eyes told her. Bridget had to be here somewhere, maybe hiding near the shed again.

With Micha right behind her, Carly combed every square foot of her yard. She looked behind bushes, even those that were logically far too small for Bridget to hide behind. They both checked and the gate was still closed. Together, she and Micha searched the shed, even though she'd blocked it off. Bridget wasn't there.

Refusing to give in to her rising panic, Carly sprinted over to the garage and yanked open the door. Even though she knew there was no way the dog could have gotten inside, Carly looked, anyway, calling Bridget's name.

"I don't understand," she said, her voice shaking as she blinked back tears. "There's no way she could have gotten out of the yard. I checked the fence and there aren't any holes. The gate is still closed."

"That's weird. Are you sure you didn't leave it open?" Micha asked, frowning.

"Yes." Puzzled, she eyed him. "Why? Do you think someone opened it and deliberately let Bridget out while we were standing just a few feet away?"

He didn't have to respond verbally. His thoughts were written all over his face.

"You think someone took her?" Heart pounding, knees weak, she stared at him, silently begging him to contradict her.

"How else would she have gotten out?" he asked instead.

"But why? Why would anyone want my dog?" But the instant she spoke, her heart sank and she knew. "The same person who blew up your rental car and shot out my front window."

Micha didn't say anything. Instead, he reached for her, no doubt intending to offer comfort. Suddenly furious, she dodged him. "Why? Why would anyone want to harm an innocent dog?"

"Carly, first off we don't know for sure that's what happened to Bridget," he cautioned. "Let's recheck the fence again. Maybe she found a hole somewhere and simply got out."

Though worry made her feel queasy, she took a deep breath to calm herself down and nodded. "That makes sense."

"Good." He pointed. "You start on that side and I'll start over here. Check every square inch, even behind bushes."

This time, instead of being in a frantic rush, she went slowly. In the overgrown areas, she got down on all fours and checked behind the shrubs, looking for any gap in her fence.

"I found something," Micha called. "Come see."

Heart in her throat, she hurried over. Micha crouched down, and pushed aside a leaved shrub. "Look."

The entire bottom of three boards was missing, leaving a jagged hole big enough for a dog to squeeze through.

Relief and worry flooded her. "This means she's somewhere in the neighborhood," she said. "Better that than having someone grab her. But we need to find her."

Micha nodded. "Grab some treats and her leash. We'll find her."

The confidence in his gravelly voice made her feel slightly better. She ran into the house with renewed purpose, grabbed a handful of Bridget's favorite treats and met Micha in the front yard.

"Here." She handed him a couple of the treats. "You go that way and I'll go the other."

"We're staying together," he said. "No way we're splitting up without knowing if…" He didn't have to finish the sentence.

She nodded. "Okay. Bridget," she called. "Here, girl."

They walked up one side of the street, all the way to the stop sign. Carly could only hope Bridget hadn't gone too far. The thought of her getting hit by a car was heart-stopping.

"Don't give up." Micha squeezed her shoulder. "She might be scared and hiding. Let's go back toward your house and stay on this side of the street before we cross over."

Two houses from hers, Carly spotted movement in a neighbor's bushes. Catching her breath, she grabbed Micha's arm. "There," she said. She'd barely gotten the word out when Bridget came trotting out, tail wagging furiously, clearly unaware she'd done anything wrong.

With a cry of relief, Carly dropped to her knees and

gathered her dog to her. She hadn't cried so far but damned if her eyes hadn't filled with tears.

"I can't lose you," she told Bridget. "I just can't."

The three of them made their way back to the house. Carly took Bridget inside while Micha went to repair the hole in the fence. He promised to double-check for any others and fix them, too.

Legs shaky, Carly dropped into a chair while Bridget got water and then curled up in her dog bed to nap. Glancing at her hands, Carly realized she was still shaking. The severity of her panic when she'd thought she'd lost Bridget stunned her.

Micha let himself in quietly. Bridget gave a quiet thump of her tail but didn't lift her head. Micha bent down and scratched her behind the ears, which made Bridget give a doggie moan of pleasure. This had Carly smiling, even though her eyes were still streaming tears. Angrily, she wiped them away, not even sure why she was crying.

"Carly?" Micha asked, crossing the room toward her. "Are you okay?"

She started to nod and then ended up shaking her head no. "I thought that psychopath had taken my dog," she said, her voice shaky. "You know things have gotten absolutely crazy when that's the first thought that comes to mind."

"I know." He gathered her in his arms and held her. She allowed herself to relax into him, inhaling his masculine scent and loving the way his strong, muscular body made her feel safe. "Carly, you really should consider staying with one of your brothers. At least temporarily, until all this blows over."

"No," she replied, without moving. "We've already discussed this. I'm not being run out of my own home."

He stroked her back, his big hand gentle. "It won't be forever. Just until we catch this guy."

Inside, she knew he had a point. Today had proved that. If something happened to Bridget because Carly continued to cling to her stubborn pride, she'd never forgive herself. "I'll think about it," she heard herself say. "But don't say anything to Jones or Heath, okay? I haven't decided anything yet, and if I do agree to go stay with one of them, I'll tell them myself."

His voice a raspy deep rumble against her ear, Micha agreed.

Now that she'd calmed down, Carly knew she needed to get ready for work. Extricating herself from Micha's arms, she glanced at the clock and gasped. "I've got to get a move on," she said. "I can't be late. I never have and I don't want to start now." She rushed off toward her bedroom, determined to get ready as quickly as she could. Being punctual had become a point of pride with her over the years. Not only did she excel at patient care, but her charting was precise and she never, ever had been late for a shift. Nor would she be today.

Somehow, she managed to pull herself together in order to leave at her usual time. As she blew into the kitchen, Micha waited by the back door.

"I'm ready," she told him. "Usual routine?"

"Of course." He gave her a quick kiss. "And please, really think about possibly staying with one of your brothers."

She nodded, even though her mind had already gone ahead to the sick children waiting for her on her floor.

She gave Bridget a quick pet and then straightened. "Let's do this," she told him, grabbing her purse and keys. "Time to start another day."

Micha reached out as she swung past, pulling her in for one more tingle-all-the-way-to-her-feet kiss. When they broke apart, they were both breathing heavily.

"Now *that's* the way to start a day," Micha said. "Give me a minute or two before you leave."

She nodded, internally shaking her head at their new routine. Watching as Micha let himself out the back door, she locked it behind him. Then, eye on the clock, she waited.

Chapter 11

As he'd done every morning that week, Micha left Carly's out the back door. He hopped the chain-link fence into the neighboring yard, and from there walked down the street to where he'd parked his Jeep. As far as he could tell, none of the vehicles parked on her street were occupied. If no one sat in a vehicle watching the house, unless they'd mounted a camera again somewhere outside, she wasn't under surveillance. Just to be safe, the night before he'd checked the numerous trees closest to her house and found nothing.

Finally, he got in his vehicle, started the engine and drove closer to Carly's house. He waited until he saw her pull out of her driveway. He then put his Jeep in Drive and followed her, allowing another car to pull in between them just for show.

When they reached the hospital, she pulled into the employee-only parking lot and Micha found a place in the parking garage, close enough that he could watch her walk in. They'd kept to this same routine every day, and he'd seen nothing out of the ordinary.

So far, so good. But Micha wasn't willing to take any chances. He'd do this for as long as he had to, until whoever was after them had been caught. No way was he letting Carly put herself in danger. That's why he really hoped she'd agree to go spend a week or two with one of her brothers. He'd breathe a lot easier once he felt she was safe.

Carly walked briskly up the sidewalk, her long blond hair up in a messy bun, her scrubs marking her as a health-care worker. Some mornings, one or two of her coworkers walked in with her. Others, like today, she made her way alone.

Micha decided to wait until Carly entered the hospital building.

And then Micha saw the man step out from behind a delivery van, clearly intent on Carly. Everything about him screamed of menace, from the too-tight line of his posture to the way he appeared to focus on her to the exclusion of everything else.

Heart pounding, Micha got out of his Jeep with a jump. He sprinted toward the door, worried the guy would take out a gun and shoot her. Instead, the man spun around at the sound of Micha's approach.

Shock and hatred mingled in the man's suddenly familiar face as he and Micha locked eyes.

Clearly unaware, Carly continued forward and slipped inside the doors, which closed behind her. The intruder ignored her, now completely focused on Micha. Something about him… Then Micha remembered.

"About time you got here," the other man drawled. "I'd hate to have to hurt that pretty little lady of yours just to get back at you."

Micha skidded to a halt, still twenty feet away. He ignored the blatant baiting. "I know you," he said. "Lieutenant Andy Shackleford. What the hell is wrong with you? Why are you here?"

"Why? You really have to ask that, after you ruined my life? You deserve to pay for what you did to me."

Pay? Micha had heard enough. "Bring it," he said, settling into a fighting stance, even though he wasn't sure if the other man might have a gun. "Let's settle this like men. No more bombs or bullets. You and me, right now."

"Not yet." Lips lifted in a snarl, Andy spun around and took off running. He raced away. Though Micha sprinted after him, the other man had enough of a head start plus a leaner build to outpace him. How did he run so fast on a prosthetic leg? Micha wondered. Andy jumped on a low-slung motorcycle, kicked it to life and roared away. Knowing there was no way on earth he'd catch him, Micha stood and watched until the bike disappeared.

What the…? Micha hadn't seen Andy for years. He hadn't even *thought* of the man since getting out of the hospital, even when the FBI had asked him if he had any enemies. They'd gone their separate ways and Micha hadn't honestly thought he'd ever see Andy Shackleford again.

Back then, Andy had hated him. Hell, he'd made no

secret of that. Lieutenant Andy Shackleford had been part of the team sent in to rescue Micha in Afghanistan. He'd been on the helicopter when it crashed. Like Micha, he'd also been badly injured. Where Micha had suffered burns and a broken back, Andy had lost his leg. Though that accident had cost both men their military careers, Andy blamed Micha, since he was the one who'd needed rescuing. Micha had assumed Andy would eventually get past that. Clearly, he had not. In the time since, that hatred must have festered inside Andy, rotting away at his insides. Now Andy apparently hated Micha enough to wish him dead.

Of course Andy had been the one who'd set up the car bomb. Again, that made sense. Andy had been an ammunitions specialist in the army. His duties had including receiving, storing and issuing conventional ammunition, guided missiles and explosives. If anyone would know how to rig a car bomb, Andy would.

Micha dug out his phone. Though he hadn't yet provided the FBI with a list of his enemies, now he had something concrete to tell them.

Special Agent Brad Howard answered on the third ring. He listened while Micha described what had just happened. After asking a series of pointed questions, he agreed with Micha's assessment of the situation.

"Did you happen to get the license plate number on the motorcycle?" Agent Howard asked.

"No, I didn't," Micha replied, mentally kicking himself. "Everything happened too fast."

"We'll start looking into it. His military records should be easy to access and we'll go from there. Don't hesitate to call if you think of anything else or if you see him again."

After agreeing, Micha ended the call. The only reason he could come up with for Andy staking out the hospital would be in hopes of seeing Micha with Carly. He must have tracked down Carly and possibly had been the one who'd been stalking her before Micha arrived.

But how had he known? A lot of time had passed since the helicopter crash, and their time at Walter Reed. Micha remembered that they'd both been in a lot of pain, and the long flight back from overseas. Micha remembered crying out for Carly. That was about all he remembered, though. Maybe Andy had pieced together something, or it was even possible Micha had said more than he knew.

A shudder ran through him. What if he hadn't come to Chicago to check on Carly? What would Shackleford have done then? Would he have enacted some sort of painful revenge against the woman he knew Micha loved?

With resolve stiffening his spine, Micha strode back to his Jeep. While he knew the FBI would be searching for his enemy, he didn't have the patience to wait too long. Especially since Andy knew he'd been made. He'd increase his efforts to take Micha down, which could also endanger Carly.

No. Micha knew he could not allow that to happen. He'd have to figure out a way to draw the other man out, preferably somewhere far from Carly, and then take him down on his own.

With no real plan other than the vague knowledge of what he needed to do, Micha decided not to go back to

Carly's house just yet. He wondered if Andy had been watching the place. No doubt he had.

Which meant Micha would just have to make sure to be seen. If he could get Andy to follow him somewhere far away from Hyde Park and from Carly, he'd take him down or die trying. He just needed to figure out a way. Until then, Micha would need to stay far away from Carly, while managing to also keep her safe.

Quickly, he dialed Jones. Without going into too much detail, he explained what he needed. "Just stay with her, please. I've got a very real lead on who's been behind all this and I need to pursue it. I absolutely need to know Carly is safe."

Once Jones agreed, Micha cut him off before he could ask any more questions. "Tell her I'll be in touch," he said, and ended the call.

Then he began thinking of ways to trap Lieutenant Andy Shackleford. Micha definitely had the advantage here, since that had been one of the things he excelled in while in special ops.

The hunter was about to become the hunted. No matter what he had to do, no matter how long it took, Micha would end the threat once and for all.

Micha discarded any idea he had for drawing Andy out that would even remotely involve Carly. He had to figure out a way to let the guy know where to find him that didn't involve being near Carly's house.

Parking in a doughnut shop parking lot, Micha started making calls. He needed to locate someone who might know how to contact Shackleford, maybe even get ahold of his cell phone number.

But none of the people he reached had seen or heard

from the guy in years. For all intents and purposes, Shackleford had become a ghost.

Micha refused to give up. But call after call, even reaching out to people who'd had extremely limited contact with him or Andy, yielded no results.

Frustrating. Gritting his teeth, Micha tried to think. He hadn't known Andy well, even though they'd shared physical therapy sessions. Each man had been focused on his own healing, as he should be. But at one point, Micha thought Andy had mentioned having a girlfriend or fiancée, maybe even a wife. If Micha could locate her, he might be able to shed more light on Andy's current location.

It was a long shot, but at the moment the only one he had.

Unfortunately, even that turned out to be a dead end.

Now what? Micha didn't want to go back to Carly's house, not yet. Now that he knew the name of his enemy, he also knew how dangerous Andy could be, especially if he escalated. From explosion to shooting, what would be next?

He worried Andy might decide to target Carly just to spite Micha. So he called Jones and, without giving a lot of details, asked him not to let Carly be alone. Jones agreed but wanted to know why. Micha had remained vague, promising to fill the other man in as soon as he knew more, and ended the call.

Now with one less thing to worry about, Micha needed to figure out a way to draw Andy out. Unfortunately, no matter which angle he used to approach the problem, they all pointed back to Carly's house.

Which meant he'd have to get her out of the house. At least for a few days.

But would Carly go? She was stubborn, a trait he usually admired in her, but not if it got her hurt. He decided he'd need to level with her. He'd slip by later tonight and let himself in after most of the rest of the world had gone to sleep. Once he explained, he felt quite certain Carly would understand what she needed to do to keep her and Bridget safe. Once Micha no longer had to worry about her, he could set a better trap for taking down his enemy.

Carly walked out of the hospital after her shift and instinctively looked around for Micha's black Jeep. While part of her thought his actions might be a tad bit overprotective, mostly she liked that he was willing to go through so much effort just to keep her safe. The police had also beefed up their patrols and it had become common to see them driving by two or three times a night.

Odd. She checked her watch. Micha must be running late.

"Carly!" Her brother Jones emerged from the parking garage, startling her. "Wait up."

A quick frisson of fear went through her. But Jones was smiling, so that meant Micha had to be all right.

"What's going on?" she asked, once Jones had caught up with her.

"Micha sent me," he explained. "He asked me to stay with you this afternoon. He said he'll call as soon as he can to explain."

"Does that mean he got a lead?"

Jones shrugged. "He didn't say. He made me promise to stay with you the rest of the day. I'm thinking he'll be back before dark, because he knows I have to head over to the brewery."

"Okay. Are you following me in your truck, then?"

Now Jones shuffled his feet, appearing slightly uncomfortable. "Micha told me to ask you to leave your vehicle here at the hospital and ride with me. I hope that's okay with you."

Intrigued despite herself, she nodded. "Sure. I'm guessing he figures it'll be safer in the employee parking lot where there are cameras. I've got to get home and let Bridget out, so let's get going."

Side by side, they walked to Jones's truck. He kept up a steady stream of conversation all the way to her house, though he fell silent as they pulled into her driveway.

"Just wait a second." Jones touched her arm. "With all that's going on, we need to be extra cautious. Look around. Does everything look normal to you?"

Curbing her impatience, she did as he asked. While she wasn't sure exactly what he wanted her to look for, she eyed the back door and the windows, which all appeared to be closed. "Everything's fine," she said. "Now I really need to let Bridget out, if that's okay with you."

Jones laughed, a short humorless sound. "Sure. Just so you know, I still have nightmares about the night your front window got shot out." He pointed to the sheet of plywood still covering it. "What if you'd been standing near there? You would have been killed."

Already out of the truck, Carly turned to look at him. "I've been trying not to think about it," she admitted. "And I've been too busy to remember to call a glass company. I need to set something up for a time either I or Micha will be here."

Jones gave her a disgruntled look. "Yes, you do."

"Now that we've got that out of the way, are you coming?" she asked, starting forward.

Once Jones had caught up with her, he walked with her to the door, waiting while she used her key to unlock it. Inside, Bridget immediately began barking a greeting, which made Carly grin. "I love hearing that," she said.

As soon as she had the door unlocked, she motioned Jones to wait and opened it, crouching low so Bridget could launch herself at her. Laughing, Carly indulged her pet's frenzied greeting while Jones looked on.

"Okay, girl." Carly got to her feet. "Let's get you outside to go potty."

Jones stayed right on her heels as she let her dog outside.

Carly shook her head, keeping an eye on Bridget. "What's going on, Jones? I'm sensing that you're not telling me everything. Why are you acting so overprotective?"

Her brother had the grace to look ashamed. "Sorry," he said. "But I promise I'm not keeping any secrets from you. Micha didn't have a lot to say, really. He just stated it was imperative that I not let you out of my sight."

"What are you going to do when you have to go into the Lone Wolf?" she asked, gesturing for Bridget to come inside. Since the dog knew her dinner would be next, she happily complied.

Inside the kitchen, Jones took a seat at the table while

Carly measured out Bridget's kibble. Since he hadn't answered her question, she repeated it.

"I don't know," Jones admitted. "I guess you can come with me if Micha's not home by then."

Carly shook her head. "I just worked a full shift. I'm tired and all I want to do is get off my feet and hang out with my dog. I'm not going with you."

"But you'll be left here without your vehicle."

She grimaced. "Then I guess you'd best take me back to the hospital to retrieve it."

"Micha better come home soon, then," Jones muttered.

"He will," Carly replied, certain.

But Micha didn't come home. The sun sank lower and lower. Jones began to pace, frequently checking his watch. She knew he liked to be at the Lone Wolf before the evening rush started.

"Go ahead and go," she urged him.

"Not until Micha shows up," he responded grimly. "Or at least calls to let us know what's going on."

Carly agreed. Waiting for Micha to call, she put off trying to reach him. "I'm afraid I might interrupt whatever he's working on," she explained.

Jones agreed. "I need to let my people know I'm running late." He sat down on the couch and spoke quietly into his phone. When he'd finished, he looked up at Carly and smiled. "They've got everything under control, at least for now." He checked his watch. "Where the heck is Micha?"

"Good question." Giving in to her growing concern, Carly relented and dialed his number. She listened as it rang several times and then the call went to voice mail.

She left a message asking Micha to call her and then eyed her brother. "Seriously, you can leave," she said. "I'm sure Micha will be here shortly. He must have gotten caught up in whatever he's doing."

Jones hesitated. "What if he doesn't show up?"

Though the thought of that happening made her stomach twist, she kept that hidden from Jones. "He will. And if he's delayed for whatever reason, I'll be fine."

"I don't like this…" Jones began.

"Go." She made a shooing motion with her hands. "I have Bridget and I have my cell phone. I'll make sure everything is locked up tight."

"What about your car? Micha really didn't want it parked here for some reason."

Carly considered and then made a split-second decision. "I'll be fine without it for now. I'm sure Micha had a good reason for wanting me to leave it at the hospital."

Still her brother didn't move. "Carly, if Micha doesn't make it back tonight, I don't want to leave you without any way to go to work in the morning."

He had a valid point. But Micha would show up eventually, wouldn't he? Unless something awful had happened to him and then… Whoa. She put the brakes on that line of thought.

"Take me to get my car," she decided. "I can run through a fast-food drive-through on the way home. I'm too tired to even think about cooking anything."

With a loud sigh, Jones gave in. "Come on," he said. "Make sure you lock up tight."

They drove to the hospital with Jones unusually quiet. As he pulled up near the gate that led to the employee-only parking lot, he turned to face her. "I don't like this, Carly. Something's going on and I don't think it's good. The fact that Micha is completely out of touch underscores that."

She thought for a moment and then nodded. "I agree. But what else can we do? We can't wait here in limbo until Micha shows up. You've got a job to go to, as do I. And I refuse to be run out of my own house."

Leaning over, she kissed her brother's cheek before sliding out of his truck. Jones sat and watched her while she got into her vehicle and started the engine. He didn't drive away until after she'd pulled out of the employee parking lot.

After a quick fast-food run and heading back home, she found herself watching her rearview mirror to make sure no one followed her. She didn't think anyone was, but to be sure she took a detour and drove down by the university and then took a circuitous route home.

Traffic ebbed and flowed, but she couldn't spot another vehicle making the exact same number of turns as she. Satisfied, she finally turned onto her street, alert to any headlights behind her.

As usual, there were numerous vehicles parked in the street. Slowing, she tried to look inside each of them without being too obvious, but in the end, she felt foolish and simply went home.

After parking, she walked up to the front door amid the wonderful sound of her dog barking a joyous greeting. She let herself in, immediately locking the door behind her, before dropping down on her haunches to let Bridget greet her as if she'd been away for hours rather than a few minutes.

The house felt strangely empty and quiet. Too quiet. Carly hadn't realized how much she'd gotten used to having Micha around.

She turned on the television, found an old movie and let it play for background noise. Though she didn't want to be one of *those* kind of girlfriends, she texted Micha. Where are you? Is everything okay?

No response. No doubt he was busy. But still, how long would it take for him to text back a simple yes? She hated feeling this vulnerable, and not because she was frightened to be alone in her own home, but due to worrying about Micha's safety.

She loved him. She'd always loved him, even when she'd believed that he'd departed this earth. Love didn't die due to the absence of a physical body. And yes, she'd been furious and hurt that he'd allowed her to believe him dead for so long, but she could also understand his reasoning. Much of that time he'd been a prisoner, then unconscious, only to wake covered in horrific burns that to him must have seemed disfiguring. In fact, she actually found those scars beautiful. A testament to Micha's resilience and, in the end, his ultimate survival.

She also understood that whoever was after him—or them, but she'd come to believe it was him—wanted Micha dead. A car bomb wasn't exactly playing around. That, and the shots through her front window, had only proved the assailant didn't care if Carly was collateral damage.

Micha hadn't wanted her to be alone. Then why wasn't he here with her?

Her sense of unease growing, she checked her texts.

Nothing. No missed calls, no messages. Trying not to panic, she took a deep breath and dialed his number.

The call went straight to voice mail. With her stomach in knots, she left a simple message. "Call me, please."

Something was definitely wrong. Acting on impulse, she called her brother. Jones picked up immediately, sounding apprehensive. "Is everything all right?" he asked. "Are you safe?"

"I'm fine," she responded. "I'm just wondering if you've heard anything from Micha."

"No, I haven't. He isn't home yet?"

"He's not. And I haven't been able to reach him." Striving to sound calm, she took a deep breath. "Did he happen to mention to you where he was going or what he planned to do?"

"No, he didn't." Jones cleared his throat. "You know what? I'm getting bad vibes about this. Why don't you come down to the Lone Wolf and let me keep you company until you hear from him?"

She glanced at Bridget, still snoozing in her dog bed. "I'd rather wait here."

"You can bring your dog," Jones said, almost as if he'd read her mind.

Momentarily, she wavered. Maybe she should go hang out at the brewery. A distraction would be wonderful right now, stop her from imagining the worst-case scenario.

But ultimately, she decided she wanted to be there when Micha walked through the door. Which she had no doubt he would. She simply needed to stop worrying.

"Thanks, but I'll be okay," she told her brother. "With

all that's been going on, I can't help but worry about him. I'm sure he'll be fine."

"I agree. If anyone can take care of himself, Micha can." In the background, someone called Jones's name. "Carly, I've got to go. Call me if you need anything."

After ending the call, Carly wandered around her house. She still found it difficult to go anywhere near the front window. In her mind's eye she could still see it shattering, shards of glass raining down to the sound of gunfire.

Shaking her head, she wandered into the kitchen. Sometimes, when she found herself stressed, it helped to bake something. Plus, she'd bet Micha would enjoy some homemade cookies or bread when he returned.

Feeling a bit better, she hummed under her breath as she got out the ingredients for chocolate chip cookies, Micha's favorite. She could just picture how his handsome face would light up as he walked in the door to the smell of freshly made cookies.

Lost in a happy reverie of measuring and mixing, she put the first batch in the oven and poured herself a glass of wine.

Two hours later, heartsick, she tried Micha's phone again. No answer, straight to voice mail. She sent a text just as a last-ditch effort, and then she took Bridget out and decided she might as well get ready for bed.

But after thirty minutes in bed, she still couldn't sleep, so she abandoned the attempt and got up. Where was Micha? She had to believe he was safe. He had to be. She couldn't lose him again.

Because he'd said she could, she called Jones, knowing he'd be at the Lone Wolf until closing time. He answered immediately. "Still all right, I hope?" he said, an undercurrent of worry behind his light tone.

"Micha hasn't come home. And he's not answering his phone calls or texts." To her absolute horror, she nearly broke down in tears. Taking a deep breath, she managed to pull herself together before she spoke again. "I need you to tell me if he told you anything about where he might have gone."

"He did not," Jones replied. "I give you my word. And, Carly, it's after one o'clock in the morning. It's not safe for you to go out looking for him at this hour."

"I know." Then she said the thing that had been lurking in the back of her mind, almost too ashamed to speak it out loud. "What if he took off, Jones?"

"Took off?" Her brother seemed puzzled. "What do you mean?"

"Disappeared." Though she knew he couldn't see her, she waved her hand in the air. "I really think he might have figured out someone was after him and leaving was the only way he felt he could keep me safe." The thought almost had her double over in pain, but if anything, these last two years had made her stronger.

"He wouldn't do that," Jones finally responded. But he didn't seem convinced. "That man is head over heels in love with you." He paused a moment again. "Though I can tell he'd do anything to keep you safe. Even disappearing if he had to."

"I can't go through this again," she said, her heart cracking. "Honestly, I won't survive."

"He'll come back as soon as he either figures out or stops the threat." Jones tried to reassure her. "I have to approve."

"Stops the threat," she repeated. "That sounds so dangerous."

"Micha knows what he's doing and he'll be careful. You know he got tons of training while he served in special forces."

"True, but there's still no reason he couldn't have told me what was going on," she argued, heartsick and beginning to feel angry. "A call, a text or even a damn handwritten note left on my table. Something, just so I know he's safe."

"You do have a point," Jones agreed. "Come up here. Being around people will make you feel better."

"No." She swiped at her eyes. "Because despite it all, I want to be here just in case he comes back."

"Just in case?" Jones sounded shocked. "Carly, snap out of it. Now I'm really worried about you. As soon as I get this place closed, I'll be over. Don't go anywhere. Promise."

Wearily, she agreed. After ending the call, she sat at her kitchen table, mindlessly scrolling through social media on her phone. Finally, she put the phone down. How could Micha not understand how disappearing, even for a night, would affect her? She'd been candid with him, sharing her devastation when she'd thought she'd lost him. Why would he do this to her again?

She had to believe he wouldn't. Which meant Micha very well could be in danger.

Chapter 12

Taking every precaution, Micha drove around, making sure to circle Carly's street at least once every twenty minutes. He only passed a Chicago PD cruiser once, about to turn onto Carly's street, which he supposed was better than nothing. Still, he'd be making another phone call and asking again for beefed-up patrols.

As he approached Carly's house, he slowed, carefully checking out the surrounding area. As usual, there were numerous vehicles parked in the street, but it was impossible to tell if anyone sat inside them. Until he made it inside the house, he'd have to assume someone might be.

Her lights were on. Ever since she'd gotten her front window shot out, she'd been antsy about being in her living room. She'd even told him she'd actually felt safer with the plywood there. He understood that. Tonight, he fully intended talking her into staying with Jones or Heath. He couldn't do what he needed while worrying about her safety. If he wanted to use Carly's house to trap Andy, she simply had to be somewhere safe.

As usual, he parked down the street from her house and got out of his Jeep, looking left to right and spotting no one. Crickets chirped and even the usual traffic sound seemed muted.

Though the fresh night air relaxed him somewhat, he still checked behind him and kept an eye on the periphery. So far, so good. The cars remained parked at the curb, and no motorcycle or gunshots disturbed the quiet. As he walked up the sidewalk, he got out his phone to call her, wanting to let her know he had arrived so he didn't startle her. He'd send her a quick text instead, so he started to type.

Looking down at his phone, he only caught the movement on the edge of his peripheral vision, spinning around to face it.

A large body slammed into him, knocking him onto the sidewalk.

"What the...?" Micha swung, landing a right hook on the other man's jaw. The streetlight revealed little, a man wearing a hoodie, but Micha figured it had to be Andy Shackleford. He must have been hidden behind Carly's large tree. For all his plans to draw him out, somehow Micha had managed to be caught unaware.

"Damn you," he cursed, twisting and blocking, all the while trying to get his pistol. But Andy beat him to it, pulling his own gun and stepping back, all the while keeping it trained on him.

"Don't move or I'll blow your head off," Andy snarled. "I mean it." He glanced sideways toward Carly's house. "How about we go inside, and you let me mess up that pretty lady of yours?"

"How about we don't," Micha responded. He couldn't let the other man know how desperate he was to keep him away from Carly. In fact, he knew talking wouldn't serve any purpose. Instead, he rushed toward Andy, ramming him in the chest with his lowered head. Somehow, Andy managed to hold on to the pistol, swinging it around and slamming it into Micha's head.

Micha went down, dropping hard and struggling to stay conscious. At least they were still two houses down from Carly's place. He could not let this madman anywhere near her, no matter what he had to do.

Somehow, he managed to push back to his feet. Lurching forward, his vision still blurry, he swung. And connected, though just barely.

Andy laughed. "Want to try that again? Come on, tough guy. You can take me. I only have one leg."

Blinking, Micha tried to focus on the other man. Not only did his head hurt like hell, but he saw double—two Andy Schacklefords when he knew there was only one. Licking his lip, he tasted blood. "Why are you doing this, man?"

"Seriously?" Disbelief rang in the other man's voice. "You know I'm entitled. After what you did to me, you *owe* me. Enough of this BS. You're coming with me."

Micha never saw the second blow coming. He slid into unconsciousness as the pavement rose up to greet him.

When he opened his eyes next, head pounding like

mortar shells had detonated inside of it, he realized his hands and feet had been bound. A rag had also been stuffed inside his mouth. He was inside the back of a van or SUV, and the motion made his injured head hurt even more. Flashes of light from passing under the occasional streetlights felt like swords into his brain.

Since he couldn't speak, he closed his eyes. Battling nausea, he felt himself slip once more into darkness.

He came to again as Andy was dragging him out of the vehicle. "Get up. Walk," Andy ordered, prodding him with some sort of stick. A cane or a baseball bat, Micha thought, struggling to clear the fog from his brain. Next, Micha fully expected to be beaten with whatever the stick was. It felt eerily familiar, as if Andy had taken a page from the playbook when the Afghanistan terrorists had taken Micha prisoner.

He suppressed a shudder. He'd barely survived then. He needed to get the upper hand now. Carly. He had to make it back to Carly. At least this bastard hadn't touched her.

Andy herded him inside a metal structure. Not a residence, Micha noted. But some sort of warehouse or storage facility. Though the darkness made getting his bearings even more difficult, Micha tried to look for landmarks. Anything to help tell him where he might be.

Prodding him again, Andy gave Micha one final shove before sliding the door closed. Despite the complete and total darkness, Micha immediately tried to work his hands free. He dropped to the floor—also metal—and realized what the absence of windows likely meant. Andy had stuck him inside of a shipping container or storage unit. No one would hear Micha if he called for help at least until morning.

Whether he was at the Port of Chicago or a trucking yard—either way there would be workers at some point, there to load the containers onto a truck or ship. Though he figured Andy would be back long before sunrise to finish enacting his revenge.

There were two things Micha had to his advantage. One, most shipping yards or storage facilities had cameras, and two, as far as Micha could tell, Andy had forgotten to strip him of his cell phone. He was pretty sure he could still feel it in his pocket. If he could manage to get his hands free, he should be able to call for help. He needed to do something before he either ran out of air or Andy came back to finish him off.

Luckily for him, he'd been in this exact same situation numerous times, both in training and in real life. It took a bit of time, some pain and maybe even blood, but he managed to get his hands free.

Finally. Flexing his fingers to try to regain some circulation, Micha untied his feet. It took a few attempts, but he finally got back enough feeling to be able to stand and move. Next, he went to where he knew the door should be. "Damn it." He remembered reading something about this. Shipping containers weren't equipped to be opened from the inside. Of course they weren't. They'd never been intended to hold people, only goods.

Since he had no idea how long the air would last in here, he tried to conserve his movements. Luckily, he'd overcome any bouts of panic-inducing claustrophobia he'd had back in Afghanistan, out of sheer necessity.

They'd kept him in a hole in the ground, maybe eight by six at the most.

The space here also felt small, though not as tiny; which meant most likely he'd been locked in the smaller size of the standard shipping containers, which he believed was twenty by eight.

Okay, so no way out on his own. However, if Andy Shackleford opened that door, Micha would be ready. He shoved his hand in his pocket, but instead of locating his phone, he came up with nothing.

Damn it. Micha figured Andy would be back sooner or later.

Either way, Micha knew he had to be prepared for when the other man returned. That likely would be his one chance to get out of this alive and back to Carly. He couldn't leave her again.

Carly. What if the reason Andy had left Micha here was because he'd gone back to do something to Carly? If he'd had even the slightest idea how much she meant to Micha, Andy would immediately figure out the best way to make Micha suffer was to hurt her.

No. Micha refused to allow his thoughts to go there. First he'd need to figure out a way out of here. Then he could get to Carly and make sure she was safe. He thanked his lucky stars that he'd asked Jones to stay with her. If Andy went there, he wouldn't be expecting her to have company.

Just in case he'd missed something, Micha once again felt his way along all sides of his prison. Nothing. No opening, nothing he could use as a tool to try to force his way out. He was well and truly stuck.

He knew he could rant and rave, pound on the metal

walls until his knuckles were raw, use up every ounce of his energy and a great deal of oxygen, all for nothing. A younger Micha might have done this once, but since then he'd learned a thing or two.

Sinking to the floor with his back against the wall, he settled in to wait. He'd conserve his strength and his air, and when the right opportunity came, he'd take it.

Time passed slowly, the way it always did when monitored. At first, he checked his watch too often, and at some point he fell into an uncomfortable doze.

A sound startled him awake. He got to his feet, not entirely certain he hadn't been dreaming, and listened.

Outside he heard voices and laughter. Teens, from the sound of them. They must be sneaking around the container yard looking for mischief.

Micha waited until they got closer. "Help," he called out. "Please help me. I accidentally locked myself in this shipping container."

The teens went silent. Micha could only hope they didn't take off running. "Please," he called out again, banging on the metal side for emphasis. "I'm afraid I'm going to run out of air in here."

"Let's go," one of the boys urged. "This could be some sort of trick."

"It's not," Micha hollered. "Who the hell would lock themselves in a small metal box and then sit around waiting for someone to show up as a trick?"

"He has a point," another young male voice said. Then, a bit louder: "Where are you, man?"

"In here." Micha banged again, a steady cadence of

tapping to let them know his location. "It's dark and hot and I have no idea where the door is."

They began talking among themselves, their voices too low for him to hear. Heart pounding, he tried to remain still, to wait out their decision.

"Bang again," the same male voice ordered. "There are, like, hundreds of these metal containers here. It's hard to tell where your voice is coming from."

He began tapping again, more softly this time, but loud enough that they should be able to find him.

A second later, he heard the sound of the door bolt sliding back and the door opened. Though it was still nightfall, there were numerous lampposts that gave off enough light to momentarily blind him.

Still, he managed to propel himself forward, stumbling out and nearly falling. Luckily, one of the kids caught him.

"Whoa." The teen stared. "You look awful. What happened to you to mess you up like that?"

Micha glanced down at his shirt and for the first time realized he was covered in blood. He reached his hand for his still-throbbing head and his fingers came back bloody from where Andy had clobbered him with the gun.

"Do any of you have a car?" he asked. "Because whoever did this to me is likely on his way to hurt my girlfriend. I need a lift to Hyde Park."

Most of the kids—teen boys, all of them—began backing away and shaking their heads. "We don't want no trouble," one said. "We're not even supposed to be here."

But one kid stood his ground, eyeing Micha thoughtfully. "You're in real trouble, aren't you?"

Slowly, Micha nodded. "I don't want him to hurt my lady. You don't even have to take me to her house, just drop me off down the street. I promise, you won't see me again."

While the teen considered him, Micha held his breath.

"Come on," the kid finally said, motioning with his hand. "Since it's my dad's SUV, I get to decide. The only thing is, you can't get blood on the seats, 'kay?"

"I won't," Micha agreed. "My head is the only thing bleeding and I'll keep it away from the seat."

Apparently satisfied, the teen led the way through the maze of containers. They finally emerged in a fenced-off parking lot, skirted the gate and went around to a back street. A large, dark-colored Suburban was the only vehicle in sight.

"You sit up front with me," the kid told Micha. "The rest of you can all fit in the back two seats."

Micha did as he was told. So did the others, who apparently looked up to their leader. "When you got here, did you happen to notice any other vehicles parked around? Specifically, some sort of van?"

"No." The boy started the car. "But I'm thinking maybe you should go ahead and call the police."

"I've got to check on my girlfriend first." The urgency in Micha's tone made all the teenagers go silent. "Please. We need to hurry." He thought again, and then decided. "I do have a friend in the Chicago PD. I'm going to call him and let him know what's happening."

Nodding, the boy passed Micha his phone. Micha

dialed Charlie Crenshaw's number from memory, un-surprised when the call went straight to voice mail. He went ahead and left a message, detailing what had happened to him and that he was on the way to Carly's house and the time. "If you get this before morning, meet me there," he said, and ended the call. All he could do now was hope he got there in time.

Bridget barked, startling Carly awake. She must have dozed off at the kitchen table with her head pillowed on her arms. Blinking, she pushed groggily to her feet and eyed her dog. Now Bridget faced the front door, her tail wagging furiously.

A moment later, her phone chimed, signaling a text from Jones. I'm here, it read. And then almost imme-diately he knocked.

Padding toward the door on bare feet, she went ahead and checked the peephole before unlocking the dead bolt. Behind her, Bridget stood furiously wagging her tail.

As soon as Jones stepped inside, Carly closed and locked the door, her racing heart settling down into its usual steady beat.

"Hey, girl," Jones said, crouching down to pet her dog. Bridget leaned into him with a groan of pleasure, her eyes half-closed while he scratched behind her ears. Straightening, he held out a cell phone to Carly. "I found this on the sidewalk in front of your house. Did you drop your phone?"

"No." Heart in her throat, she took it from him. "I think that's Micha's," she said, turning it over in her hands. "In fact, I'm positive it is."

Jones cursed. Carly raised her gaze to his. "This means Micha is in danger."

"We don't know that," Jones argued. "Do you know his passcode to unlock his phone? We might find some more info there."

"I don't," she said thoughtfully. "But I bet I can guess." She typed in 0922, which had been the date she and Micha were originally supposed to get married. The screen vibrated but the phone didn't open. "That wasn't it." Considering, she tried Micha's birthday. "Nope."

Jones watched her with a mixture of concern and amusement. "Not as easy as you thought, I take it?"

"I'll figure it out," she replied. "Clearly, guys think differently than women. How did you decide on your passcode?"

Jones shrugged. "Do you remember the date you and Micha first met?"

"Of course." Without waiting, she typed that in. And just like that, the phone unlocked. "I'm in. Good job, Jones. But how did you know?"

"Just a lucky guess." Jones grinned. "What's open on the screen?"

"It looks like Micha was in the middle of texting me," she said. "He'd typed, About to be… About to be where? Or what?" She frowned. "What did he mean?"

"Maybe, about to be home?" Jones suggested. "Since it looks like he was texting you on the way toward your front door."

"Which means he was grabbed?" Heart beginning to pound, she stared at her brother in horror. "Should I call the police?"

"Not yet." Jones held out his hand for Micha's phone.

"Let me take a look and see if I can find any other clues."

She stood close, watching as he scrolled through the list of recent calls. "He's been busy," Jones commented. "He made several calls this evening. Several of them out of state. Let's check his web browser."

Though doing all this felt like a huge invasion of Micha's privacy, Carly nodded. She didn't see where they had any other choice.

"There are a couple of websites still open. Look." Jones showed her. "A few army ones, and he did a search for someone named Andy Shackleford. Does that name ring a bell with you?"

Carly shook her head. "No. Micha never mentioned him."

"What I think we should do next is call some of the numbers that Micha did. Maybe a few of those people might have some insight as to where he's gone or what he was doing."

Again, Carly had to quash back her uneasiness. "Do you want to call them or should I?" Glancing at the clock, she winced. "You realize we'll be waking all of these people up."

Jones patted her shoulder. "It's for a good cause. I'll do it. I don't mind."

She thanked him. "Do you want something to drink? Water, tea?"

"Do you have any coffee?" he asked. "I know it's after two in the morning, but I just got off work. I'll be up for a long time yet."

"Sure. I can make you a cup."

He followed her into the kitchen, still scrolling

on Micha's phone. "He made all of these phone calls much earlier today. There hasn't been any activity since around ten-thirty."

Eyeing him while the coffee brewed, she shook her head. "Maybe we should let the police handle this. I doubt any of those people had anything to do with Micha disappearing."

Watching her, Jones slowly nodded. "You're probably right. Let's call January's fiancé, Sean, since he works in Homicide, alongside Detective Joe Parker, who is also on the case. I'd rather deal with someone we know rather than Dispatch and then whichever officers happen to be on duty."

"I agree." She took a deep breath, calling on her nurse's training to remain calm. "I've been dealing with a police officer named Charlie Crenshaw. He's one of Micha's friends. I'm going to speak to him while you're talking with Sean."

"Sounds like a plan." Jones gave her a brotherly hug. "It's all going to be okay. If there's anyone who knows how to take care of himself, it's Micha."

Though she nodded, she couldn't help but think of the car explosion and the person who'd shot out her front window. Whoever had Micha meant him serious harm. She could only hope Micha would survive this. She couldn't lose him again.

"I love him," she said out loud, shaking her head. "I really, really love him."

Jones stared at her. "Well, duh. Why do you sound so surprised? The entire family knows how much you and Micha love each other. Just like January loves Sean and Heath loves Kylie." He shook his head. "Now let me make my call and you make yours. The sooner we get law enforcement working on this, the sooner we can find Micha and get him back home safe."

"I agree." Turning her back to Jones, she located the number Charlie Crenshaw had given her and called it. As she'd suspected it would, due to the lateness of the hour, the call went straight to voice mail. Carly left her name and number and a quick description of what they thought might have happened to Micha. Right before she was about to end the call, she remembered to add the name Andy Shackleford.

When she'd finished, she turned around to find her brother clearly doing the same thing and leaving his own message.

"No one wants to take a call at this time of the night," he said, shrugging. "But at least the messages will be there whenever they check."

Bridget growled, the hair on her back rising. She rose from her dog bed, eyeing the front door.

"What's wrong, girl?" Carly asked.

Jones grabbed her arm. "Come on," he said. "Out the back door right now."

"I'm not leaving my dog." Quickly, Carly clipped a leash on Bridget's collar. Then, with Jones urging her along, they all rushed out the back door, down the steps and into the yard.

"I want you to hide in the storage building," Jones told her, giving her a gentle push.

But Carly refused to budge. "Not without you. Come with us."

"I'm going to double around and see who's out front,"

he told her. "Please, Carly. Micha would never forgive me if I let something happen to you."

Reluctantly, she ducked into the storage shed, bringing Bridget with her. "Be careful," she told her brother. "Because I won't be able to live with myself if anything happens to you, understand?"

Jones nodded once, and then slipped off into the darkness on the side of her house. Heart pounding, feeling like the worst kind of coward, Carly crouched in the darkness, petting her dog, hoping to keep her from barking.

But although Bridget appeared restless, on edge, she kept quiet. Other than occasionally growling low in her throat. She crouched low, allowing Carly to hold her, though she never took her gaze off the exit.

After what felt like forever, Jones finally appeared. "It's okay to come out," he said, slightly out of breath. "False alarm. I checked all sides of the house and up and down the street. Didn't see another person. Let's get back inside."

Carly exhaled. "I'm beginning to think Micha might have a valid point about me going to stay with you or Heath," she said, her voice shakier than she would have liked. "I can't live like this."

"I can't tell you how relieved I am to hear you say that. But come on." Jones took her arm. "I'll feel safer once we're all behind locked doors."

Agreeing, Carly ran for the back door, Bridget keeping low to the ground but not leaving her side. Jones made up the rear.

Inside the brightly lit kitchen, Carly turned the dead bolt. "There," she said, slightly out of breath. "We're safe."

Still on the leash, Bridget snarled, baring her teeth as she faced the hallway. The back of Carly's neck prickled as she followed her dog's gaze. A man wearing military fatigues and body armor stepped into the kitchen. He had a huge military type of gun pointed directly at her.

"Nobody move," he ordered. "Lady, keep your dog under control or I'll kill it."

Nodding, heart pounding so hard the blood roared in her ears, Carly kept a tight grip on the leash. Bridget continued to snarl, struggling to lunge toward the stranger. "Bridget!" Carly ordered. "No."

To her surprise and relief, the dog instantly quieted, though she never took her intent gaze from the man with the gun. Carly suspected Bridget would bite him if she got the chance, but Carly couldn't take the chance of allowing her dog to be hurt or worse.

Eyeing the man, Carly recognized the pain behind the anger in his eyes. She'd seen it too many times before in the NICU, in both men and women as they tried to deal with the cruel blow dealt to them by fate as their newborns struggled to live.

"Did you know Micha over there in Afghanistan?" Carly asked, hazarding a guess. "Are you Andy Shackleford?"

Surprise flickered across the other man's face, though he quickly buried it. Emotionless, he stared at her, keeping his weapon pointed in her direction. "Shut up. Both of you, back against the wall."

Ignoring him, Jones stepped in front of Carly, his body language making it plain the man would have to go through him to get to her. "What do you want?" he asked. "Micha's not here."

Andy Shackleford—if that's who he was—bared his teeth in a semblance of a smile. "I know he's not here," he said, the twisted grimace on his face making him appear to be in a weird combination of pain and glee. "Because I have him locked up. I'll deal with him after I make him watch me slowly kill the woman he loves."

Carly gasped. She pushed around her brother so she could see the other man. "Why? Whatever Micha did to make you hate him, killing me won't change anything. You have to know this."

Eyes narrowing, he shrugged. "Maybe not. But at least I'll get to make him pay for what he did to me."

"You are Andy Shackleford, aren't you?"

"I am." His response came without inflection. "Have you heard of me?"

Behind her, Jones grabbed her arm and squeezed, his way of warning her to be careful. While she understood his concern, she figured their only chance right now would be to keep this guy talking. At some point, Sean or Charlie would have to listen to their messages. Hopefully before morning.

She lifted her chin, deciding to respond without really answering his question. "Tell me what he did to you, Andy Shackleford. I at least deserve to know the reason you want to hurt me."

Unblinking, he considered. "I'm sure he's told you the story. He thought he was some big hotshot spy, but he got captured. I was part of the rescue mission to get him out."

"And the chopper crashed." Eyeing him, she put two and two together. "You were also injured in the crash."

"I was." He gave a jerky sort of nod. "Lost my leg.

Nearly died. And that was the end of my military career. I was going places and it was over, just like that. Because of Micha. Now the time has come to make him pay."

Chapter 13

The kids dropped Micha off at the end of the block, per his request. He thanked them, dug out a twenty and handed it to the driver. "For gas," he said. He stayed put, watching them as they drove off, wondering if he'd made a mistake by not calling 911. For all he knew, Charlie Crenshaw might be on vacation.

Too late now. Second-guessing himself would only make him less effective.

When he reached Carly's house, he was relieved to notice Jones's vehicle parked out front. Good. At least Jones had stayed with her, so she wasn't alone. Between her brother and her vigilant dog, she'd have plenty of protection. And who knew, maybe Micha was wrong by trying to guess what Shackleford would do next.

As a precaution, Micha swung around to the back.

As he'd suspected, yellow light from the kitchen spilled into the backyard. Moving as quietly as possible, Micha noticed the back door hadn't been closed all the way. He'd just reached for the handle when he heard voices.

"Because of Micha. Now the time has come to make him pay." Andy Shackleford. Crossing to the window where the video camera had been placed, Micha peered into the kitchen. Jones and Carly faced the window, luckily. Shackleford should know better, Micha thought, standing with his back to the door like that. He must have gotten overconfident, complacent. Which again would work in Micha's favor.

Then he saw the gun. He recognized it immediately. It appeared to be a Ruger SR-556, an AR-15-style semi-automatic rifle. Overkill for something like this, but he remembered Andy Shackleford had never been subtle.

Damn. Judging from the way the other man held the weapon, Micha figured Andy's finger hovered right over the trigger. If Micha went with his original plan and rushed him, Andy could easily squeeze off multiple shots and hurt or kill both Carly and Jones.

Not acceptable odds.

He'd have to come up with another plan.

Inside, a cell phone started ringing. Judging by the ring tone, Micha figured it was his. No one answered. Micha could only hope Charlie Crenshaw had gotten his message and was now trying to call him back.

That gave Micha an idea. He slipped back around to the front and rang the doorbell, then dashed around to the back door. Bridget started barking and Carly's voice sounded frantic as she tried to calm her pet. Jones added his voice to hers, which led Micha to believe Andy must have threatened to hurt the dog.

Andy cursed. And cursed again. "Who is it?" he demanded. "Who the hell comes to visit after two o'clock in the morning?"

"I don't know." Carly kept her tone calm. "If we don't answer, they'll probably go away."

"Good." Andy turned and motioned toward the back door. "We'll give them a few minutes to leave and then we're going."

"Going where?" Carly asked.

"To reunite you with your beloved," Andy said. "We three have a lot of catching up to do."

Looking toward the window where Micha crouched, Jones must have caught sight of him. His eyes widened, but that was the only reaction he showed. He turned away, stepping in between Carly and Andy. "You're not taking her anywhere without me," he said, arms crossed.

"Such devotion," Andy mocked. "And all for nothing. Are you really willing to die for your girlfriend, knowing she's messing around with another man?"

"She's my sister," Jones replied. "And you'll have to go through me if you intend to try hurting her."

Andy laughed. "Brave words from an unarmed man. You're lucky, though. I still haven't decided what to do with you." With his back to Micha, he motioned to Jones. "Kill you or bring you along with me, that's the question."

The single, staccato whoop of a police siren sounded out front, making even Micha jump. A second later, someone pounded on the front door.

"Chicago Police. Open up."

"Out the back door, now." Motioning wildly with his rifle, Andy herded Carly and Jones toward the exit. Micha knew if he was going to get a chance to take Andy down, this would be it. Andy appeared to be barely able to hang on to the edge of his shredded self-control.

The back door flew open. First Carly, then Jones, ran out; Carly took off left, Jones right. While Andy tried to track them, Micha jumped him.

Andy went down, rifle flying. Jones scrambled for it as Andy rolled, swinging wildly to dislodge Micha. His elbow connected with Micha's jaw, snapping Micha's head back. Before Andy could take another punch, Micha hit him, hard. Once, twice and a third time. He forced Andy's hands behind his back and sat on him, figuring it wouldn't be long until law enforcement showed up.

"Chicago PD." Two armed officers burst through the back door, weapons out. One focused on Jones, who held the rifle loosely. "Drop the gun."

Jones immediately complied, slowly lowering the weapon to the ground before raising his hands up in the air. Carly emerged from the direction of the storage shed, also with one hand up and the other holding tight to Bridget's collar. She walked the dog over toward the house, putting her inside. Then, both hands raised, she sat down on the back porch.

Though Andy continued to try to struggle, Micha had a good grip. He glanced up to see his friend Charlie Crenshaw grinning at him. "Looks like you just about had everything under control," Charlie said.

Micha shook his head. "Could I get a little help here, please? Some handcuffs would be nice."

A moment later, with Andy cuffed and scowling, Charlie helped Micha up off the grass. Carly rushed over, wrapping her arms around Micha's waist so tightly he could barely breathe, and held on. Micha hugged her back.

"We'll need to get statements," Charlie said. "And I'm assuming you want to press charges against this guy?"

"Yes," Carly answered. "And not just for breaking and entering, but kidnapping. He had Micha locked up somewhere."

"In a shipping container," both Micha and Charlie said simultaneously.

"He left me a detailed message," Charlie clarified. "I take it this is Lieutenant Andy Shackleford?"

"Yes." Still holding Carly close, Micha regarded his enemy grimly. "He not only set the bomb that blew up my rental car, but he's the one who shot out Carly's front window."

"Attempted murder, too?" Crenshaw sounded almost gleeful.

"Chicago PD!" another voice shouted, and Sean Stafford ran into the backyard. He'd clearly come here straight from bed, as he looked as if he'd just gotten up. Right behind him came Carly's cousin January.

"Carly! Are you all right?" She rushed over, wrapping up Carly's other side in a partial hug.

"She was supposed to wait in the car," Sean said sheepishly. "I'm just glad you guys took care of everything before we got here." He glanced at Charlie. "I called it in, though. There should be a few more guys here shortly."

They all filed inside, filling up Carly's small living room. Cuffed with his hands behind his back, Andy glared at everyone sullenly. His face had started to swell, the bruises purple where Micha had hit him.

Carly gasped when she got a good look at Micha. "Your head," she said, her eyes wide and worried. "The back of your head is all bloody."

Grim-faced, Charlie eyed him. "I'm going to radio for a couple of EMTs."

"No need," Micha started to say. But Crenshaw shook his head and ignored him.

Carly put her small hand up along his cheek. "That needs to get looked at. At least let the EMTs clean it and see if it needs a few stitches. What did he hit you with?"

"I'm not sure, but I'm thinking the butt of the rifle." Though he felt a little bit foolish, Micha had to admit his head hurt like hell.

She winced. "There's an awful lot of blood. I can start getting it cleaned up and take a look at it."

"Since you're a nurse, I'd rather do that," he agreed.

Her stern look coaxed a smile from him. "I still want the EMTs to look at it. Promise me you'll let them."

Since he could deny her nothing, he agreed.

Two more uniformed officers arrived after everyone had gone inside, ringing the front doorbell. Carly let them in and they took custody of a still-sullen Andy, escorting him to their squad car.

"He'll be held downtown," Sean told Micha.

"Locked up, right?" Carly asked. January had finally

pried Carly off Micha and stood with her arm around her cousin's shoulders, clearly trying to comfort her.

The EMTs walked right in, making Carly realize the front door sat wide open. Shaking her head, she went to close it, then led the paramedics over to Micha.

"There's better light in the kitchen," she told them. "Follow me."

They had Micha sit at the kitchen table. With a gentle kind of competence, one of the men got to work checking out his wound while the other took his blood pressure. He almost protested that, but one glance at Carly's steely gaze had him holding his tongue. She went and got a bowl of warm water and a clean washcloth and began carefully cleaning up his head wound.

"Are you sure you don't want to let us take him to the hospital so they can do that?" the EMT asked.

"I'm a nurse," Carly replied. "And I know he won't go."

"He might need antibiotics," the man continued. "And as you know, only a doctor can prescribe those."

"We'll be all right," Carly said, smiling. "I work at the hospital, so I can get him in to see a doctor if necessary."

The man nodded. He shone a small light into Micha's eyes. "You probably have a concussion," he said, getting to his feet. "But if you're absolutely against letting us run you to the ER, I think you're in good hands here."

Micha mumbled his thanks. Carly got up to let the two men out, and they spoke quietly for a moment at the door. He let his gaze follow her as she made her way through the still-crowded living room, the pounding in his head making him ache to close his eyes. He resisted, partly because he seemed to remember something about not going to sleep with a concussion, but mostly because he didn't want to look away from Carly.

"Are you in pain?" Carly asked when she reached him. "Don't even answer that. Let me get you something."

She left again, returning to hand him a couple of pills and a bottle of water. "Nothing prescription," she said. "But they should still help with the pain."

The steady hum of voices from the other room made him long for quiet. As if she understood, Bridget scooted over under the table and rested her head on his leg. Micha stroked her head, glad to have her company.

More than anything, Micha wanted everyone to finish their business and leave so he could be alone with Carly. Soon, he told himself. Despite his aching head, he wanted to hold her and kiss her and show her exactly how much she meant to him. Catching him watching her, the heat in her gaze told him she wanted the exact same thing.

Charlie had Jones in the hallway, taking notes while Jones finished giving his statement. Judging from his exhausted expression, Carly's brother couldn't wait to get out of there and go home.

"Carly, I'm ready for you next," Charlie said, motioning her over. She nodded but went to Jones first and gave him a huge hug. He hugged her back, his gaze meeting Micha's over the top of her head. Once she released him and walked over to talk to Charlie, Jones dragged his hand through his hair and headed toward the front door. Micha pushed to his feet to join him.

"Thank you," Micha told him, walking him out.

"For what?"

"For keeping Carly safe. I don't know what Andy would have done to her if he'd caught her here alone."

Jones shuddered. "That guy is seriously unhinged."

"Yeah." Micha considered his next words. "Some of what happened over there really messed with a lot of the guys' heads. I didn't know Andy all that well, but from what I was told, before the crash he was career military. They said he put all of his focus on an upward track. The chopper crash kind of ended that for him."

"I understand being bitter about that," Jones said. "But why blame you? Why not blame the pilot?"

"The pilot was killed," Micha replied, his voice quiet. Even now, remembering the crash brought back a lot of pain. "And I guess Andy needed someone to pin his anger on, so he chose me. After all, if I hadn't been captured, there wouldn't have been a rescue mission at all."

"That's flawed thinking." Jones shook his head and unlocked his truck. "I'm going to head home now. I've got a lot of unwinding to do before I can even think about going to bed."

"Thanks again, man," Micha said.

"You take care of yourself and my sister," Jones said, giving a two-fingered wave before getting in his vehicle and driving off.

Micha watched him go and then turned around to head back inside. He made it as far as the front porch steps before he slid to the ground as everything went gray and then black.

Answering all of Officer Crenshaw's questions, Carly kept one eye on the door waiting for Micha to return. Even though the danger appeared to be past, he had a beast of a head wound. She'd even begun to rethink making him go to the hospital. In fact, once the questions were over, she thought she'd just go ahead and drive him to the ER herself.

When ten minutes had passed and still Micha didn't return, part of her wondered if he might still be talking with Jones. But she'd seen how tired her brother appeared to be and knew how badly he'd wanted to go home. In addition, Micha could barely stand. There was no way he was still out there chatting it up with Jones.

Something was wrong.

Cutting off Charlie mid-question, she took off for the front door, motioning for him to follow.

When she caught sight of Micha slumped on her porch, she let out a low keening cry of worry and rushed to him.

"Do you want me to call for an ambulance?" Charlie asked.

"If we can get him into a squad car, I think it'd be faster to take him that way," she said. "If we could run lights and sirens, that is."

Charlie eyed her doubtfully. "Micha's a big man. I don't know if I can lift him."

"My cousin's fiancé is still here. He's a homicide detective with Chicago PD. If we enlist his help, I'm pretty sure we can get him into a car."

Without waiting for an answer, she ran back inside.

Working together, Sean and Charlie managed to get Micha into Carly's vehicle. Then, with Charlie escorting her, police lights flashing, they headed to the hospital. Sean and January followed close behind.

Once there, Charlie ran inside and alerted the charge nurse. Two orderlies were sent out with a wheelchair, though Carly informed them they'd need to come back with a stretcher instead. Meanwhile, Carly checked Micha's pulse, which was steady, not weak. She wished she had the equipment to check his vital signs. The fact that he'd passed out after a blow on the head had her extremely worried.

After what felt like an eternity, the orderlies returned with two more. All four of them managed to get Micha on the stretcher and inside to triage.

Once inside, Carly was allowed to go back and wait with Micha until the doctor ordered tests, which would be an X-ray and an MRI. "The X-ray will show the bone," the doctor explained. "While the MRI will show the bone as well a soft tissue, so I can take a look at the brain."

Carly nodded. Though she already knew this, she appreciated the doctor taking the time to explain.

While Micha was off having his scans, she returned to the waiting area to let January and Sean know. "Charlie had to go," Sean said. "He wanted me to tell you he'd touch base with you later today."

The small waiting room had free coffee, though Carly knew from experience that it tasted pretty foul. She checked her watch and guessed she really didn't need to ingest caffeine at this hour of the morning. She wasn't scheduled to work today, so she might get some sleep at some point.

Right now, she felt too antsy to sit, so she settled for pacing the waiting room and hallway.

"Did Micha ever wake up?" January asked on her way to get a cup of coffee.

Carly thought about warning her, and then decided her cousin was old enough to make her own choices. "Not that I know of," she said.

Half an hour dragged on by. Carly knew all too well how long things could take in busy hospital ERs, though the near-empty waiting room gave her hope.

"Carly…" January called her name, inclining her head to where the doctor in his white coat had entered, carrying a clipboard.

Heart skipping a beat, Carly hurried over. January and Sean gathered behind her, offering their physical support.

"Mr. Harrison has a linear skull fracture," the doctor said, smiling slightly.

Carly breathed a sigh of relief. "Those are the most common," she told January. "All that's required is usually an anti-inflammatory and rest."

The doctor eyed her approvingly. "That's correct. We feel quite confident that this will heal itself. How did you know?"

"She's a nurse," January answered for her.

"I work in the NICU next door," Carly elaborated.

"Nice to meet you." The doctor smiled again. "He's back in the room, though he was still sleeping so I haven't been able to give him the report. Let us keep an eye on him for a little bit longer, and then we can discharge him to go home with you. I'm thinking another hour or so. Will that work for you?"

"Of course." Carly sagged with relief. Seeing, January put her arm around Carly's shoulders, letting her know without words that she'd help hold her up.

"May we go see him?" Carly asked.

"Certainly." The doctor waved his hand in the general direction of the room. "I'll fill out the paperwork and pre-sign the discharge papers, though I'll make sure the nurse knows he can't leave for at least thirty to forty-five minutes."

Which in hospital-speak meant an hour or more. Carly thanked him.

Once the doctor had left, Carly led January and Sean down the hall to Micha's small room. Micha appeared to still be sleeping, though numerous machines beeped while taking his vital signs. She allowed herself to drop into the hard plastic chair next to the bed. January came over and began to rub Carly's shoulders. "It's going to be all right," she murmured.

Carly's phone, which she'd silenced, began to vibrate, indicating an incoming call. Since it was still way too early for most people to even begin stirring, she figured it might be Jones, calling to check on things. When she saw Heath's number on the caller ID, she shook her head. She might as well go ahead and answer, since Heath wouldn't give up until she did.

"Hi, Heath." She let every bit of her exhaustion show in her voice. "What's up?"

"I just talked to Jones," Heath said. "And as soon as he told me what had happened, I went by your house, but no one was there. Are you okay? Where are you?"

"At the hospital, but wait," she interrupted him before he could speak. "Micha was injured. He has a skull fracture, but luckily it's not anything requiring surgery.

The doctor was just here and said Micha will be discharged soon."

"Do you want me to come up, anyway?" Heath asked, as she'd known he would. "I can be there in thirty minutes."

"No need." Carly didn't bother to suppress her yawn. "We're all exhausted. January and Sean are with me, but as soon as we get to take Micha home, all I want to do is sleep."

"That's understandable." Heath's tone softened. "Are you all right, Carly? Is there anything I can do to help you?"

Carly had never loved her oldest brother more. "Thanks, Heath. Nothing right now, but if I need anything, I know I can count on you."

"Promise me you'll call me."

"I will."

Ending the call, Carly raised her head to find Micha had opened his eyes and was watching her.

"Hey, there," she said, leaning in closer. "How are you feeling?"

Slowly he reached up and felt the bandage on his head. He winced. "What the heck happened?"

"You took a dive on the front porch," she said, leaning in to take his hand in hers. "Turns out when Andy hit you, he fractured your skull."

His eyes went wide. "What?"

"It's okay." Squeezing his hand, she carefully kissed his cheek. "They expect it to heal on its own. The doctor was just in and he's discharging you today. You'll have to take it easy for a while."

"Andy's still in custody, right?"

She nodded. "It's over, Micha. It's finally over."

"At least that part of it is," Micha agreed. "Now they just need to find your father's and uncle's killer."

Touched that he'd thought of her family in the middle of his own crisis, she started to tell him not to worry about that right now but Sean pushed forward.

"We've got multiple people and agencies working on that," Sean said. "Sooner or later, the murderer will make a mistake. They always do. And then we'll have them. Right now it's a matter of trying to make sure no one else gets killed. There's always a fine line in cases like this."

"Thanks," Micha replied, his eyes drifting closed.

Carly turned to her cousin and her fiancé. "I'm a little concerned about Simone," she said, keeping her voice low. "She seems obsessed with finding our fathers' killer. I'm worried she might get herself in trouble."

"I agree." January grimaced, her expression troubled. "When Simone fixates on something, she doesn't give up until she's resolved whatever it is."

"I'll talk to her," Sean promised. "I'll try to make her understand there are numerous professionals working around the clock to solve this case. Hopefully, once she gets that reassurance, she'll stand down."

Privately, Carly doubted that. January caught her gaze and gave a tiny shake of her head, letting Carly know she felt the same way. After all, she knew her sister.

"Thanks for coming," Carly told them, motioning toward the door. "Since we're just waiting to be discharged, why don't you two go on home and get some rest."

"Are you sure?" January asked, appearing unconvinced.

"I am." Carly shooed them away. "I'll be fine. I really appreciate you both coming."

Exchanging glances, January and Sean quietly said their goodbyes and left.

Alone in the room, Carly sat by Micha's side and watched him sleep. She couldn't believe how close she'd come to actually losing him a second time.

He was her person. The one who understood her, loved her and had her back. Despite two years apart, they still got each other's jokes, understood when certain occasions called for what kind of food.

And the chemistry... One glance from his brown eyes was enough to send her pulse into overtime.

Once, she'd thought they needed to take things slow, to get to know one another again. Now she understood all too well how fleeting and fickle time could be. And she and Micha had always been on the same wavelength. None of that had changed. Neither time nor distance had been able to take that from them.

Micha had opened his eyes again by the time a nurse appeared with his discharge papers. Carly hunted down his clothes, which had been placed in a plastic bag under the bed, and helped him get dressed. The nurse brought a wheelchair, waving off Micha's protests that he could walk. "Standard procedure," she and Carly said at the same time.

"I'll go get the car." Carly took off, almost running.

She pulled around and opened the front passenger door, watching as Micha stood and gingerly got in.

All the way home, Carly drove slowly and carefully, not wanting to jostle him in any way. Once they reached the house, she parked and went around to help him get out. "You can lean on me," she offered.

"I can walk," he insisted, though he let her slip her arm around him with her shoulder under his arm.

Inside the house, Bridget wiggled and wagged, clearly glad to see them. "Just a minute, girl," Carly told the dog. "Let me get Micha settled and then I'll take you out."

In the bedroom, Micha sat gratefully on the edge of her bed and allowed Carly to help undress him. Clad only in his boxers, he climbed in between the sheets. Carly brought him a glass of water and went to take care of her pet.

Once she'd returned, Carly allowed exhaustion to claim her. She downed a glass of water, double-checked all the door locks, turned out the lights and went back to her bedroom with Bridget following at her heels. Bridget got settled in her dog bed, heaving a contented sigh that made Carly smile.

Grabbing her oldest, softest oversize T-shirt, she climbed into bed next to the man she loved. Moving carefully so she wouldn't wake him, she debated on whether or not to spoon him. In the end, she decided just to let part of her arm rest against his back, touching him, yet not enough to disturb him.

"Come here," Micha rasped, rolling onto his side to face her. "You know I can't sleep unless I'm holding you."

This made her happier than it should have. This, with him spooning her from behind, was how she wanted to sleep for the rest of her life. She'd tell Micha that in the morning.

Chapter 14

Micha awoke sometime in the morning with a curvy, soft woman in his arms and a raging hard-on. He also had a killer headache, which should have been enough to destroy any amorous thoughts.

But his body apparently had other ideas.

He tried to ease away, to roll over so Carly wouldn't notice the proof of his desire pressed so heavily against her.

Instead, Carly tightened her arms around him and burrowed deeper into the covers. Her even breathing indicated she was still asleep.

Closing his eyes, Micha tried to clear his mind, to focus on something else, anything else but the aching need to bury himself inside her. The throbbing in his head finally outweighed everything else, and he slipped off to sleep.

When he woke again, he was alone in the bed and sunlight streamed through the window. His headache had gone. Stretching, he stood. He thought he almost felt normal. Though the clock on the nightstand showed it was after ten in the morning, he could hear Carly moving around in the other room, long after she should have been at work. A twinge of unease had him pushing to his feet.

"Carly?" he called out. "What's going on?"

Carly appeared in the bedroom doorway, her expression troubled. "I'm glad you're awake. You got a phone call while you were asleep. I probably shouldn't have answered it, but I didn't want to disturb you, so I did." She took a deep breath. "It was your mother, Micha. Your father is in the hospital. She didn't go into too many details. She asked for you to call her back. It sounds like she wants you to come home."

Micha froze. He started to shake his head, but a jab of pain stopped him, reminding him of his head injury. He hadn't spoken to his mother in person since his brother's death, though he'd kept every letter she'd sent him. He'd supposed the military had notified her of his supposed death, the same way they'd told Carly.

Since his father had already declared Micha dead to him long before the helicopter crash, Micha hadn't seen any need to inform his parents of his ultimate survival. He figured his actual death might have finally given them both peace.

"My mother called?" he repeated, still trying to process Carly's words. "How is that even possible? Where would she get my number?"

"Since clearly she knows you're alive, it seems likely

someone in the military gave it to her." Carly came closer, putting her arm around him gently. "And she wants you and your father to patch things up while there's still a chance."

Micha sat back down on the edge of the bed. Carly dropped down next to him. She silently handed him his phone. Feeling hollow, he accepted it, turning it over and over in his hand. "I'm not sure what to think," he began.

"Don't think, feel." Carly laid her hand on his arm. "We've been given a second chance, you and I. Maybe your parents deserve one, too."

Pushing to her feet, she left him there, alone with his thoughts and his phone.

Micha thought of the last time he'd seen his father, of the anguish that had darkened the older man's brown eyes as he'd prepared to bury his firstborn. He'd been so proud of his two boys, serving their country. He'd already been struggling to keep the farm going, pinning everything on Brian's promise to take over when he'd completed his military service.

All of that had been gone in a flash.

Micha had been just as stunned and hurt as his parents, maybe even more since he'd idolized his older brother. The ruin of his parents' hopes and dreams had hit them hard, but after losing Brian, Micha had actually begun to question the wisdom of copying his brother's life choices. At least as far as joining the military.

In the midst of all this grief and uncertainty, Micha's parents had asked him to give up all his dreams and essentially become Brian.

The things his father had said to him when he refused were the kinds of words that could never be taken back. And to this day, so many years later, Micha had not forgotten them.

But there were other times Micha could remember. The county fair, prize calves and the carnival rides after. Every year without fail, his father had taken his boys and let them ride every ride, eat as much cotton candy and as many hot dogs as they wanted, until they'd gotten so tired they'd fallen asleep in the truck on the way back home to the farm.

When Micha had gone on his first date with pretty Sally Fromm from town, his father had sat Micha down and had *the talk* with him. He'd slung his work-roughened hand around Micha's shoulders and they'd talked and laughed and Micha had gone away feeling good about what it meant to be a Harrison man.

Memories came rushing back, one after the other, and to his surprise Micha felt tears pricking at the back of his eyelids.

The events of the last two years—being captured, the helicopter crash, the burns, almost dying and the long slow climb back to recovery. He hadn't dared to even hope for Carly's forgiveness, or to once again have her love. And yes, he'd also missed his parents, his family. He'd even missed that damned dairy farm.

In fact, he'd made a carving of his parents, standing with their arms around each other, and with their family dog at their feet. He thought of that now and went to get it, running his thumb over the smooth and polished wood.

Hands shaking, he pulled up the recent call list and hit Redial to call back the same number he remembered from his childhood, the landline that his parents had clearly hung on to.

His mother answered, sounding so much older he caught his breath and could barely get out the word "Hello."

"Micha," she said, recognizing his voice. She started to cry. "I'm so glad you called."

"It's good to hear from you, Mom," he said cautiously. "What's going on with Dad?"

She told him about his father and the stubborn man's refusal to go to a doctor for regular checkups. As a result, she'd walked into the kitchen one morning and found him nonresponsive. He'd had a stroke. Only her panicked phone call to 911 and their quick response had saved his life. He'd spent ten days in the hospital and had just been moved to a rehabilitation facility. She'd spent much of that time trying to track Micha down.

"Is he going to be all right?" Micha asked, stunned.

"He's got a long road ahead of him," she replied. "He's relearning how to walk, and his speech was also affected. The doctors have been cautiously optimistic about his recovery, but he won't ever be the same man he was before."

Micha wasn't sure how to respond. He was still trying to process the unexpected swell of emotion he'd felt upon hearing the news. His father had always seemed larger than life, invincible.

"Will you come visit?" his mother asked. "Please. I know he'd love to see you, as would I."

Though his first instinct was to hold on to his pride and refuse, the trials he'd been through had made him rethink many things. Holding grudges served no purpose other than to deepen the hurt and bitterness. "Would he want me there?" he asked, even though he wasn't sure he was ready for the answer.

Though she could have lied, Micha's mother gave him the truth. "Though I'd like to think he would, I'm not sure. He has no clue that I called you. But know this, ever since he said what he did at Brian's funeral, he's regretted those words. He deserves a second chance. We both do."

"I'll come," he said, making an instant decision. "But I'll be bringing someone with me. I'd really like you to meet her."

"I'd love that," she said instantly. "I figured there was someone special when she answered the phone. In fact, I'd be honored to meet her. Please tell me about her, where you met and how long you two have been together."

Micha took a deep breath. He allowed the love he felt to show in his voice as he spoke about Carly. He went back to the beginning, to his initial proposal, their plans to marry and then what had happened to him in Afghanistan.

She gasped when he told her about being captured and then went quiet when he talked about his burns, the scars, and the years of physical therapy and recovery.

"We learned when they told us you were alive that you'd been hurt," she said softly. "We just didn't know the extent of it. I called, but because you hadn't put me on the list of people authorized to receive information, they wouldn't tell me anything."

"Wait," he interrupted. "They *told* you that I was alive?"

"Yes, of course. They'd sent two men in uniform to announce your death. Those same two came back to let us know there'd been a terrible mistake."

Stunned, he shook his head. "They didn't correct the misinformation with Carly," he said, bemused. "All this time, she truly believed I was dead. She was furious with me for not reaching out and letting her know."

"I can't say I blame her," she agreed, a hint of reproach in her voice. "That must have been very painful. I know it was for me."

He swallowed back the urge to remind her that she'd stood by his father when they'd said Micha was dead to him. Even now, that hurt. He'd had lots of time to reflect on those words, both while captive and while in the hospital and rehab. He'd finally thought he'd managed to forgive, but he'd known he'd never forget.

"I made a mistake. Shutting Carly out of my life was the worst one."

"I made a mistake, too," his mother said softly. "I can only hope you'll forgive me the same way Carly clearly forgave you."

Those words…she was right. He turned the carving over in his hand, thinking how much he'd like to give it to her. To them.

From the corner of his eye, he saw Carly slip into the room. She sat down next to him and put her hand on his shoulder, offering her physical support. Turning slightly, he placed a kiss on the back of her hand.

"We all make mistakes," his mother continued. "And we all have regrets. If she had known, would you have let her visit you in the hospital?"

Even now, he wasn't sure. He'd been in a lot of pain,

had been told he was disfigured for life, and severe depression had taken hold.

"I didn't want anyone to know what had happened to me," he said, his voice breaking. "Not even Carly. And she's the love of my life."

Next to him, he registered Carly's swift intake of breath. Glancing at her, he mouthed, *As if you didn't know.*

When his mother spoke again, he could hear the tears in her voice. "When can you be here?"

Though he wanted to say they'd leave immediately, he knew he had to check with Carly about her work schedule. It wasn't even a bad drive, right around five hours. "I'll have to let you know. Oh, and Carly's dog will be coming with us. I hope you don't mind."

"Of course not. But please, hurry."

"I'll call you when we're on our way," he said. After ending the call, he dropped the phone on the bed and turned to Carly, taking both her hands in his. "My father had another stroke. It's not looking good," he told her. "My mother wants me to come see him, and her. I agreed." Swallowing, he looked deep into her eyes. "Carly, I'd like you—and Bridget, if that's okay—to go with me. It's time for me to mend old fences and I want you to meet my mom. I know you have to work, but—"

Leaning forward, she kissed him, effectively cutting him off. "Let's go. I already asked for four personal days off due to your head injury. Since I never use my time off, it was granted. So let's get packed and head out."

"I need to shower," he began.

"Fine, just don't let that bandage on your head get wet. Maybe take a sponge bath instead for now." She pushed to her feet, and then turned around and kissed him one more time for good measure.

"Bossy," he muttered, smiling against her lips.

"You betcha." Smiling back, she tossed her head. "By the way, I'm driving. No way I'm letting you near the driver's seat with that skull fracture." She shot him a sideways glance. "I'm looking forward to driving that new Jeep. A road trip is just what it needs to break it in."

As she swept from the room, he found himself grinning. Carly paused at the doorway and wagged her finger at him. "Now shower and pack," she ordered. "I bet we can be ready to go in less than an hour."

Impressed, he nodded and took himself off for the bathroom. Deciding to do as Carly had directed, he took a sponge bath, careful to keep his head and bandage dry. He got dressed, trying to imagine seeing his parents and the farm again after being away for so long and couldn't. Since he'd told his mother he'd let her know when they were on the way, he gave her a quick call before grabbing his rolling duffel bag and beginning to pack.

Carly waited for him in the kitchen when he towed his bag in there twenty minutes later. She'd just finished packing dog food and her own bag sat by the front door. "I've let both my brothers know where I'll be," she told him. "And I was going to make sandwiches for lunch, but now I'm thinking we can just get fast food along the way."

She'd left her long blond hair down and the sunlight streaming through the kitchen window lit her up in a golden glow. Her bright blue eyes and serious expression only made him ache for her. He always had and figured he always would.

As if she knew his thoughts, she met his gaze. A slow smile blossomed across her face, lighting her up from within.

He went to her and took her into his arms. Holding her close, he breathed in the light floral scent of her, marveling at what a lucky man he was to have her.

"You're the love of my life, too," she said softly. "I want you to know that, Micha. I'm glad you came back to me."

Then, just as he was debating kissing her, maybe even try to convince her to go back to the bed for a bit, she stepped away and heaved a sigh. "Mushy stuff over," she said with mock severity. "We need to get on the road," she said, her voice brisk. "I'll carry everything out and get it loaded in your Jeep."

Bemused, he managed a nod, though damned if he was going to sit around and watch her do all the work. He'd injured his head, not his arms. As she went out the door, he grabbed his bag and followed her.

Though she raised her brows when she saw him, she only shook her head and held out her hand for his keys.

Gripping the steering wheel, Carly warred between nerves and exhilaration. Bridget had settled down in the back seat and quickly fallen asleep. "How are you feeling?" she asked Micha, driving 90 South toward Indiana.

He shrugged, trying for nonchalance, but she could see the tension in the way he held his shoulders. "I'm not sure. My father is dying. I haven't seen either of my parents for years. So much wasted time, all because of my father's stubborn pride. And now I'm going to see him when it's too late to try for any kind of meaningful relationship." He swallowed hard. "I'm not going to lie. It hurts. Like hell."

The sorrow in his voice had her aching for him. He'd been through so much and somehow managed to emerge from everything with more strength and compassion than any man she'd ever known, with the exception of her brothers and her late father and uncle.

"You'll get through this," she promised. *"We'll* get through this."

Micha nodded but didn't comment. He'd put the address into the Jeep's navigation system for her and turned his head to look out the window. About an hour into the trip, Carly could tell by his even breathing that he'd fallen asleep. She figured this had to be a good thing. That way, he'd at least be well rested, which would hopefully give him strength to deal with what lay ahead.

Alternating between watching the road and checking on Micha, she realized there was something very important she needed to do before meeting Micha's mother. The thought made her feel as if drunken squirrels had taken up residence in her stomach. But the longer she drove, the more she came to understand this was the right thing to do. She just wasn't sure when. Since she had no actual plan, she figured she'd simply have to play it by ear. As long as Micha continued to sleep, she didn't have to worry about it, so she pushed it to the back of her mind.

A little over two hours from when they'd left Chicago, she took the exit toward a town called Goshen, Indiana, simply because she liked the name. Cruising down Main Street, she eyed the refinished storefronts, enjoying the warm, welcoming feel of the small town. She pulled into the parking lot of a place called Hopper's Pike Street Grill, and parked under the shade of a huge oak tree.

When she did, Micha blinked and sat up. "Where are we?" he rasped.

"Goshen, Indiana. This seemed like a good time to stop for lunch. A lot of the downtown places appear to only open for dinner, but this one looks like they have lunch."

He nodded, covering a yawn with his hand. "I've been asleep the whole time, haven't I?"

"You have. I'm thinking you must really need the rest." *Now? Should she ask him now?* Her heart started to race and she took a deep breath to calm herself. Maybe after lunch.

"Do you mind getting something to go?" Micha asked. "I'm not sure I'm up for going in to eat right now."

"I understand." Reaching over, she squeezed his shoulder. "That was actually my plan. But I also need to stretch my legs and visit the ladies' room, plus let Bridget out. Are you sure you don't want to get out and walk around, too?"

Micha considered, finally giving a small nod. "That might not be a bad idea."

After taking Bridget on a leash to relieve herself, Carly poured some bottled water into a plastic bowl she'd brought so her dog could get a drink. "Though it's not really hot, I'm not comfortable leaving Bridget in the Jeep," she said. "You go ahead in and when you come back out I'll take a turn."

Micha touched the bandage on his head. "Do you think they'd believe it if we said she was my service dog?"

Considering, Carly shrugged. "It's worth a shot, even though we don't have a vest on her or anything. Some restaurants let dogs eat out on the patio. Maybe they have one out back."

With Bridget at her side, Carly and Micha walked into the restaurant together. Immediately, the delicious smell of fried chicken made Carly's mouth water. "I'll meet you back here at the entrance," she told Micha. "Then I'll see if I can place a to-go order."

Turning, Micha frowned. "I've changed my mind. Let's sit down and take a few minutes to eat. The break will be nice. That is, if they let my service dog stay." He spoke loudly enough so that the hostess looked up, eyed him and Bridget, and gave a quick nod.

Since the lunch rush had clearly already happened and the restaurant seemed mostly empty, this no doubt influenced the hostess's decision. Carly held the dog while Micha went to the men's room and he did the same when her turn came.

When they were all together again, the hostess found them a booth in the back of the room near the window and brought them menus. Bridget settled quietly under the table. "She's the perfect dog," Carly told Micha.

The waitress came and took their drink orders, asking them if they knew what they wanted or if they needed time to look at the menu.

Checking out the lunch specials on the back page, Carly ordered the fried chicken. Micha did the same. To her relief, Micha's gaze appeared to be a lot more focused than it had been earlier.

"Are you feeling better?" she asked, trying to push back her nervousness so she could put out there what needed to be asked. Was now the right time? Her stomach churned, making her realize she couldn't do this and eat, so once again she decided to wait.

"I am." He studied her intently. "But are you? You seem worried or upset."

Though she knew he'd see through her fake smile, she smiled, anyway. "I'm fine. Maybe a bit nervous about meeting your mother." Which was the truth, just not all of it.

Their food arrived, the golden chicken crispy. It tasted as wonderful as it smelled.

Once they'd finished up, when the waitress arrived with the check, Micha snatched it. "My treat," he said, ignoring Carly's protests.

Back in the Jeep, Micha fell asleep almost immediately. Carly watched him, slightly concerned, but also aware sleep helped the body heal.

This time, he only dozed for thirty minutes, waking and giving her the sexiest, sleepy smile she'd ever seen. "Sorry about that," he rumbled, stretching. "I promise I'll try to stay awake now. All that food…"

Stifling her own yawn, she nodded. "I know. It's been a struggle."

This made him sit up straighter. "Really? Do you want me to take over?"

She laughed at that. "Nope, I'm good. We only have a few more hours to go."

Finally, a sign appeared announcing they had reached Rawson, Ohio. "Home sweet home," Micha drawled. "Though the farm is really on the outskirts, kind of in between Rawson and Mount Cory."

Shutting off the GPS, Micha gave directions, pointing out where he'd gone to school and some of the places where he and his brother, Brian, had hung out. Since he rarely ever even spoke his brother's name out loud, she caught her breath and waited to see if he'd say more.

"There were city kids and country kids," he mused. "Brian and I desperately wanted to be city, but of course we weren't."

Keeping silent, she nodded. She could hear him trying to rein in the raw emotion in his voice. She wondered if he'd ever properly grieved his brother, or if that, too, was catching up with him as he tried to come to terms with his father's serious illness. In this, she knew she could only be there for him if he needed her. He had to face this on his own, though she planned to be standing by his side.

They left the small downtown and he directed her in what seemed like complicated turns out on a dirt road in the middle of rolling fields as far as the eye could see.

"It's so green," she said. "I didn't know what I expected, but it's..."

"Boring, I know." He gave her a rueful smile. "I couldn't wait to get out of here when I was a teenager. Brian was the same way."

She caught her breath. This was the third time he'd said his brother's name, a major difference for a man who'd struggled to even utter Brian's name. Once, when she'd asked, he'd said there were some things he just couldn't talk about. So she didn't press, even now. Especially now, though Micha appeared to be opening up. It was his story to tell, and she figured he'd do that when he was ready.

Simply nodding, she waited to see if Micha would continue.

"Brian was always the star," he said. "The most popular guy in school, and outstanding athlete, and the girls loved him. His one major flaw was that he would say whatever he thought people wanted to hear, even if it wasn't true. He told my parents he would come back and take over the ranch once he served his four years in the army. They believed him, of course, and it did take a lot of pressure off me."

"How do you know he didn't mean it?" she asked, unable to help herself.

Micha grimaced. "Because he told me and everyone else he knew that he considered the army his ticket out of here. He was right. That's why I enlisted as soon as I graduated high school."

Carly didn't comment, figuring she didn't need to point out that maybe Brian had simply told Micha what he'd wanted to hear also.

"None of it mattered in the end," Micha continued. "Because Brian went and got himself killed. Damn, I was pissed at him."

Even now, so many years later, she could hear the grief in his voice.

Micha must have noticed it, too. He shook his head and dragged his hand through his hair. "Sorry. Enough of talking about the past. Look around. What do you think? Have you ever been to Indiana or Ohio before?"

"It's pretty," she said. "Very green with lots of trees. And no, I haven't."

Now, she thought. Now would be the perfect time to ask him the question she'd been wanting to ask since they'd left Chicago. Heart pounding, palms sweating, she tried to think of exactly what she wanted to say.

"Let's not talk about anything else that's serious," Micha told her, effectively canceling out her short but to-the-point speech. "Okay?"

What could she do but agree? Her question would have to wait until later, but since they weren't too far from Micha's parents' place, Carly knew she didn't want to wait much longer. She couldn't. She needed to have things clear in her head. And she could only hope once everything was settled, the end results would match her heart.

Chapter 15

During his time as a captive and later while in the hospital recovering, Micha had often wondered if he'd ever see his childhood home again. It had felt odd to feel nostalgic for a place he'd only wanted to escape, but he figured that was part of human nature. Until he'd joined the army, the farm had been the only place he'd ever lived. He even pictured it, most often in the context of him simply driving down the gravel road in his vehicle, looking out over the familiar green fields that would be still unchanged from his childhood, and maybe even taking a picture of the front of the house he'd grown up in. This hadn't ever included him seeing his parents in person.

Surprisingly, seeing his parents again made him feel both nervous and eager. Meanwhile, he took in the familiar scenery and allowed a place inside of him that he hadn't even known was broken to slowly heal.

Then something new and unfamiliar made him sit up straight.

A sign advertising a new housing development sat at the corner of his parents' private drive and the now-paved main road.

"What the…?" he wondered out loud, just as they crested the small hill and he caught sight of several large houses in the area where his family had once grazed cattle.

"Nice houses," Carly said, fidgeting. She seemed antsy for some reason. He put it down to nerves at meeting his mom.

"They are nice," he reluctantly admitted, admiring the clean lines of the houses. "Though they're out of place here."

"Maybe this will soon be an up-and-coming residential area." Hands on the steering wheel, she practically bounced in her seat. "And look at the size of their yards."

He shook his head. Carly always made small talk when she was nervous. It was part of her way of processing stress.

"If I was in the market for a new home in this part of Ohio, I'd definitely consider one of those," she continued. "I bet they're a lot less expensive here than in Chicago."

Though Micha found their presence in what had been unspoiled farmland unsettling, he swallowed hard and agreed.

The road curved, and once they'd left the subdivision behind him, the rolling, treed hills he remembered took over.

Finally, his parents' house came into view. Still painted a cheery yellow—his mother's doing—the single-story ranch house looked a little more weathered than he remembered. Carly pulled the Jeep up in front of the two-car garage and parked. She killed the engine and turned to face him, wiping her palms off on the front of her jeans.

"Nervous?" he asked, wondering if she'd find it comforting that he was, too.

"A little." Carly nodded, fidgeting in her seat. "Though not about what you think. At least not entirely." She took a deep breath, the worry in her wide-eyed gaze making him want to comfort her. "Listen," she continued. "Before we go in there, I need to ask you something important."

"Anything," he said, meaning it. "What is it?"

"Just a second." To his surprise, her hand appeared to be shaking as she reached for a delicate silver chain she wore around her neck. Her gaze locked on his, she pulled it out of her shirt. "This," she told him, showing him what she wore dangling at the end of the necklace.

He caught his breath. "Is that…?"

"Yes. The engagement ring we picked out together before you went back to active duty. I wore it on my finger for a year after I was told you died."

Touched, he swallowed hard. "You kept it."

"Yes. Once I stopped wearing it on my hand, I wore it on this chain, tucked inside my clothes so no one could see. I just took it off and put it in my jewelry box right before you came back. I put it back on this morning. This ring means that much to me. It's a symbol of our love."

Their love. Hope bloomed within him, unfurling in his chest.

Then, while he struggled to figure out the right words to say, she unclipped the chain, removed the ring and held it out to him.

Throat aching, furious with himself for actually daring to hope, he froze, eyeing the ring as if it were dangerous. In a way, it was.

She was giving it back. Now, as he prepared to face one of the most difficult times in a life that hadn't been easy in a long, long time, Carly Colton had decided to stab him in the heart.

"No." He refused to believe it, his chest aching. "It's yours. You keep it. I don't want it back."

"What?" Tilting her head, she eyed him as if she thought he'd lost his mind. "You thought… Oh, Micha. I brought the ring back out to ask you if you wanted me to wear it again." She lowered her hand. "That's what I get for being presumptuous. I wanted you to put it back on my finger."

Thoroughly confused now and almost afraid to dare to believe he'd heard her properly, he looked from her beautiful blue eyes to the sparkling ring and back again. He thought his heart might explode from his chest. "Do you mean…?"

"Yes. I'd like to go back to being engaged," she said primly, though a tiny smile hovered at the corner of her mouth. "That is, if you still want to marry me."

"If I still want…" He sucked in his breath. "Carly Colton, are you proposing to me?" he asked, blood roaring in his ears. "Because if you are, the answer is yes. Definitely, unequivocally yes!"

"Well, technically I'm asking if we can reinstate our engagement," she began. Then her eyes widened. "Yes?" she repeated. "Does that mean we…"

"Have a wedding to plan." Leaning over, he kissed her. Not a long, deep kiss like he longed to do, but a quick one due to them being parked outside his childhood home. "I love you," he said. He took the ring and, gazing in her eyes, slowly slipped it over her finger. "Back where it belongs. Engagement reinstated."

"You know what?" she asked, her expression suddenly solemn. "I love you, too, Micha Harrison. I always have and I always will."

Now he knew he could face anything. "Let's go inside and meet my mother."

"Yes." She nodded. "Now I'm ready to meet my future mother-in-law."

Her simple choice of phrase made his throat close. The thought that his father might never get to know the wonder and beauty that made up Carly Colton hurt. But he couldn't focus on that now. His mother needed him. And too many years had passed since he'd hugged her.

Pushing aside all raw emotion, he nodded. "Let's go."

They got out of the Jeep at the same time, linking hands to walk up the sidewalk. They made it halfway when the front door of the house opened and his mother stepped out onto the front porch. She wore a pair of faded blue jeans, work boots and a cotton, button-down shirt. She looked the same, he thought, except she now wore her silver hair in a stylish short cut.

"Micha!" She cried out his name and opened her arms.

Micha stepped into them without hesitation. Carly remained a few steps back, quietly watching.

Clinging to him, his mother wept. "It's so good to have you home."

"It's good to be here," he replied.

"What happened to your head?" she asked, pulling back far enough to peer at his bandage.

"That's a long story," he told her. "I'll save it for later, if that's okay with you."

Expression troubled, she searched his gaze, exactly the same way she'd used to when he was a teenager and she was trying to ascertain if he was telling the truth. "But you're all right, aren't you?"

He hugged her tight. "I'm all right, Ma. I promise."

When she finally released him, Micha turned her around and introduced her to Carly. "Mom, this is my fiancée, Carly Colton."

More hugs, more weeping, and finally his mom ushered them both inside the house. She kept checking back over her shoulder to make sure they were following her.

Inside, the place appeared the same as he remembered, untouched by time. The familiar floral wallpaper decorated the kitchen walls, and the same metal-and-vinyl kitchen table and chairs sat under the same stained-glass light fixture. It felt like stepping back into the past.

Except now he knew his father wouldn't come stomping in through the kitchen door, having left his dirty boots on the back stoop, wanting nothing more than a hot shower and a good meal.

Micha waited until they were all sitting around the

old kitchen table sipping on his mother's freshly made lemonade before asking about the subdivision.

"We had to sell off some of our land," his mother explained, only slightly apologetic. "With your father slowing down due to age, we were struggling to keep the ranch running. Finally, we decided to just hang on to the house and ten acres. Even that was a lot, though. Right before Al had his stroke, we were even talking about moving into Lima since it's less than a half hour away."

"Dad is considering living in town?" Micha asked. Next, he halfway expected her to tell him pigs could fly.

His mom nodded. "He's sick, but technically he's living in Lima now. He was at Saint Rita's Medical Center, but yesterday they moved him into a rehabilitation facility. They said he'd be there a few weeks."

Rehabilitation. His dad must hate that. Al Harrison had always taken such pride at being a man's man, big and weather-roughened, his large hands calloused from hard work. Micha couldn't imagine how he'd deal with being weakened by a stroke. "Will we be able to visit him?"

"Yes." Expression troubled, his mother placed her hand over his. "But I should prepare you. He's in and out of consciousness. I'm not sure he'll even recognize you."

He hadn't expected that. He swallowed hard. "I hope he does. There are a few things between us that we need to settle once and for all."

Though she nodded, his mother once again started to cry. Carly, with her big heart, got up and went to her, wrapping the older woman in a tight hug. "It's going to be all right," she murmured. "You'll see."

Though she nodded, his mom's bleak expression indicated she wasn't sure anything would ever be all right again.

"We've received an offer on the house and remaining ten acres," she finally said. "By the same people who built that fancy subdivision. Though your father and I were only considering it before he had the stroke, I'm likely going to accept it now."

For a moment, Micha couldn't catch his breath. But then he realized she was right. He hated the thought of the two of them struggling to run the ranch. Who knows, maybe they'd be open to moving closer to Chicago. He decided to bring that up at some point before he left.

After finishing their drinks and refusing his mom's offer to make them something to eat, they got Bridget settled in the kitchen and then they all piled into Micha's Jeep to drive to Lima. After all these years away, Micha would finally see his father again. He only wished it were under different circumstances.

Thoroughly charmed by Micha's mother, who'd asked her to call her Beth, Carly kept quiet and stayed in the background while Beth and Micha reconnected. For as long as she'd known and loved Micha, he had buried his emotions deep inside regarding his family. Seeing him now, clearly hurting yet full of love, only made her realize she'd made the right choice in reinstating their engagement.

As if she'd ever doubted. Even when she'd been furious and hurt over the way he'd let her think he'd died, she'd still loved him with every ounce of her being.

Micha had let his mother ride in the front seat and he'd taken the back while Carly drove. Pulling up in front of the rehabilitation hospital, she parked. The single-story brick building appeared welcoming.

Carly glanced at Beth and then Micha. "Should I wait out here?" she asked, willing to give them all the privacy they needed.

"No," Micha answered immediately. "I want you with me."

Beth wisely stayed out of the discussion, rummaging in her purse for something.

Carly got out, motioned at Micha to do the same. "I think you should talk to your father privately at first. Once you're comfortable, you can bring me in and introduce me."

Opening his mouth as if to argue, Micha considered. He exhaled. "Maybe you're right."

"You and your mother," Carly urged. "I don't want to intrude right now. I'm sure they have some sort of lobby. I'll sit there and wait."

Though Micha still appeared uncertain, he nodded. Inside, he waited until Carly had gotten settled in a chair before offering his mother his arm. Together the two disappeared down one of the hallways.

Her phone chimed, indicating a text. It was Jones, just checking to make sure she'd arrived in one piece. They texted back and forth for a little bit, and right before he said he had to go, he reminded her to let Heath know she was okay. She did that, received a brief, I'm glad, in response, which meant her eldest brother had to be too busy to chat.

She checked social media, scrolling through her feed, when she looked up to see Beth had returned.

"I'm letting them have alone time," the older woman stated, dropping into the chair next to Carly. "Al has been in and out of it since they moved him here. He's sleeping a lot, though they tell me they've been able to get him up out of bed in a wheelchair. Micha is talking to him, hoping his father will respond to the sound of his son's voice."

Carly nodded. "Has he been awake much with you?"

Slowly, Beth nodded. "A little bit," she said. "It's been really frightening, not knowing if my husband is going to recover."

Reaching over, Carly hugged her. "It'll all work out. Sometimes these things just take time."

Once Carly let go, Beth eyed her curiously. "You sound awfully confident. How do you know?"

"Because I'm a nurse." Carly smiled. "Pediatrics, though. I work in the Neonatal Intensive Care Unit. Time, along with modern medicine, often bring about surprising healing. Now I don't know your husband's particular medical situation, but I'm sure his doctor can give you a lot more information."

"Oh, he has. He actually said something similar to what you just did. We need to give Al time and see what functions he regains. The therapy here is supposed to help with all that, too."

"I'm sure it will."

Both women looked up as Micha reappeared. He seemed composed, Carly thought.

"Dad woke up," Micha told his mother. "Not for long, but I'm pretty sure he saw and recognized me."

Beth's gaze searched his face. "Did he say anything? I know it can be kind of hard to understand him."

"No. He just looked at me and smiled. Then he closed his eyes again."

"How long are you staying?" Beth asked, her tone guardedly hopeful.

Micha glanced at Carly. "I'm not sure. We haven't actually discussed it yet."

"I see. Well, you're both welcome to stay as long as you like. Please, at least another day," she pleaded. "We have so much catching up to do."

"We'd planned to spend the night," Micha replied. "Beyond that, I'm not sure."

"I'm glad. That's a start." Beth got up slowly, relief shining in her eyes.

Carly's heart went out to her. If Micha wanted to stay a couple of days, she'd be willing.

Once they arrived back at the farm, Beth informed them she would be making something special for supper, including dessert, so she asked them to please save their appetites. She showed them the room she'd given them to use, asking if they wanted to stay together or in separate rooms.

Micha tugged Carly close. "What do you think?" he asked, only half teasing.

"If you're okay with it, Beth," Carly replied. "Together. We've actually been living that way at my place for a little while."

"I don't mind." Smiling, Beth turned to go. "We'll

probably be eating at six. Why don't you two rest up a little and then join me in the kitchen?"

Once she'd left, closing the door behind her, both Carly and Micha dropped down on the bed and sat, legs dangling off the side.

"I haven't heard anyone call dinner supper outside of a television show," Carly mused. "I like it."

"We're country folks," Micha said. He looked around. "This used to be my bedroom growing up," he. "It's been painted and fixed up, but that actually looks like my bed and old dresser."

Unable to resist, Carly wiggled her eyebrows. "I bet you never slept with a girl in it. Or have you?"

He laughed. "No. This will be the first time."

"And the last," she pointed out. "We'd better make it matter."

Hauling her up against him, Micha kissed her. "Oh, we will. I can promise you that."

By the time he released her, she couldn't stop smiling. "I'm so glad we came," she said, resting her head against his shoulder.

"Me, too." He tucked a wayward strand of her hair behind her ear. "Before we go back home, I'd really like you to meet my dad."

Carly nodded. "I'd like that, too."

He hesitated, his expression serious. "I'm thinking of talking to my mom about them both moving to Chicago after they sell the farm. I think it'd be better for everyone if they lived closer to us."

"I agree." Heart full, Carly nodded. "And I'd really love for them to meet my family, too." One large, blended family.

"Me, too." Micha kissed her again, another slow and sensuous promise of what the night would hold later.

From her spot on the floor, Bridget woofed, wagging her tail.

"See, even our dog agrees," Micha said, smiling broadly.

Our dog. Carly liked that.

"Come on." Micha pulled her up to her feet. "Let's go see if there's anything we can help with in the kitchen."

"You go." She shooed him with her hands. "I want to freshen up a bit. I'll be out there shortly."

He kissed her again, a quick one this time, and left. Once the door had closed behind him, Carly dropped back onto the end of the bed. Bridget got up and nudged her with her nose so Carly would pet her.

Stroking her dog's silky fur, Carly exhaled, reflecting on how much her life had changed in such a short time. The love of her life had come back to her, she'd gained a dog and now would be adding in-laws to her family. Maybe even, someday, she and Micha would have children. The thought made her smile.

The only thing that could make her life complete would be for her father's and uncle's killer to be caught and brought to justice.

After washing her face and brushing her hair, Carly headed toward the kitchen with Bridget padding along at her side.

She'd barely reached the end of the hallway when the scent of something heavenly reached her. "Lasagna?" she guessed, stepping into the kitchen.

Beth grinned. "Yes. My specialty from an old family

recipe. When Micha was younger, he requested I make it for every birthday."

"That and your amazing cheesecake," Micha added, looking hopeful. "I don't suppose you happened to make one of those, too?"

Instead of answering with words, Beth simply went to the refrigerator and opened it. She held up a beautiful cheesecake decorated with cherries on top.

"Of course!" Micha laughed. "Thank you so much, Mom. I seriously used to daydream about your lasagna and cheesecake."

After closing the refrigerator, Beth turned to face him. Her eyes had filled with tears. "I almost lost you twice. Once at Brian's funeral and then again when the army told me you were killed. Naturally, I'm going to make your favorite foods for you."

Pushing to his feet, Micha hugged her. "I love you, Mom."

She hugged him back. "I love you, too." Holding out her other arm, she met Carly's gaze. "Get over here, Carly. I want a group hug with my daughter-in-law-to-be."

Touched, Carly joined in. To her surprise, she even teared up a little.

"Sit, sit." Beth motioned toward the table. "Lasagna takes time to cook. I've made salad that we can eat beforehand if you're hungry."

"We can wait," Micha said. "Sit with us, Mom. Carly and I want to talk to you about considering a move closer to Chicago."

Stunned, Beth pulled out a chair and dropped into it. She looked from Micha to Carly. "Are you serious?"

"Yes. At least think about it, why don't you? Since you're selling the farm and planning to move, anyway, why not live closer to us?"

"Plus, the Chicago area has a lot of top-notch doctors," Carly added. "I work at one of the hospitals there, so I can help you with referrals. I know how difficult finding a good doctor can be."

After looking from one to the other, Beth covered her face with her hands, crying now in earnest. "I'd love that," she finally said, smiling through her tears. "And I'm sure your father would, too. I'll talk to him about it, when he's able to understand."

Micha nodded. He reached into his pocket and put a small, highly polished carving on the table. "I made this for you," he said.

Beth sniffed, reaching for it. When she picked it up, she began crying again. "This is beautiful," she managed. "And looks just like us, right about the time you left for the army. You say you made this?"

Slowly, Micha nodded. "I kept it with me for years. Now I'd like you to have it."

She smiled through her tears. "I'll treasure it always."

The stove timer dinged.

"Oh!" Beth jumped to her feet, wiping at her eyes with her hand, before grabbing a tissue and blowing her nose. "The lasagna is done. It will need to sit on top of the stove for a few minutes. Carly, do you drink red wine? Would you like to eat your salads?"

Declining Carly's offer to help, Beth bustled around the kitchen, clearly in her element.

Later, after devouring the most delicious lasagna

Carly had ever tasted, bar none, along with garlic bread and salad, Carly nearly groaned when Beth got out the cheesecake. "I'm too full," she protested.

"You have to just try a bite," Micha insisted. "Even if it's just a sliver. I promise you, you've never tasted anything like it."

With a sigh, Carly gave in. Both Micha and Beth watched, beaming, as Carly cut into the fluffy dessert with her fork and opened her mouth. She'd expected good, but this was better. Melt in your mouth, light and sweet and perfect. "That's the best cheesecake I've ever tasted," she said, unable to conceal her amazement.

Clearly pleased, Beth laughed.

"I told you," Micha said, before turning his attention to his own plate. He devoured his own slice, as did Carly.

Then, stuffed and sleepy, Carly finished her wine and jumped to her feet. Ignoring Beth's protests, she began taking care of the dishes. "You and Micha go on and let me clean up," she said. "I'll join you both in the living room when I'm done."

Bridget woofed, reminding Carly she hadn't been fed.

By the time Carly took care of her dog and the dishes and poured herself another glass of wine, thirty minutes had passed. She carried her wine into the living room and took a seat on the couch next to Micha. He put his arm around her and tugged her close.

Beth watched them both with a dreamy smile. "I never thought I'd see this day," she mused. "Thank you, son."

"For what?" Micha asked.

"Forgiving me and your father our mistakes."

Micha appeared stunned. "We all have made choices we regretted later. Me in particular. If Carly hadn't forgiven me…" His voice broke.

Carly kissed him, snuggling into his side. "I think the best thing to do is keep looking toward the future," she said. "We cannot change the past."

The three of them chatted for a few more hours. They turned on the evening news and watched that, too. Finally, Beth excused herself to go to bed.

"We'll be visiting your father again tomorrow," she reminded Micha, stifling a yawn. "I'd like to go in the morning, so I can bring him doughnuts from his favorite place. I'm thinking we can leave around eight."

Micha used the remote to turn off the TV. He got up, gave his mother a hug and kissed her cheek. "We'll be ready. I'm hoping Dad will feel well enough tomorrow to meet Carly."

Beth's smile never wavered, despite the sadness in her eyes. "Sleep well, you two. I'll see you in the morning."

After Beth left, Micha and Carly turned off the lights. Carly took Bridget outside one last time and then they made their way to their room.

As quietly as possible, they got ready for bed. Bridget turned circles on the dog mat Carly had brought for her, heaved a sigh and settled down to sleep.

"This has gone better than I expected." Micha climbed into bed, propping his pillow up behind his back. "Everything I could ever have dreamed of, with the exception of my father having had a stroke."

"He'll get better," Carly said, hoping she was right.

"I think so, too. I can't wait to introduce you to him as my bride-to-be."

The satisfaction in his voice made her smile.

"Do you want a long or a short engagement?" she asked, getting into bed next to him.

Micha shot her an incredulous look. "Are you kidding me here? I want to marry you as soon as is humanly possible."

Turning to face him, she took both his hands into hers. "I agree, but I'd prefer to wait until your entire family can be there. Your father needs time to heal."

Clearly touched, Micha held her gaze and slowly nodded. "I agree. But I don't want to wait forever. It's already been way too long."

"Let's see how your dad does in rehab. Your mom said she'd keep us posted."

Micha nodded. "That sounds like a plan. But you know what? Your family isn't going to want to wait. As soon as they see that engagement ring on your finger, you know they're going to start planning big-time."

This made her laugh. "You're right. But at least I have a good excuse to make them give us a month or two."

"You do," he agreed. "But before we leave tomorrow, I'm going to tell my dad he'd better work hard so he doesn't hold up our wedding too long."

Carly wasn't sure what to think about this. "Are you sure that won't be putting too much pressure on him?"

"Nope." He kissed her, his eyes lighting up. "He thrives on a challenge. He always used to say what motivated him the most was someone telling him he couldn't accomplish something. He's got this, Carly. I know he does."

She nodded, then reached over and turned off her nightstand lamp. "We got this, too, Micha Harrison," she breathed, nibbling on his ear. "Now turn off your light so we can show each other how much we do."

With a strangled laugh that turned into a moan as her mouth moved lower, he did as she'd requested.

"Turns out you're right, Carly Colton," he murmured as she settled her body over his. "We got this."

* * * * *

Don't miss the next exciting story from the Colton 911: Chicago miniseries:
Colton 911: Hidden Target
by Colleen Thompson

You'll love these other thrilling books by Karen Whiddon:

The Widow's Bodyguard
Snowbound Targets
Texas Ranch Justice
The Texas Soldier's Son

WE HOPE YOU ENJOYED
THIS BOOK FROM

ROMANTIC SUSPENSE.

Danger. Passion. Drama.

These heart-racing page-turners will keep you guessing to the very end. Experience the thrill of unexpected plot twists and irresistible chemistry.

4 NEW BOOKS AVAILABLE EVERY MONTH!

He thought she deserved the full truth.

And I can't give it to her here and now.

"It's a complicated situation," he stated, hearing how
weak that sounded even as he said it.

"Like Lockley?" Norah replied.

"She's a different animal completely."

The voices started up again, and Norah at last relented.

"Okay, I believe you need my help, and I'm willing to
hear you out," she said. "Let's go."

Jacob didn't let himself give in to the thick relief.
There was genuinely no time now. He spun on his heel
and led Norah back through the slightly rank parking lot.
When they reached his car, though, she stopped again.

"What are we doing?" she asked as he reached for the
door handle.

"I'd rather go over the details at my place. If you don't mind."

"You don't live here?" she asked, sounding confused.

"Here?" he echoed.

"I guess I just inferred…" She gave her head a small shake. "I'm guessing it's complicated? Again?"

He lifted his hat and scraped a hand over his hair. "You might say."

He gave the handle a tug, but Norah didn't move.

"Changing your mind?" he asked, his tone far lighter than his mind.

"No. But I need you to give me the keys," she said. "I want to drive. You can navigate."

"I thought you believed me."

"I believe you," she said mildly. "But that doesn't mean I come even close to trusting you."

Jacob nodded again, then held out the keys. As she took them, though, and he moved around to the passenger side, he realized that her words dug at him in a surprisingly forceful way. It wasn't that he didn't understand. He wouldn't have trusted himself, either, if the roles were reversed. Hell. It'd be a foolish move. It made perfect sense. But that didn't mean Jacob had to like it.

Don't miss
The Negotiator *by Melinda Di Lorenzo,*
available May 2021 wherever
Harlequin Romantic Suspense
books and ebooks are sold.

Harlequin.com